# Bolan fired

A barely audible whoosh of gas sounded at the end of the Iver-Johnson's barrel as the .22 flew across the theater. Suddenly the speaker stopped shouting and froze.

Bolan pulled the trigger once more.

This time, the subsonic round hit the speaker squarely over the heart. The water glass fell from his grip to shatter on the wooden floor of the stage. Tennessee State Representative Patrick McGinney clutched his chest with both hands and leaned forward.

*Other titles available in this series:*

# DON PENDLETON's
# MACK BOLAN.
# SHOWDOWN

## A GOLD EAGLE BOOK FROM
# WORLDWIDE.

TORONTO • NEW YORK • LONDON
AMSTERDAM • PARIS • SYDNEY • HAMBURG
STOCKHOLM • ATHENS • TOKYO • MILAN
MADRID • WARSAW • BUDAPEST • AUCKLAND

First edition December 1995

ISBN 0-373-61445-4

Special thanks and acknowledgment to
Jerry VanCook for his contribution to this work.

SHOWDOWN

**Printed in U.S.A.**

Assassination has never changed the history of the world.

—Benjamin Disraeli 1804–1881


No one should get away with attempting to influence the fate of a nation by such brutal acts as assassination. The perpetrator of such an outrage must pay the steepest price possible.

—Mack Bolan

# PROLOGUE

Thunder exploded through the moonless sky as Colonel Shim Sang watched the tall man standing next to him just inside the tree line unzip the collar of his light rain parka, unroll the hood and pull it over his head. The tall man jerked the strings tight around his throat as lightning followed more thunder, briefly illuminating the rustic lodge in the clearing.

The door to the lobby of the two-story stone structure stood open, and through it Shim could see lodge guests seated in rustic wooden furniture. Behind them, against the wall, stood a floor-to-ceiling fireplace.

The tall man turned to Shim. "You sure it's just the two of them?" he asked.

Shim raised his eyes to the lodge's second floor, stopping briefly on a dark window next to the third door from the left, then returning his gaze to the man at his side. Another flash of lightning showed him a wild shock of white hair and pale, near-transparent skin. "Yes, Won Kwang," he said, still amazed that the American unhesitatingly answered to the Korean name after all these years. "Senator Thomlinson and his wife returned the children to their daughter and her husband this morning."

The rain predicted by the thunder and lightning finally came, and Shim pulled his windbreaker higher on his neck. "There is a song about this, is there not?" he asked.

The American glanced down at him again. "A song?"

"Yes, a song about it raining at night in Georgia?" Shim said unsurely.

The American nodded. "Yeah, in fact, that's the name of it. 'Rainy Night in Georgia.' But Samuel Johnson said something that fits our situation even better."

"Really? What was that?"

"'Rain is good for vegetables, and for the animals who eat those vegetables.'" He turned to face Shim as he finished. "'And for the animals who eat those animals.' That's from Boswell's *Life.*"

Both men laughed. "How very appropriate," Shim said.

The sound of tires crunching over the gravel road from the lake filtered through the falling rain. Shim shifted his gaze toward a dark pickup as it turned into the parking lot and parked next to a black BMW. A canoe had been lashed down in the truck bed, and as more lightning flashed, the aluminum sides reflected the light toward the men in the trees.

Shim took a step deeper into the trees.

The tall American chuckled softly. "Relax," he said. "Nobody can see us if we don't move."

Shim watched three men barrel out of the truck's cab and pull golf bags from the bed. They hurried toward the door to a room on the first floor.

"It may not happen until morning," the American said. "In this rain the senator may decide to eat here at the lodge."

Shim Sang shrugged. "Tonight, tomorrow, it makes no difference," he said.

"Not to you, maybe. But I don't care to spend the night out here in this if I don't have to. The romance of shit like that went away during my first week in Nam."

Shim started to answer, then stopped when a light appeared in the window he'd been watching. He held his breath as the shades were drawn back. He let the breath out and smiled when he saw the gray-haired man who had just drawn the curtains staring out into the rainy night.

The man was knotting a tie around his throat. Behind him, a woman, roughly the same age, was buttoning a pleated white blouse.

"The senator's wearing a tie," the American said. "That means they aren't eating at the lodge. They're going to town, Shim. And that means the car."

Shim nodded silently.

The gray-haired man moved away from the window, allowing the elderly woman to be seen more clearly. She tucked the tail of the blouse into a dark skirt and reached for a matching blazer.

Shim glanced at the bed next to her. The covers had been thrown haphazardly down to the foot of the bed and the sheets were wrinkled. He smiled. "Do you suppose, Won Kwang," he said, "that it is still good when one is that old?"

"What?" the American asked.

"Sex," Shim said.

"I don't know. Ask me when I get that old."

Shim and the American both laughed, knowing they would not be heard over the rain and thunder. "For the senator's and Mrs. Thomlinson's sake, though," the American said, "let's hope they both came, and came good, this one last time."

Shim reached into his jacket pocket and pulled out a shiny metal flask. He unscrewed the lid, tipped it to his lips, then handed it to Won Kwang. "To their orgasms," he said.

The American had just taken the flask when the upstairs door opened and the elderly man and woman appeared in matching gray raincoats. They hurried along the second-floor walkway, then down the rough cedar steps.

Shim watched Senator William G. Thomlinson open the door for his wife, then hurry around the car and jump behind the wheel.

A moment later an explosion louder than thunder rocked the night. Fire shot from the BMW toward the sky and the entire lodge lit up from the flames.

"What in the world did you wire it with?" Shim asked, shaking his head. "A neutron bomb?"

The American laughed as people began sticking their heads out of the other rooms of the lodge. "Just a little C-4," he said. He raised the flask and took a drink. Then the two men started off through the woods.

# CHAPTER ONE

The hunter had become the hunted.

Mack Bolan limped slowly along Prince Street, the sturdy oak cane in his right hand tapping the way ahead. His eyes squinted as if each step caused pain.

But they missed nothing.

It wasn't just Bolan's eyes that were on alert. His ears, his nose—every sense in his body—were tuned to what was happening around him. The time was 2019 hours on Prince Street, a time when Flushing should still be hopping with street life. But it wasn't.

Bolan limped on, the smells of paprika, fennel, sesame oil and mango chutney filling his nostrils as he passed deserted fruit-and-vegetable stands. The scene reminded him of something out of a postholocaust movie, after almost all human life has vanished. As he passed the front of a small restaurant, he saw an elderly Oriental man busily preparing the hot Korean salad known as kimchi. The man glanced up quickly, nervously, then returned his attention to his vegetables.

Bolan shook his head and walked on. Here was a man who, like most of the people in this area of Queens, knew the rules and decided it was healthier to abide by them. What were those rules?

The first stated that no one would be on the streets at eight o'clock when the Anju Dragons made their "victory lap" through Flushing.

Bolan scanned the window of the Rick Pak market as he limped by, seeing sheets of dried seaweed and bottles of Korean rice wine. The front door opened suddenly, and a short, balding Oriental with a wispy mustache looked out at him with frightened eyes. "You come in!" the little man said. "Not safe out there! You come in!"

Bolan smiled, shook his head and walked on. Behind him, he heard the noise of an iron grate being rolled down over the doorway. The man slammed the door again, and a dead bolt thudded.

Bolan couldn't argue with the man as he continued his private tour of Flushing. It *wasn't* safe out here.

That's why Bolan, better known to the world as The Executioner, had come.

For all of his adult life, Mack Bolan had fought evil and injustice the world over—first in the uniform of a United States Army Special Forces soldier, then in a more private war in which he wore civvies. But regardless of how he was dressed, the Executioner had always been a soldier.

And he was a soldier tonight. Even during this masquerade as a helpless old man.

A hard smile curled the warrior's lips as he limped past a deserted stand piled high with taro roots, bok choy and cuttlefish. Rule number two stated that by 8:30 tonight, the proprietor and the other vendors on Prince, Main and Union streets could return to the sidewalks. Business as usual could resume. Anything missing from their stands would be considered part of the weekly "protection" fees they paid the Anju Dragons. At least on the surface, Flushing would return to normal. But the knowledge that the Dragons were always there, always watching, would still hang in the air with a smell more foul than rotting cuttlefish.

A sudden gust of cool summer wind whipped around the corner of a side street, and Bolan pulled the collar of his new lightweight raincoat tighter around his throat. The expensive coat, together with Gucci loafers and the solid-oak walking stick with the brass duck-head grip, made him stand out in this section of Queens.

Bolan's clothes shouted "victim" as loudly as if he'd draped hundred-dollar bills from the pockets. They were the bait, and as he shuffled along, he caught the scent of the sharks.

The Executioner continued along the deserted street, exaggerating the limp even further. It wasn't easy for a man of his size or obvious physical prowess to look like an easy mark for a street mugging, but the hobble in his gait helped. The loose raincoat hid the heavy muscles in his shoulders and arms, and the gray he had streaked through his hair added to the illusion, as did his stooped posture.

But the clincher, the Executioner knew, was not anything he had worn or even done. What would ensure that the Dragons selected him as prey was the simple fact that there was strength in numbers.

No matter how big or tough one man might be, the Anju Dragons would have enough men to overpower him. The Dragons, like gangs the world over, were brave in groups but cowards when alone, and they never took their "victory stroll" in detachments of less than ten.

The Executioner had just passed the closed curtains of the House of Seoul restaurant when unseen footsteps sounded from a side street. Voices speaking a mixture of Korean and English echoed with shrill laughter through the silence.

Bolan limped on, instantly deciding on one of the several escape routes he had reconned that afternoon. As he reached the corner, he glanced to his right and saw a dozen young men wearing green silk jackets.

The laughter and chatter among them suddenly stopped.

The Executioner ignored them, stepping off the curb into the intersection. He was halfway across the street when he heard someone yell, "Hey!"

With a quick glance over his shoulder, Bolan quickened his pace to the stagger of a frightened old man. As he reached the far curb, he heard footsteps pound up behind him. A hand clutched the back of his arm and he was whirled around to face the gang.

Bolan's eyes fell on a golden dragon embroidered on the green jacket of the man who held his arm. He let his eyes travel up to the gangster's face and saw the fury in the drugged-out eyes.

The young man was in his early twenties and wore his black hair cropped into a short flattop. He dropped the Executioner's arm and spoke rapidly in Korean.

Bolan shook his head. "I don't understand," he said in a meek, rattling voice.

A wicked smile began to creep over the Dragon leader's face. "Why are you here?" he said in perfect English.

The Executioner shrugged, casually letting his fingers fall just below the duck-head grip and circle the oak cane. "Just out for a walk," he said.

"An expensive pastime," the Dragon said, and the other members of the gang laughed.

Bolan let his eyes wander quickly over the young men. Here and there he saw bulges under the green jackets. Korean martial-arts weapons. Or weapons borrowed from the Okinawan arts. He had already seen one end of a nunchaku hanging under the leader's open coat, and knew the other stick fastened to it by either a cord or chain would be down the man's sleeve, ready for a quick draw with the opposite hand.

The Executioner looked closer. Some of the bulges were smaller: guns. There would be pistols hidden on the bodies of the Dragons, as well. Contrary to what the press led the public to believe, AK-47s and Uzis were too hard to conceal to make them a weapon of choice among street gangs.

"I like your coat," the leader said. "I want it."

"It's too big for you," Bolan said, and watched the smile fade from the young man's face as the subtle insult sank in. The Executioner glanced quickly around the rest of the Dragons one last time. This was not the place to take them out. When the fighting started, and they realized they had chosen the wrong opponent, some of them could flee down the open streets. He needed them penned into an enclosed area where escape would be impossible.

And the Executioner knew just the place.

As the Dragon leader reached into his jacket for the nunchaku, Bolan stepped forward, bringing the duck-head grip straight up under the man's chin. A loud crack echoed along the deserted street and the Executioner felt bone crush beneath the brass. His left hand grasped the cane three-quarters of the way down, and as the young man's head rocked back, he drove the rubber covered tip into his groin.

The Dragon leader shrieked like a woman.

Bolan slid his right hand down the cane, brought it around like a baseball bat against the side of the leader's face and heard the jaw splinter. Drawing the cane back, he jabbed it as if it were a spear, and heard the Dragon leader's larynx crack.

The warrior took a half step to the side as a stocky Korean gangster drew a *kusarigama,* gripping the handle of the sickle in his hand and whirling the lead ball attached to it by a chain. The ball was on its way toward Bolan's face when the duck-head grip crashed into the thickset man's nose.

Bolan ducked under the twirling chain and let the ball sail over his head, then turned down the street. With most of the Dragons still in shock at the "old man's" fighting skill, the Executioner sprinted away. A second later he heard shouts of anger, and once again the Dragons' feet pounded after him.

The Executioner had a half-block lead when he turned into an alley, ducking quickly behind a Dumpster. Pressing his back against a brick wall, he looked deeper into the dark shaft between the buildings. In the dim glow of an alley light, he could see a twenty-foot fence less than ten yards away.

The first Dragon rounded the corner into the alley and flashed past the Dumpster. Bolan let him go. He counted nine more as they raced toward the fence. Gone now were the martial-arts weapons, and in their place the Executioner saw revolvers and pistols.

The man in the lead caught himself on the fence, cursed in Korean and looked quickly around as the others joined him. "Where is he!" he screamed angrily. "He could not have climbed the fence so fast!"

The voice that came from his side was not so sure. "You saw what he did to Kwang and Bong," the man gasped. "He *might* have."

Bolan stepped out from behind the trash bin and drew the sound-suppressed Beretta 93-R from under his raincoat. His thumb dropped the selector to semiauto as he lined the sights up on the nearest Dragon.

The Beretta coughed softly and the man fell to the pavement of the dirty alley.

As the other Dragons turned toward their fallen comrade, the Executioner swung the 93-R toward a gangster with a shaved head and goatee. A second near-silent 9 mm slug from the Beretta drilled through the curving tail of the gold dragon embroidered on the front of his jacket.

The man fell facedown next to his friend.

Bolan took out two more Dragons before the others pinpointed his location. He dived back behind the trash bin, a cluster of rounds piercing the thin metal. Rolling to his belly, he switched the Beretta to 3-round-burst mode and let the sights fall on a gang-banger aiming a stainless-steel revolver at the Dumpster.

The trio of 9 mm hollowpoints hit the gunner mid-chest, driving him back against the fence. He slumped to the ground.

A drug-crazed Dragon rushed forward, blindly firing a Smith & Wesson semiauto. Bolan dropped him with another burst, then swung the Beretta toward a man wearing faded blue jeans and high-topped basketball shoes.

A duo of .40-caliber rounds chipped the concrete next to the Executioner's shoulder, forcing him to roll away from the Dumpster. He came to rest on his belly again, tapping the trigger and sending three subsonic missiles into the man's sternum.

The Beretta emptied the last of its sixteen rounds into a fat Dragon firing a Glock with both hands. With the element of surprise now long gone, Bolan jammed the quiet Beretta back into shoulder leather and drew the mammoth Desert Eagle .44 Magnum from his hip.

Only two of the men who had chased him into the alley still stood as the Executioner rose to a kneeling position. The man who had questioned Bolan's ability to climb the fence fell first. As the big Magnum exploded like a nuclear bomb in the narrow confines of the alleyway, 240 grains of steel-jacketed lead blew a hole the size of a softball out his back. Blood dripped down the fence behind him as Bolan rose and pointed the Desert Eagle at the last Dragon.

The 1911 Government Model in the man's hands shook uncontrollably as he fired wildly, the rounds missing the warrior by ten feet. Bolan took his time, lining up the front blade sight between the two posts on the slide, and centering them on the man's forehead.

Behind the sight picture, he saw death in the eyes of the Dragon even before he squeezed the trigger.

Suddenly the only sounds in the alley were the mammoth Magnum echoes still bouncing off the bricks.

BOLAN RELOADED BOTH the Beretta and Desert Eagle, then hurried out of the alley, jogging back up the street. According to classified U.S. intelligence, the Dragons were more than just another of the many Oriental street gangs that had appeared in America's major cities during the past two decades. Comprised of North Korean agents masquerading as refugees, they had direct ties to Pyongyang's Communist government. Their activities in the U.S., which included not only extortion but drug smuggling, hijacking and robbery, had a twofold purpose: to create as much havoc as possible and to provide revenue for the faltering North Korean economy.

The Executioner slowed as he neared the two Dragons still on the ground at the corner. The leader—the man with the close-cropped hair—was lying on his back, as dead as a man could get. The other was also on his back, moaning as blood streamed from his swollen, broken nose. Hearing the Executioner's footsteps, he rose to a sitting position and reached under his green jacket.

A quick side-thrust kick sent new blood spurting from the man's nose. He screamed and fell back to the pavement.

Bolan dropped to one knee between the two men. He jerked a Colt Commander out of the screaming man's hand, patted him down and found no other weapons. The Executioner drove a hard right cross into the man's jaw, ending the howls of pain.

Turning to the leader, Bolan ran a hand around his waist and came up with a Rossi .44 Special. He stuck both guns in his belt as doors up and down Prince Street began to open.

The shopkeepers timidly peeked out.

A search of the Dragon leader's pockets produced a billfold, a set of keys and an opened envelope. The address on the front of the envelope matched that on the driver's license, but when he pulled out the single page, Bolan found the letter was written in Korean characters.

Hushed noises began to sound up and down the street, and Bolan turned to see that several of the shopkeepers had worked up the courage to step out onto the sidewalks. One man, small and wiry and dressed in slacks and a short Oriental-style robe, walked cautiously forward.

Bolan rose slowly so as not to frighten the man. As soon as he was within hearing distance, the warrior extended the letter. "Can you translate this?" he asked.

The lean figure reached out tentatively, taking the piece of paper as if it might bite. His aged eyes ran across it quickly, then he looked up at Bolan. "It is from the leader of the Anju Dragons in Philadelphia," he whispered, then glanced nervously around.

"What does it say?"

The old man squinted at the page. "He is thanking him—" he indicated the man on the ground at Bolan's feet "—for taking care of some business for him. That business is not named."

Bolan nodded. "Anything else?"

The old man glanced down at the letter. "They are close friends," he said. "They grew up together in Pyongyang."

The Executioner eyed the unconscious Dragon on the ground. He and other Dragons in this part of Flushing would seek revenge when they learned what had happened here tonight. This had been only one contingent of the gang operating in this neighborhood, and the shopkeepers along Prince Street would need protection.

Bolan slowly pulled the Rossi out of his belt and handed it to the little man.

The old man knew what it was for. He smiled, then bowed his thanks as several other Korean men arrived to stand next to them. Two of them stooped to retrieve the nunchaku and *kusarigama* from the sidewalk. A third stepped between Bolan and the others. "Somebody call police," he whispered. "They coming."

As if to punctuate the warning, a siren sounded in the distance.

Bolan nodded and handed the man the Colt Commander as the rest of the shopkeepers suddenly appeared in droves to surround him. Many of them chattered in Korean. Those who could extended their thanks in English. Then a teenager wearing a New York Mets baseball cap elbowed his way through the crowd.

The boy's accent betrayed New York rather than Korean birth. "The cops are here, dude," he said. "You better take off."

The pistols Bolan had given the old men and the two Oriental weapons disappeared under shirts. Somewhere on the other side of the crowd, the Executioner heard two car doors slam. He turned to look up the street.

The clothes he was wearing were more suited to Wall Street than Prince, not to mention that he was the only Caucasian in sight, so running would only draw more attention. Bolan stooped over slightly, leaning on the cane, and suddenly the elderly potential mugging victim was back.

The crowd parted as two blue-uniformed patrolmen made their way through.

Bolan turned and, with several of the Korean shopkeepers flanking his sides, shuffled off into the night.

IN THE GLOW from the streetlight outside the window, Jerry Wayne Waack inspected the Sako TRG-21's trigger group. Damn, he liked this rifle. It had served him well. And it would be a shame to say goodbye to such a friend.

But Waack didn't see any way around leaving the weapon here when he was done. Not if he wanted to get out of this deal with his ass still in one piece.

The skin along Waack's arms felt hot as he finished assembling the weapon. Even though he'd been in the shade of the thick Georgia pine much of the day before, he'd picked up too much sun and his skin had taken on a warm pink burn. He set the rifle on the table, rolled both sleeves of the plumber's coveralls to his elbow and ran his hands across his arms. That helped. At least some. He moved his hands back to the TRG's adjustable butt plate and ambidextrous pistol grip, hoisting it into the air.

Waack smiled at the rifle. The TRG-21 had originally been developed for the Finns, who wanted a long-range competition rifle that could also perform military sniper duty. Well, he couldn't speak personally about the TRG's competence as a bench-rest piece, but he knew damn well that it took out people just fine, thank you.

Waack turned in his chair and looked across the coffee table he'd pulled in front of the window. Four stories below, across the street in Central Park, he could see the wooden platform under the temporary light poles that had been set up. People had begun arriving and were being kept at a distance from the stand by ropes. The ropes were reinforced by uniformed NYPD officers and plainclothesmen whom Waack knew were both cops and private bodyguards. The bodyguards made him smile.

Politicians were taking their safety more seriously since last night.

Careful to stay far enough from the window to remain in the darkness, Waack placed the Sako on the floor next to him and unbuttoned the top two buttons of his striped coveralls. The sunburn wasn't the only problem in this condominium—the old bitch who owned the place kept it hotter than hell on the Fourth of July. And even with a temperature that had to be in the nineties, she had been wearing a shawl when she let him in earlier.

Waack shrugged in the darkness. Your blood slowed down when you got that old, he guessed.

From the kitchen, he heard the sound of pans clanking against each other. He glanced that way, remembering that the old woman had been washing dishes when he'd knocked on her door earlier, her hands and wrists covered with soapy water. Turning his attention back to the window, he pulled his collar farther away from his neck. He shouldn't complain, he supposed. The sunburn wasn't her fault, and the heat was the only thing wrong with this site.

Waack had studied the windows along the building that morning and found that this fourth-floor window on the corner afforded the best angle of trajectory. It also provided the shortest range: two hundred yards, maybe two-ten, tops.

It was time to find out for sure.

Lifting the range finder to his eyes, Waack took the reading: 203 yards from his eye to the wooden podium at the top of the stage. "Ah," he said loud enough to be heard in the kitchen. "The kid's still got it." He got no response.

Setting down the range finder, he lifted the Sako. He checked to make sure the scope was mounted securely in place, then flipped the bipod down, steadied it on the coffee table and looked though the lens. The cross hairs rested on the top of the podium for only a second before he whisked the Sako away from the window. His eyebrows lowered as he studied the faces of the cops and agents below. None of them had seen a thing.

That knowledge brought another smile to his face. Yes, this should not be a hard shot at all. He had perhaps the best rifle-scope combination known to man, and he was still the best. He had been the best sniper to operate behind enemy lines in North Korea, and he'd been the best in Vietnam before that.

Waack's stomach suddenly turned sour. Well, maybe not the best in Vietnam. There had been that other bastard, Mack Bolan. Sergeant Mercy, they had called him. They said he was the best. And he had been good—Waack knew that. But Jerry Wayne Waack had never doubted that he was better.

Waack reached into the toolbox in which he'd transported the rifle, pulled out the radio receiver and set it on the edge of the coffee table. He glanced through the window again, toward the carefully tended bushes just to the left of the stage. By now several hundred people had gathered to block his view, and an occasional glimpse of green through the throng was all he could see of the shrubs.

But seeing the shrubs didn't matter. He had thrown the pop bottle containing the transmitter into them early this morning before security had been set up. The cops and bodyguards weren't the Secret Service, by any means, but they might well have been smart enough to check the bushes since then. If they had, the bottle might have been removed.

Waack flipped the switch and smiled when he heard the voices of the men and women below. The bottle hadn't been noticed, or if it had, the men below had determined it wasn't a bomb and decided that trash collection didn't fall within their duties.

More people arrived carrying signs and banners. Among them, he saw Shim, who carried a folded newspaper that contained a backup transmitter, just in case. But now it wouldn't be necessary. The Korean didn't look toward the window—he was far too professional for that. Waack watched him disappear into the throng and felt a warm glow of friendship.

The crowd continued to grow, spreading closer to the street and farther into the park. Waack could see he'd have a three-quarter frontal shot of the podium once Reardon took his place.

Jerry Wayne Waack settled in to wait. He listened to a small brass band suddenly strike up their rendition of "You're a Grand Old Flag" as several limousines arrived on the street directly below the window. More men in dark suits and sunglasses got out, scanning the area with their hands near their open coats. A moment later Senator Patrick Reardon's balding head popped out of the middle limo. Six men crowded around him as he walked away from Waack toward the platform, waving at the crowd.

The din from the transmitter grew more excited now, with some of the people chanting "Reardon! Reardon!" Others had come to heckle the congressman. They shouted "Communist!" or "Socialist!" with a few obscenities thrown in for good measure.

Senator Patrick Reardon sat on the stage as one of the New York City councilmen introduced him. Then he finally moved under the bright lights behind the podium. Waack noticed the little black dots on top of his head where hair had been transplanted.

Without taking his eyes off the hair transplant, Waack raised the Sako. "'Take away the self-conceited and there will be elbow room in the world,'" he quoted, then paused to think. "Benjamin Whichcote, if I remember correctly."

The only response from the kitchen was the soft splash of water in the sink.

Waack found himself chuckling at Reardon's opening joke about two politicians and a goat. The senator's next witticism led into an oration favoring more gun control, and Waack's chuckle became a full-blown laugh as he made the final adjustments on the Sako. He had smuggled more guns into the U.S. than he could remember, and no laws on the books had stopped him. The fact was, no law yet had stopped smuggling of any kind, and new laws weren't about to keep weapons out of the hands of those who wanted them. He was sitting right smack-dab in the middle of New York City, the birthplace of gun control in the form of the Sullivan Law, and the only people who paid any attention to it or the new Brady Bill were the ones who didn't shoot people, anyway.

"I'm all for you, senator," Waack said aloud. "Take the guns away from those sons of bitches. Who knows, one of them might shoot back at me some-day."

The rattling of pans came from the kitchen again, then Waack heard the crash of a plate falling to the floor. He ignored the noise and set the Sako down on the coffee table.

He had to work quickly now. This close to the glass, the weapon might well be visible in the light from the street. Certainly it wouldn't be easy to identify as a rifle, but it could be spotted by some sharp cop or bodyguard as something that hadn't been there a moment before.

Waack moved his eye to the scope and let the cross hair center just below the front of Reardon's hair transplant. Reardon had launched into a tirade against what he called "international arms trading" by the time Waack got the stock positioned against his shoulder. "We cannot allow the nuclear capabilities of North Korea to continue to go unchecked!" the senator thundered from his podium. The crowd applauded. "If the UN is blocked from taking action by China, we take action ourselves!"

Yes, Senator, Waack thought, what a damn fine idea. Then he shut all sound, all hearing, all taste and all smell from his consciousness. For a brief moment, no world existed for Jerry Wayne Waack save that which consisted of his index finger, the Sako's trigger and the dots that formed the hair transplant just above the cross hair within the scope.

As always, the detonation of the round surprised Waack when it came. As it should be, he thought, to the trained and skillful shooter. By the time the thought ended, he had whisked the rifle away from the table, dropped it on the floor and was squinting through the window.

The uniformed cops below had drawn riot batons and were shoving the screaming crowd away from the stage. The bodyguards—pistols and submachine guns in their hands—had gathered protectively around the prostrate body behind the podium. They looked first one way and then another, not yet aware of the shot's origin.

Waack examined the window. The .308-caliber hole in the glass was small but would eventually be noticed. It was time to go. He stood up, turned and started toward the door.

A sudden shadow appeared from the kitchen, causing Waack to jerk the SIG-Sauer P-226 from inside his coveralls. He lowered the weapon to his side as the old woman's overfed cat stepped off the tile and onto the living room carpet. Waack saw the bubbly film of soapy dishwater on the cat's face as he squatted to scratch the animal's ear.

The cat purred softly and rubbed against his knee.

"So that was you making all that noise in the sink, was it?" Waack chuckled in a low voice. "Got thirsty, huh?" He rose. "Well, hang on. Let me get something for these arms and then I'll take care of you."

He walked down the hallway, the cat following. In the bathroom, as the cat rubbed up against his leg once more, Waack opened the medicine cabinet and dug through the bottles of prescription drugs until he came across a tube of zinc oxide. He spread the thick white cream up and down both forearms and around his neck, then stuck the tube in his pocket.

Waack cut down the hall to the kitchen, the cat trailing with a series of meows. In the refrigerator he found a quart of milk and poured some into a soup bowl. He set the bowl on the floor and listened to the lapping tongue as he searched the kitchen cabinets for cat food. Not finding any, he opened a can of tuna, dumped it onto a plate and set it next to the milk.

Jerry Wayne Waack leaned over, gave the cat a final stroke from head to tail, then walked out of the kitchen. "Got to watch those plumbers," he said, stepping over the old woman's body in the middle of the living room floor. He opened the front door, stepped out into the hall, then closed it behind him.

# CHAPTER TWO

The lights of Elizabeth, Rahway and New Brunswick flashed by as Bolan, in a rented Buick Century, rolled south into New Jersey. Night traffic had been light once he'd left New York but had picked up each time he neared one of the smaller cities.

Five miles north of Princeton the warrior rounded a curve and saw a long line of vehicles stacked up two hundred yards ahead. Beyond that he could see the flashing red lights of several New Jersey State Police cars blocking the road.

Bolan slowed, glancing across the highway to where several more of the white police cars had parked along the shoulder. Engines running, they were ready to give chase to any car that decided a U-turn was an option.

Bolan muttered under his breath. He didn't have time for delays. He had already formed a plan of attack for the Dragons in Philadelphia, but its success depended upon his arrival before the gang got any detailed accounts of what had happened in Flushing.

Pulling to a halt behind an Oldsmobile, Bolan leaned back, settling in for the wait, inching the Buick forward as the Olds moved. By the time he was six cars from the barrier, he could see the troopers in their blue shirts and dark trousers with yellow stripes. Heckler & Koch P-7 pistols hung from their belts, and rounded peaked caps sat atop their heads.

The Executioner continued to wait while four more cars passed through the stop, then watched the officers pull a drunk from his vehicle and handcuff him. The Oldsmobile pulled up to the men with the H&Ks, and a tall trooper with graying hair approached the driver's window.

As the Olds pulled away, Bolan reached into the pocket of his sport coat, producing a California driver's license bearing his picture. He lifted his foot off the brake, let the Buick roll forward, then stopped next to the tall trooper.

"License, registration and proof of insurance, please," the man in blue said in a formal tone, leaning into the window. His name tag read Hall and the stripes on his sleeves told the Executioner he was a sergeant.

Bolan handed the driver's license through the window and watched Hall move his eyes from the face behind the wheel to the picture. The sergeant's hand dropped closer to the P-7 on his hip as Bolan leaned toward the glove compartment. Standard procedure. Hall had no idea whether a vehicle registration and insurance papers, or a gun, were about to emerge from the dash.

Bolan flipped the catch and the glove compartment swung open. He looked inside to find an empty compartment.

The Executioner cursed softly under his breath, angry at both the rental agency for not keeping the papers where they should have been, and at himself for not checking. He sat up straight in his seat and turned toward the window. "This is a rental," he said. "And the papers aren't here."

"Step out of the car please, Mr. Belasko," Sergeant Hall said, using the name he'd seen on the driver's license. "And keep your hands in plain sight." He stood back from the door, and now his hand slid to the grip of the P-7.

Bolan reached through the window and opened the door from the outside, keeping his other hand visible on the frame. As he exited the Buick a gust of wind caught the tail of his jacket, blowing it back over the Desert Eagle.

A split second later Hall's 9 mm pistol was out of the holster and aimed at Bolan's heart. Two seconds after that, three more H&Ks and two Remington 870 shotguns had joined the party.

Bolan heard the dull clink as the slides on the shotguns jacked 12-gauge shells into the chambers. He held his hands up and to the sides. "Relax, guys," he said. "I'm on your side."

Hall stepped in cautiously. "We'll see," he said. He reached in and jerked the Desert Eagle from Bolan's hip, then stepped back again, glancing down at the huge pistol. "I don't know any agency—federal, state, county or city—that issues cannons like this," he said.

By now another trooper had patted Bolan down and come up with the Beretta 93-R. Hall glanced at it, handed the Desert Eagle to a comrade and holstered his own weapon. He stepped in quickly, spun the Executioner around and locked a set of cuffs over Bolan's wrists. "Machine pistol, complete with silencer," he said. "If you're on our side, I'm the Pope."

Bolan shook his head. "Look in my right shirt pocket," he said.

Hall hesitated, then stepped in again, pulling out the thin leather-bound U.S. Department of Justice credentials. He stepped to the side, frowning, still unconvinced. Finally turning to a short trooper holding one of the shotguns, he said. "Put him in the back of one of the cars. I'll check it out." He paused. "DeSalvo, take over the checkpoint."

Two of the men in blue moved in, taking Bolan by the arms, leading him to a police car and shoving him into the back. Two troopers sandwiched him in the middle while Hall got behind the wheel and jerked the radio mike from the mount on the dashboard.

The sergeant keyed the mike. "John 43, headquarters," he said.

"Go ahead," replied a gravelly male voice.

"Affirmative, headquarters," Hall said. "I need a confirmation of credentials, U.S. Department of Justice."

The voice chuckled over the airwaves. "There's a night number, but it'll be morning before they can confirm, I imagine."

Hall turned in his seat. "You heard the man. Looks like you'll be spending the night with us." He turned to the trooper next to Bolan. "Take him on in."

Bolan blew air between his clenched teeth as the trooper opened the door. "Wait a minute," he said, and the trooper halted, half out of the car. "I can give you a home number to call."

Hall shook his head. "Won't fly," he said. "You could give us Fidel Castro's number, for all we'd know, and by the looks of those guns, that might just be whose it was." He turned back around and started to get out.

Bolan felt himself getting irritated and had to remind himself that these men were just doing their jobs. "It's the home number of the Justice Department's Director of Sensitive Operations," he said. "Harold Brognola."

Hall turned back suddenly. "Hal Brognola?" he said. "I know him. At least I met him at a training seminar a few months ago." He stared at Bolan, then said, "Okay, who knows. Maybe you are who you say you are. Give me the number. We'll see what Brognola has to say."

Bolan rattled off Brognola's home number and Hall relayed it to headquarters.

All four men sat back to wait, the troopers' eyes still glued to the Executioner. Bolan knew what they were thinking. Hal Brognola was something of a public figure, and it wouldn't take too much work on the part of a smart con to have someone waiting at a phone to play his part.

As they waited, Bolan watched through the window as the officers manning the roadblock administered another test for intoxication, then handcuffed a woman with high-piled bleach blond hair, tight blue jeans and cowboy boots. He turned to Hall. "This roadblock. Just a random check?"

Hall turned and rested his arm over the seat. "You didn't hear about what happened in Central Park?" His attitude was slightly less formal now that Brognola's name had entered the picture, but Bolan could tell he was still skeptical about his credentials.

Bolan shook his head. "I've been busy this evening. Haven't listened to the news."

"Senator Patrick Reardon got shot," Hall said. "Sniper."

The Executioner's eyebrows lowered in concentration. Bill Thomlinson, a senator from West Virginia, had fallen victim to a car bombing the night before. There had to be a connection. Reardon's assassination explained the roadblock and the fact that his nonissue guns had created such excitement. While hardly a sniper's weapon, the Beretta did appear to be more the weapon of a killer than a cop. And Hall was right—no law-enforcement officers carried the Desert Eagle. The big .44 Magnum was primarily a hunting pistol and had too much recoil in combat situations for most men.

The radio squealed suddenly and the same rocky voice said, "Headquarters, John 43." There was a short pause, then, "I've got Mr. Brognola on the line."

Hall grabbed the mike. "Patch him through."

The trooper evidently recognized the voice. "Mr. Brognola, Sergeant Dennis Hall. Met you in Trenton last year at your undercover seminar." Brognola didn't respond, so Hall got back to business. "I've got a guy here who claims to be one of yours," Hall said. "Belasko, Mike Belasko. Big guy, dark hair. Carrying some pretty strange weaponry I know Justice doesn't issue."

Brognola cleared his throat. When he spoke again all trace of drowsiness was gone, and his tone had changed to one of forced amiability. "You familiar with my title, Sergeant Hall?" he asked.

"I remember, sir. You're the Director of Sensitive Operations."

"Right," Brognola said, his tone still cheery. "Now, don't you suppose the word *sensitive* might just imply that things are done a little bit differently in our section?"

"Well, sure—"

"And wouldn't it follow then, Sergeant, that the equipment we employ might also be unusual?"

"Yes sir," Hall said quickly. "Just wanted to make sure." He held Bolan's Justice Department ID card under the dome light. "Want me to read you Belasko's commission number?" he asked.

"No," Brognola said, and now his voice had grown curt. "I don't doubt it's him. He's the only agent I've got careless enough to get stopped by you. Put him on the line."

Hall shrugged and stretched the cord back over the seat.

Bolan took the mike and thumbed the red button on the side. "Go ahead, sir."

"Hello, *Mike*," Brognola said irritably. "Is everything straightened out now or should I put the coffee on and plan on staying up the rest of the night?"

Brognola was playing his part well, and Bolan had to subdue a chuckle. He glanced at Hall.

Hall shrugged. "You're free to go. Brognola's word is good enough for me."

"I think we're okay," the Executioner said into the mike, then handed it back to the sergeant.

"Okay, Mr. Brognola. Thanks for your help," Hall said.

"Tell Belasko to report directly to my office at 0800 tomorrow," Brognola ordered. "And good night."

Bolan repressed a grin. He had awakened Hal Brognola in the middle of the night too many times over the years to keep count, and the Justice man had never objected; it was part of his job, and Brognola took it in stride. His irritation tonight was just another part of the act to convince the state police that Bolan was actually a Justice Department agent.

The Executioner looked up at Hall, who was handing the Beretta and Desert Eagle over the seat. "You're free to go," the sergeant said. "Sorry for the inconvenience." He grinned. "And I'm sorry for the ass chewing you're gonna get tomorrow morning."

Bolan nodded. "It'll be bad, Sergeant Hall," he said, stuffing his guns back under his coat and getting out of the car. "But somehow I'll live through it."

TRAFFIC PICKED UP AGAIN on Highway 611 as Bolan spotted the lights of Greater Philadelphia ahead. Entering from the north, he passed through Wakefield, Stenton, Huntington and Fern Parks, then entered the city proper. Little activity could be seen around Temple University as he passed, and even less was taking place at the Philadelphia Museum of Art.

The City of Brotherly Love was asleep at this early-morning hour.

At least most of it.

Here and there as Bolan neared the center of one of America's oldest cities, he saw the street people. Some had made camp under overpasses. Others walked aimlessly down the access roads, waiting until daylight to close their eyes, knowing that public slumber in the darkness meant the chance of getting their throats cut for the meager possessions they carried in beaten suitcases, shopping carts and paper sacks.

Bolan saw an occasional police car as he drove through the darkness, but they were few and far between. It was the same in most big cities across the nation. Budget problems had resulted in forced reductions and sent hundreds of experienced officers to the end of the employment line. Low entry salaries meant many young men and women who would have considered law enforcement now looked elsewhere for careers.

The Executioner felt a mixture of melancholy and anger as he passed through the semisleeping city.

He knew that the system no longer took care of the men and women in blue, on the front lines of the new Civil War. Many retired early or took other employment. Police forces across the nation were losing the best and the brightest potential recruits. And the young, intelligent, talented men and women who could have represented the future of law enforcement were never fitted for a blue uniform.

Bolan saw the gas-station sign off the next exit and pulled onto the ramp, halting at the stop sign before circling under the highway. He pulled into the lot, seeing a Chevy van at one of the pump stations and pulling up to the other. Sticking the unleaded nozzle into the gas tank, he flipped on the automatic cutoff switch as three teenaged men came out of the office-convenience store.

Bolan kept the young men under observation as he walked to the phone booth at the corner of the lot. Thirteen, fourteen years old at the most, they wore no gang colors but had all the other trappings. Their baseball caps were worn backward or at angles, their ill-fitting shorts hung below the knee, their leather boots were ankle high and their plaid flannel shirts were fastened at the collar but unbuttoned the rest of the way down.

The Executioner shook his head. These boys were no gangsters—at least not yet. They were "wannabes" who had somehow gotten off track, choosing to follow the wrong role models.

Bolan watched them move to the van. The tall, slender black kid who walked with the easy poise of a point guard was at least two years shy of a driver's license, but he slid behind the wheel of the van nonetheless. The door still open, he and his friends spoke in hushed tones, occasionally glancing toward the Buick, then to the Executioner.

Bolan kept one eye glued their way as he pulled the envelope he'd taken off the body of the Dragon leader from his pocket and read the name again: Choi Bong. Pulling the letter from the envelope, Bolan set it on the shelf under the phone, then searched his pocket for a quarter.

The old man who had translated the letter for Bolan had accompanied him out of the Flushing area to an all-night Chinese diner. Bolan had ordered dinner for them both, and watched the elderly gentleman down egg rolls with one hand while he deciphered the Korean writing in more detail with the pencil in his other.

It was the English version of the letter that Bolan looked at now. The page had been signed by one Kim Hyuk, and a phone number was printed below the name.

The three boys at the van eyed the warrior as he dropped the quarter into the slot and tapped in the number. He turned to watch his car as the line connected and rang.

The phone was picked up on the third ring. "Kim."

There was loud music, laughter and Korean chatter in the background. Holding the phone to the side, Bolan cleared his throat. Earlier he had needed to look old. Now he planned to sound young. And at least slightly frightened. "Kim Hyuk?" he asked.

He got a reply he couldn't understand.

"I don't speak Korean," Bolan asked.

"I then talk you language," the voice said in broken English. "This Kim Hyuk. Who you and what you want?"

"I'm . . . I'm a friend."

"Round eyes?"

"Round as a wheel," Bolan said, laughing softly.

"Then you not friend. Acquaintance, maybe. Maybe business associate. No friend."

Bolan saw the tall kid behind the wheel of the van pointing at the Buick. He and the white boy seemed to be arguing.

"Okay, make it a business associate, then," the Executioner told Kim. "I've got something for you." He waited, but got no answer. "You heard what happened to Choi Bong and his boys this evening?"

"I get phone call." Kim paused. He must have motioned to the people in the background because the music and other noise suddenly went dead. When he returned to the line, he said, "You kill Bong?"

"No, no...of course not," Bolan said, keeping the apprehension in his voice. "I didn't have anything to do with it. In fact it screwed up a deal I had going down with Bong." He paused. "Look, I didn't kill him, but I was there. I saw who did."

"Who?" Kim demanded. "You tell me now."

In the parking lot, Bolan watched as the tall black kid stepped down from behind the wheel of the van, grinned toward the phone booth with nervous bravado, then started toward the Buick.

The other two wannabes turned to Bolan and flashed gang signs.

"Not so fast," Bolan told Kim. "I'm sitting on a load of crank that Choi was supposed to take off my hands. I don't have a buyer. You interested?"

"I interested in who kill Choi Bong."

"Buy the crank from me, at the same price I was offering it to Choi, and that information comes free."

The line went silent for a moment, and Bolan took advantage of the break to open the phone-booth door. The tall boy had pulled the nozzle from the Buick's gas tank and was replacing it in the pump.

On the phone line, the Executioner heard voices whispering in Korean. Then Kim came back on. "What your name?"

"Belasko will do," the Executioner said.

"Okay, Belasko. We deal. You in town here?"

"I'm here," Bolan said. "Tell me how to get to your place."

More whispering. "No. We meet you somewhere."

Bolan chuckled silently. He had expected this. For all Kim Hyuk knew, the man he was talking to could be a Philadelphia PD narc or a member of a rival gang trying to locate the Dragons' base. "Okay," he said. "Where?"

Across the lot, the tall kid now opened the Buick's driver's door and looked in, then turned to his friends and shook his head. Bolan watched them huddle together again as Kim gave him directions to a thickly wooded park in a residential area just south of Connie Mack Stadium. "You driving car?" the Dragon leader asked.

Bolan shook his head in disbelief at the minidrama unfolding on the lot in front of him. Then, turning his attention back to the phone, he said, "I didn't walk from New York."

"You funny guy," Kim said. "Some houses across the street from park. You leave car there. Walk down first trail you see in trees. You understand?"

The tall boy turned toward the phone booth, took a deep breath, then started forward, the other two at his heels. "I understand," Bolan told Kim. "What do I do after I'm on the trail?"

"You walk. We find you. You come alone and bring crank. No guns or we shoot."

Bolan couldn't suppress another short laugh. Alone and unarmed, and bring the speed. Under those conditions he might as well just give them directions to the drugs, shoot himself in the head and not waste the time and energy it took to get to the park. "How do I know I can trust you?" he asked, forcing himself to sound nervous.

"You trust me," Kim said. "It go fine. We deal again. Okay?"

Bolan paused, then said, "Well . . . okay. When?"

"One hour," Kim said. "We talk then."

The Executioner hung up as the three boys stopped in front of the phone booth.

"Give us your car keys," the tall boy said, his voice unnaturally low.

Bolan smiled. "Why do you want my keys?"

"So we can take your car, dude," the white kid said. He stuck his chest out, bouncing lightly up and down on the balls of his feet.

Bolan shook his head. "Sorry, boys," he said. "I'm going to need the car tonight."

The white boy quit bouncing, reached under his flannel shirt and produced a sharpened screwdriver. A length of steel pipe, the end wrapped in black electrician's tape, appeared in the hand of the tall kid. A click echoed into the phone booth as the third boy opened a lock-blade folding knife.

"Give us the keys, asshole," the tall kid said. "You don't, we gonna fuck you up good."

"Well," Bolan said, patting the side pockets of his jacket, "looks like I don't have much choice." His hands went to his pants pocket. "Now where'd I put them?" He let his other hand disappear under his coat. "Nope, I guess they're lost." The hand reappeared holding the Desert Eagle. "But since I've lost the keys, how about this instead?" He aimed the .44 Magnum just above the nose of the tall, slender kid.

Three sets of eyes suddenly grew wide and round.

"Tell you what," Bolan said. "Instead of me giving you my keys, why don't you all be good little boys and give me your toys?" He held out his other hand, palm up.

The knife came first, then the pipe. Then the white kid set his screwdriver gently down in Bolan's palm.

Bolan stared at each boy in turn, watching them shrink visibly before his eyes. "You're trying to play in a league you aren't ready for yet," he said in a low, menacing voice. "And besides that, you're on the wrong team." He looked into the terrified eyes.

These kids weren't Dragons or even Crips or Bloods. They were little boys trying to grow up too fast, too tough, and going about it all wrong. Maybe they'd realize how close they'd come to death tonight, maybe they wouldn't. Maybe there was still hope for them, or maybe it was already too late. The Executioner didn't know. But saving them from the future they were prescribing for themselves was worth a try.

"Go home," Bolan said. "It's way past your bedtime."

The white kid stared at the mammoth hole at the end of the Desert Eagle. "Yes, sir," he said.

The other two kids nodded, their eyes also glued to the weapon. They turned and started toward the van.

"Hey," Bolan said.

All three of the wannabes turned around.

"That van belong to you?" the Executioner asked.

They shook their heads.

"Then leave it."

The kids cut sideways across the lot and disappeared onto the dark streets of Philadelphia.

The Executioner paid for his gas, revved the Buick, and disappeared into the night.

THE TALL LIGHTED TOWERS of the radio station had been visible for several miles when Bolan cut the Buick's headlights and pulled into the parking lot. A half dozen vehicles—belonging to the station's nighttime skeleton crew, he assumed—had been parked against the building. The warrior pulled in next to them, got out and closed the door.

Bolan walked quietly behind the building, stopping to glance up at the quarter-moon. Visibility would be mediocre, at best. But that could possibly work to his advantage.

Seeing no curious eyes behind the radio station, Bolan pulled a small metal tin of camouflage makeup from the pocket of his raincoat. A moment later his face and hands had been blackened. With a final glance around, he dropped the tin back into the coat and broke into a jog across the grass.

A half mile to the east, the Executioner could see a cemetery. Beyond that, a brightly lit sign announced the Trinity Christian Church Family Life Center. A large metal building that likely housed a gym and rec facilities, it sat at the end of a long concrete drive a hundred yards off the street. A lone car was parked just behind the building.

Beyond that stood the wooded area to which Kim had directed him.

The Executioner shrugged out of the raincoat as he ran, revealing his skintight blacksuit. Across his back he wore a black leather shoulder rig that held the sound-suppressed Beretta 93-R under his left arm, with a magazine carrier and sheathed Tanto under his right. The big Desert Eagle stayed in place as he ran, secured in the black thigh-drop holster that fell from the ballistic nylon belt around his waist. Assorted other equipment was hidden in the pouches on the belt and various pockets of the blacksuit.

Bolan reached the edge of the radio-station lot and leaped the short fence that separated it from the cemetery. He sprinted past a tall marble marker, dropping to concealment behind a winged angel cradling a baby in her arms. Looking out past the marble and granite gravestones ahead, he picked out a zigzag route that would keep him hidden during his run toward the Family Life Center.

The man in black rose swiftly, racing through the dark night, dodging the markers as he went. He took refuge again, this time behind a small mausoleum, stopping to catch his breath and search for any changes in the surroundings. Finally reaching the other side of the cemetery, he dropped to a squat behind a red granite stone and drew a deep breath.

Rising once more, the Executioner stepped out from the marker, took a step, then dove over the fence onto the grounds of the Family Life Center. He hit the grass on his shoulder, rolled to a halt on his belly, then stopped. From here he could see the woods beyond the metal building. Just outside the thick trees, on the side nearest the street, a deep gully had been eroded by poor flood control.

At least fifty yards of open space separated him from the Life Center. After that he would have to cross another expanse of open land beyond the ribbed metal walls.

Pulling himself by his elbows, the warrior started forward, belly-crawling quickly across the grass and then the driveway to the Life Center. He rose to his feet and sprinted the last few yards to the building, then pressed his back against the cool corrugated steel as he drew the Beretta from under his arm.

Far away on the street, he heard a car putter by. The only other sound was the howling of a dog at a nearby house.

The Executioner walked silently to the front of the building. Peering around the corner toward the street, he saw several swing sets and a slide. A dark figure sat on the concrete bench of a picnic table under a small open pavilion. The man faced the houses on the other side of the street, the amber glow of a cigarette moving back and forth to his mouth.

A sentry. Kim expected him to park his car across the street and enter the trees on the trail.

Kim had a big surprise waiting for him.

Bolan ducked back behind the building, then moved swiftly toward the other end. He passed a glass door and glanced in to see billiard and Ping-Pong tables, and through an inner door beyond, the dark silhouette of a net hanging from a basketball goal. Reaching the corner, he saw that the car parked behind the building was a two-door Chevy Lumina. Bolan ducked low and hurried to the window. The vehicle had been deserted.

On his belly again, the Executioner crawled across the last few yards to the woods. Hard laborious breathing came from the trees as he neared. Rising to a squat, he moved quickly into the foliage and took refuge behind a thick pine. A quick glance around the edge revealed a small clearing.

A man sat on a large rock in the middle of the clearing, facing in the opposite direction. Bolan frowned.

The man wore a gray business suit. The bald patch in the back of his head told the Executioner the man was middle-aged.

He was no Anju Dragon. So what was he doing out here in the middle of the night?

Drawing the Beretta again, Bolan moved swiftly out into the clearing. His left hand slipped around the balding head to cover the man's mouth.

A stifled scream pressed against the Executioner's fingers as he took the man neatly to the ground, rolling him over and climbing on top. He kept his hand over the man's mouth as a pint bottle of vodka tumbled to the ground.

The man's fluid-filled eyes looked up into the warrior's. Bolan leaned close, whispering into his ear. "I'm going to take my hand away. Don't scream, don't yell. Answer my questions in a whisper." He pressed the Beretta's sound suppressor into the man's forehead. "Do you understand?"

The man's head bobbed up and down.

Bolan took his hand away. "Quietly now," he whispered. "What are you doing here?"

"Jus'...havin' a drink," the man slurred.

"Why here?"

"My wife," the man said, barely loud enough to hear. "Shend me back to A.A."

Bolan nodded to himself. The car behind the Life Center must belong to this man. He had snuck off to get away from his wife and get crocked.

Deeper in the trees, Bolan heard a muffled voice. He glanced up. The Dragons were close. He looked back down to the drunk beneath him. He had to do something with the man or he stood a good chance of taking a stray bullet.

There was only one answer.

Bolan transferred the Beretta to his left hand, raised his right and brought his fist down hard against the drunk's jaw.

The Executioner rose. The drunk would have quite a headache tomorrow, but he'd have had one, anyway. And a headache was preferable to a bullet.

Bolan crept softly over the bed of pine needles that covered the ground, moving through the trees toward the noises he had heard. When he spotted a walking trail, he stayed back in the foliage, paralleling it as other voices joined the first. He heard quiet laughter as the voices grew louder, then stopped when he saw the glow of another cigarette through the leaves and branches.

The distinct odor of marijuana smoke drifted into the Executioner's nostrils as he dropped to one knee, letting his eyes focus on the area around the burning ash. In the center of a small clearing, he saw a dozen bodies sitting in a circle around the charred remains of a camp fire. Empty quart bottles of malt liquor and other trash littered the ground. The amber end of a hand-rolled joint passed from hand to hand, each of the Dragons drawing smoke deep into his lungs as Bolan crept closer.

The Executioner stopped again ten feet from the break in the trees. His eyes fell on a dark figure with the sleeves of his shirt rolled high over his elbow. The Dragon's belt had been cinched around his arm, and the point of a hypodermic needle was penetrating his flesh.

The voices were more distinct now, but they spoke in Korean. As his eyes dilated to the low light even further, Bolan saw two other figures. A boy who looked to be in his late teens lay on his side in the middle of the circle of Dragons. His hands had been tied behind his back. He didn't move.

Next to him, also on her side, lay a female shape. The buttons had been ripped from the girl's shirt. The tails of the torn blouse were pulled back over her ribs, and her white bra reflected the soft moonlight dripping through the trees.

The Executioner felt his fist tighten around the Beretta as one of the Dragons moved toward her, running his hand across her exposed ribs. The girl shrieked but the gang-banger's free hand stifled the noise. His hand moved from the girl's ribs to fumble with the clasp at the front of her bra.

From the side of the circle, the Executioner heard several harsh words barked in Korean. He recognized the voice. Kim. Turning, Bolan saw a thick-shouldered man wearing a white T-shirt. The sleeves had been ripped high to expose powerful barbell-built biceps.

The Dragon fumbling with the girl's bra heard the words, as well. He let her go and moved back.

Bolan didn't have to speak Korean to understand what was transpiring. The Dragons had stumbled across these teenage lovers upon arriving at the woods to meet Bolan. They were anxious to have their fun with the girl, and by the looks of her blouse they had already started before Kim ordered them to wait until after the meeting with "Belasko."

The Executioner fought back the anger that threatened to alter his judgment. This girl he saw before him would not be raped. At least not tonight, with him there. But how many other young girls had the Dragons molested in the past? How many would they violate in the future?

Bolan answered his own questions as quickly as he asked them. He didn't know about the past, and could do nothing about it if he did. But the future of these modern-day Neanderthals was in his hands, and he vowed they had already performed their last outrage.

The Executioner flipped the Beretta from 3-round burst to semiauto, raised it to the end of his outstretched arms and squeezed the trigger. A 9 mm subsonic hollowpoint shot from the chamber.

The man who had tried to unfasten the girl's bra had been sitting cross-legged. Now he lay on his back.

A few muffled snorts came from around the circle of men. One of them held up a half-empty quart of malt liquor, pointed to the Dragon who'd just taken the bullet and laughed out loud, thinking the would-be rapist had passed out.

Bolan shot him next.

The voices grew more alarmed as this man fell face forward and the Dragons sensed something was wrong. But in their foggy drug-and-alcohol-infested brains, exactly what that something was hadn't yet congealed. The Executioner swept the Beretta across the circle to Kim, letting the front sight fall on the side of the leader's head. The trigger moved back once more.

But as it did, the man sitting next to Kim started to stand up. The bullet meant for the Dragon leader's head caught him in the shoulder. He screamed, and sat back down.

The reality that they were under fire finally sank in, and Philadelphia's Anju Dragons drew guns and other weapons as they scrambled for cover.

Bolan flipped the Beretta back to 3-round burst and caught one of the shadowy forms as it bolted for the trees. Dead before he hit the ground, the gangbanger's trigger finger froze on an unseen gun, and a lone round shot off harmlessly through the trees. The shadow fell over a pile of dried sticks, sending sharp crunching sounds echoing through the forest.

The Executioner stepped from the trees, swinging the Beretta to his right, taking out another fleeing shadow. A tall, skinny Dragon ran headfirst into the trunk of an elm. A pistol fell from his hand as he bounced backward in time to take three 9 mm slugs in the neck. He fell forward into the tree, rolled to the side, then toppled out of sight in the grass.

In the corner of his eye, the Executioner saw the stocky specter he knew had to be Kim pull a large revolver from under his torn T-shirt. Twisting away from the circle, the Dragon leader took off through the trees.

Bolan used the Beretta as a club, swiping the suppressor across the face of a Dragon who charged foolishly forward with a knife, then put three rounds into the man's chest. Raising the 93-R, the Executioner took out three more gang-bangers with as many taps of the trigger, then holstered the near-empty Beretta and raced after Kim.

Bolan drew the Desert Eagle as he ran, sidestepping the tree trunks and leaping over rocks and rain fissures carved into the forest floor. Kim was no longer in sight, so the Executioner tracked by sound, timing his own footsteps between those of the thunderous stomps that were hurrying in the direction of the street.

The Executioner ran on, conscious of the fact that the Dragon leader might decide at any moment to stop, take cover and ambush him. But he had no choice. He had to press on. To hold back now would mean losing Kim—and the only link he had to further Dragon operations.

A high-pitched scream suddenly split through the woods ahead. Bolan quickened his pace, anxious to take advantage of whatever unforeseen obstacle Kim had encountered. Lights from the street appeared as he neared the edge of the trees. He raced into them and suddenly his feet were kicking thin air as if swimming.

The Executioner reached back over his shoulder, twisting, trying vainly to catch a limb of the tree he'd just passed. At the same time he remembered the gully on the street side of the trees, which he had spotted from the Family Life Center.

As he fell through the night, Bolan turned and saw Kim on his back at the bottom of the ravine. Preparing to hit and roll, the Executioner silently prayed that no sharp tree stumps or other impediments lay directly below him.

Bolan hit the ground with his feet and knees together, executing a modification of the basic parachute landing fall. The balls of his feet touched the ground first. He rolled to the side of his right calf, then to his thigh, then to the side of his back, thus distributing the impact evenly throughout his body. His nylon combat boots rolled up into the air, then back down again.

The Executioner popped back to his feet. Low, painful moans came from the man on the ground. The Desert Eagle leading the way, the Executioner walked to Kim's side. The Dragon leader's hands were clasped around his left foot, the knee pulled tightly against his chest.

A series of exposed tree roots shot from the damp earth next to Kim. He had hit them on his descent, and had either sprained or broken his ankle.

The Executioner stooped, lifting the Smith & Wesson Model 29 from the dirt next to the ailing gangster and shoving it into his belt. "Can you walk?" he asked.

Kim shook his head. Tears poured down the tough guy's cheeks.

"Let's see for sure," Bolan said. He reached down, grabbed the man's arm and jerked him to his feet.

Kim screamed in agony. As soon as Bolan released him he fell back to the ground.

"Good," the Executioner said. "It'll save me tying you up. I'll be right back—so don't go away."

Turning, the Executioner pulled himself up out of the deep ravine and hurried back through the woods to where the teenagers still lay tied on the ground amid the littered Dragon bodies. He dropped to one knee as he unsheathed the Tanto, for the first time getting a good look at the two. The girl was pretty, with fiery red hair and freckles. The boy had long blond hair and a light complexion. Neither of them could have been over twenty.

Bolan sliced through the coarse ropes that had bound them, then helped the girl to her feet.

"Thank you!" she cried, embracing and pressing her sobbing cheek against his chest. "They were going to—" The girl stopped in midsentence, pulling back to arm's length and running her eyes up and down Bolan's blacksuit. "Are you a . . . policeman?" she asked.

Bolan smiled. "Next best thing," he said.

The boy rose to his feet and looked up at the warrior as he rubbed his wrists. "Whoever you are . . . thanks."

Bolan nodded. "How old are you?" he asked.

"Nineteen," the boy said.

"Eighteen," said the girl.

"Then you're old enough to know better than to come out here at night."

Both teenagers looked down at the ground.

"You have a car?"

The boy nodded. "It's parked behind the Life Center."

The Executioner nodded. He had figured the car belonged to the drunk, but now it looked as if the man sleeping it off in the woods had probably walked over from the housing area.

Bolan looked the teenagers in the eye. "You're the second group of kids I've come across tonight who should be home and in bed. I'm going to tell you the same thing I told them. *Go home.*"

Bolan took them each by the arm, escorted them to their car and watched them drive away. Hurrying back to the gully, he found Kim still moaning in the same position as before.

"You . . . take me doctor?" the Korean whimpered.

"Maybe," the Executioner said, hauling the Dragon leader to his feet again. "That is if you're a good boy. But first I want to go say hello to some more of your friends."

## CHAPTER THREE

The Dragon's lair lay less than three blocks away.

By the time Bolan had gotten Kim into the Buick and driven to the site, the injured gang leader's wimpish moans had settled down to a tolerable level. The Executioner parked three houses down and scanned the neighborhood with battle-trained eyes. What he saw was a community of near identical, pre-World War II duplexes constructed of red and gray stones that had been bonded with cement. Broken windows had been mended with plywood scraps or cardboard. Wheel-less cars rusted away atop concrete blocks. Worn out washing machines and other appliances took up space on porches, and mangled tricycles and bicycles littered front yards.

Bolan's eyes finally settled on Kim's house up the street. Two vehicles—a Jeep and a late-model BMW—stood in the gravel driveway. "You guys have both sides of the duplex?" he asked Kim.

"Yes."

"How many men inside each one?"

In his peripheral vision, the Executioner saw Kim shrug. "I don't know."

Bolan turned to face him. Kim turned away.

"Look at me," the Executioner ordered.

Kim turned and fixed his eyes on the steering wheel.

"No," Bolan said. "I said look at *me*."

The Dragon leader's eyes rose to meet those of the Executioner.

Bolan met his stare. "Would you like me to drag you out of this car and use that ankle as a trampoline?" he asked.

Kim's face paled. "You . . . would do that?"

The Executioner's eyes didn't waver. "Lie to me again and watch. Now I'll ask you one more time. How many men in each side of the duplex."

Kim's hands trembled in his lap. "Two on left side," he said. "Right . . . I not know. I promise. Not know."

Bolan turned back to the stone houses. "Is there an inside door from one side to the other?"

Kim shook his head. "No. Separate units."

Bolan studied the house. It had been built long before cities had adopted the stringent building codes they had today. The builder would have been under no obligation to construct a concrete fire wall to separate the two sides of the duplex, which meant the barrier probably consisted of nothing more than wallboard or perhaps plaster and lath.

Not much soundproofing. He would have to move from one side to the other *fast*.

"Let's go," the Executioner said. He opened the door, walked around the Buick and grabbed Kim's arm as the gang leader got out. Pushing the limping Dragon ahead of him with his left arm, he drew the Beretta with his right.

The Executioner stopped Kim in front of the left-hand door as soon as they'd mounted the two steps to the porch. He took up a position just to the side, the

Beretta ready in front of him. He had shoved a fresh magazine into the weapon on the drive over, and now flipped the selector to semiauto.

Rap music, the lyrics in Korean, blared from the door on the other side of the porch, but the unit they were about to enter was silent. Bolan glanced to the window. Faint light seeped around the edges of the closed shade, and on the dirty brown carpet he could see a smashed cigarette butt.

Bolan turned back to Kim and nodded. The Dragon leader reached out, twisting the knob.

The Executioner gave Kim a one-step lead, then ducked around the corner. He caught a quick flash of two men lying on the tattered carpet. The one on the right held a crack pipe to his lips.

The other man saw the figure in black behind his leader and rolled across the floor toward an AK-47 propped against the wall.

Bolan's near-silent 9 mm hollowpoint split the man's spine midway up his back as he rolled toward the weapon. Elbowing Kim out of the way, the Executioner turned the gun toward the man with the pipe as he jerked a small automatic pistol from his belt.

Two rounds hammered from the Beretta, the first catching the crack-stoned Dragon in the chin and snapping his head back. The second drilled through his Adam's apple, and he fell to his back on the floor.

The living room contained two rear doors, and Bolan dropped into a combat crouch, aiming the Beretta at a point on the wall halfway in between. He waited several seconds, but meeting no resistance, he reached down and pulled Kim to his feet. Grabbing the back of the gang-banger's torn T-shirt, the Executioner steered the man in front of him toward the side door.

Bolan shoved Kim around the corner, then peered around the door frame into a kitchen. Empty. His hand still full of dirty T-shirt, he jerked the Dragon leader back out of the room and directed him toward the other door.

This doorway led to a short hallway. Bolan saw a tattered tapestry hanging on the wall that joined the duplexes. The scene depicted an Arab on a horse, riding away with a captured woman in a veil and harem pants. Opposite the tapestry was a closed door.

Bolan pushed Kim to the door. "Open it," he whispered.

"It is just—" Kim whispered back.

"Open it." The Executioner jammed the Beretta into his ear.

Kim did as he was told, revealing the green metal box around a heating unit.

Bolan shoved the man down the hall, checking two small bedrooms, the bath that separated them and the closets.

Kim had told the truth. Only two men were on this side of the duplex. The Executioner twirled the Dragon leader around and pointed him back toward the living room. They had drawn abreast of the heating closet when the Executioner saw the tapestry move.

The barrel of a rifle poked into the hallway.

The Executioner raised the Beretta. Aiming an inch above the front sight of the rifle barrel, he squeezed the trigger and the 93-R coughed. The rifle barrel jerked to the side, moving the tapestry further.

Behind it, Bolan saw the ragged hole chopped out of the wall. Standing in the middle of it was a short, wiry Oriental with shoulder-length black hair. Blood poured from a hole in his lower chest. As he stared at the Executioner, the Winchester Trapper 30-30 in his hand finally exploded, the round flying to Bolan's side.

The Executioner heard Kim grunt as he tapped the Beretta's trigger again, sending another round into the man's face. The Dragon took two steps back and slid to the floor.

The tapestry fell closed again.

Bolan glanced down to his side and saw Kim's dead eyes staring blindly at the ceiling. Behind the tapestry, he heard frantic movement. Voices chattered madly in Korean. The Beretta still aimed at the tapestry, he moved quickly into the living room and grabbed the AK-47 leaning against the wall.

Bolan checked the magazine. Full. He worked the bolt, chambering a round, then holstered the Beretta and turned the rifle toward the tapestry.

A full-auto burst of 7.62 mm rounds blew through the Arab and the woman wearing the veil. The tapestry fluttered, then swung into the ragged doorway as screams sounded on the other side. The tapestry swung back out, and Bolan briefly glimpsed some running legs.

The Executioner moved closer to the makeshift doorway, held the trigger back again and swung the barrel of the assault rifle back and forth across the hole. The magazine emptied and he dropped the weapon to the floor, drawing the Desert Eagle.

By now only shreds of material hung over the opening. The Executioner peered through the ragged strips and saw three dead and two wounded men littering the floor.

Ripping what remained of the Arab and his captive from the wall, Bolan looked into another short hallway. The house on the other side of the wall was a mirror image of the house he was in, and a half step to the side provided him with a partial view of the living room.

It also provided a man wearing a green Dragon's jacket with a target. The nickel-plated .45 in the Dragon's hand jumped with the recoil as a bullet zipped past the Executioner and bored into the wall. Bolan fired from the hip, point-shooting the big Desert Eagle. The Eagle roared in his hand, sending a round into the Dragon's belly.

The man staggered backward.

Bolan raised his point of aim and pulled the trigger again.

The second explosion thundered off the narrow walls on top of the first as another big Magnum slug split the gang-banger's sternum.

The Executioner stayed close to the wall as he stepped into the living room. He saw a flash of green in the kitchen and hit the floor, the Desert Eagle gripped in both hands. A fist gripping a revolver suddenly appeared next to the doorframe outside the kitchen.

Bolan shifted his sights six inches and tapped two rounds through the wall. He heard a shriek inside the kitchen, then another Dragon toppled into the doorway. Behind the man, the Executioner heard the crash of metal.

Moving swiftly, Bolan looked into the kitchen to see that one of his rounds had penetrated the Dragon's body and struck a toaster on the counter, sending it to the tile. Hearing a noise, he whirled toward the bedrooms.

Two men stood abreast just inside the first bedroom. One held a Government Model .45. The other, standing sideways, was trying to maneuver a long-barreled shotgun in the narrow confines.

Bolan's first round blew through the would-be shotgunner's ribs, eliciting a shrill screech. The Executioner swung the .44 to the man with the Government Model and put two rounds into his chest.

The Desert Eagle's reload took less than a second. Bolan thumbed the magazine release and had a fresh load in the grip before the partially empty mag hit the filthy carpet. He moved cautiously over the bodies in the hall and into the first bedroom. Inside, he saw only a bare mattress on the floor. The closet, bathroom and other bedroom were also empty.

Holstering the Desert Eagle, the Executioner started in the far bedroom, systematically searching a chest of drawers and a bureau for leads to other Dragon bases. Stony Man Farm Intel provided that there were branches in most major U.S. cities, but most of the exact locations were unknown.

Moving from the bedroom, the Executioner gave the rest of the rooms a quick search, then moved back through the wall to the side of the duplex where he and Kim had entered. Stepping over the dead Dragons who littered the floor, he moved from the kitchen and living room into the larger of the two sleeping areas.

This bedroom held a king-size bed, a desk with a computer and two chests. Bolan moved first to the desk, his eye falling on a thick envelope that rested on the keyboard. As he opened the envelope and identified the contents as photographs, he heard a police siren. Somebody—one of the neighbors—had heard the gunfire and called the cops. By the wail of the siren, he had only seconds.

With envelope in hand, the Executioner hurried into the living room. He saw the flashing red lights around the edges of the shades. Pivoting on the balls of his feet, he hurried back down the hall and into the smaller bedroom.

The window rose easily. Bolan dived through the opening and hit the ground, rolling to his feet facing the alley.

"Police officers!" screamed a voice behind him. "Freeze!"

The Executioner ran. Without looking over his shoulder, he sprinted to the alley, leaped over a short fence and ran to his right. As he raced down the dark alleyway, he heard footsteps and heavy breathing behind him. But gradually, the footsteps faded.

A MIXED STENCH of garbage, urine and factory smoke filled the air of the inner city. As dawn broke over

Philadelphia, the bricks of the buildings in the alley lightened from a dark gray to a deep reddish brown. From a distance came the bangs and clanks of trash cans being dumped into trucks.

Bolan slowed to a walk. He had run for twenty minutes, keeping to the alleys and dodging patrol cars as he crossed the intersections. But he had seen none of the black-and-white cruisers for several blocks now, and guessed he must be over two miles from the Dragon's duplex.

That didn't mean his troubles were over, however. With the light of day, and the increased activity it brought, concealment was about to become a major problem. Men wearing skintight black combat suits and toting huge automatics and sound-suppressed machine pistols tended to draw attention.

Bolan crossed a side street quickly and started down another alley. Ahead, he saw a series of cardboard boxes turned onto their sides and lined up against the bricks. He stopped at the first—a refrigerator carton that read Westinghouse on the side.

Leaning down, the Executioner looked inside to see an elderly woman wrapped up in blankets. She snored softly, oblivious to her house guest. He moved on to the next box. Inside this makeshift shelter, he found a boy in his late teens or early twenties with an orange mohawk and wispy beard. The boy, too, slept on.

Bolan's luck changed at the third "street home." A tall, thick man in a frayed wool overcoat, maybe thirty years old, maybe sixty, lay on his side, snoring like a clogged chimney. He clutched an empty bottle of wine to his breast with both hands. The cardboard box smelled as if it had been dipped in a tank of gin.

Bolan tapped his boot against the man's foot.

One eye opened.

"Good morning," the Executioner said.

The other eye opened, then both of them stared at the blacksuit and weapons. "My God," the man said, sitting up inside the box. "They sending the SWAT teams after us now?"

The Executioner chuckled. "Not exactly," he said. "Come on out. I've got a business proposition for you."

The man scooted slowly out of the box. He rose to his knees, grunted painfully, then struggled to his feet. Clasping his head with both hands, he weaved back and forth.

Bolan studied him. A big man, he stood only an inch or two below the Executioner. He wore at least three shirts under the coat, and unless Bolan missed his guess, there were several other pairs of pants beneath the frazzled tweed slacks that were held up by suspenders.

"A business proposition, huh?" the man said. He grinned slyly, the week's worth of beard moving up on his face like a herd of black ants. "Don't let the nice clothes fool you, buddy. I didn't come for a job interview."

Bolan laughed. "Don't worry," he said. "I'm not offering you work—"

"Well, thank God for that."

"What I want is to buy your coat from you."

The man frowned. "I need this coat."

"You can buy a new one with what I give you."

The man looked skeptical. "Why would you want it?"

Bolan shook his head. "How about if I keep that to myself and add to the price?"

The man in the overcoat shrugged. "It appears that my assumption that you represented a police agency was incorrect," he said. "You, sir, are fleeing from the law. A fugitive from justice. Tell me I'm wrong."

"You're half right."

"And that's better than being half wrong anytime," the man said. He frowned again. "Okay. But I must warn you, this is a very special coat. Belonged to my father, and his father before that, and—"

"How much?" Bolan asked.

"For you, twenty dollars."

Bolan shook his head. "I'll give you a hundred."

The man had the coat off in a flash. "Would you happen to hold an MBA or any other business degree?" he asked as he slipped out of the sleeves. "I should like to know. I wish to avoid whatever university bestowed it upon you."

Bolan caught himself chuckling again as he unzipped a pocket in his skinsuit and pulled out a hundred dollar bill. This man was intelligent and obviously well educated. There had to be quite a story behind his present condition, but the warrior didn't have the time to find out.

Bolan took the coat. "How many pairs of pants are you wearing?" he asked.

"At last count," the man said, stuffing the money into his shirt pocket after a quick look around for prying eyes, "four."

"The top pair will get you another hundred."

The man's tweed slacks came off almost as fast as the coat. Beneath them, he wore a stained pair of khakis. "Can I interest you in a tie and shirt to go with that?" he asked.

"I don't think so," Bolan said, handing him another hundred.

"We're running a special on shoes today," the man said, looking down at the ragged cowhide covering his feet. "Twenty percent off."

Bolan shook his head, fighting another laugh. "No, I think that's it." He slid the tweed slacks over his blacksuit and slipped into the overcoat. Stepping to the side, he caught his reflection in a window. He wasn't going to be signing any modeling contracts with *Gentlemen's Quarterly* today, but the coat and slacks did their job. The blacksuit, Beretta and Desert Eagle were hidden, and it looked as if he were wearing a black turtleneck beneath the overcoat.

Bolan turned to walk away, then turned back. "Make me a promise," he said.

"One free promise with every purchase," the man said.

"Buy another coat and some decent clothes before you go to the liquor store."

The man saluted stiffly. "On my word of honor," he said, smiling again.

Bolan left the alley and walked down the street, stopping under a striped awning as a middle-aged woman unlocked the door to a small café. She smiled wearily as he entered, waved him to a steel-and-linoleum table in the middle of the room, turned on the lights, then disappeared into the kitchen.

The Executioner pulled out a chair and took a seat facing the door. The woman returned wearing a pink-and-white waitress uniform and carrying a pad and pencil. "Coffee?" she asked.

Bolan nodded.

The woman scribbled on the pad, then said, "What else?"

The Executioner ordered scrambled eggs, bacon and toast and watched her walk through the swinging door to the kitchen. As soon as she was out of sight, he reached under the overcoat to his blacksuit and pulled out the envelope full of photos. Holding them in his left hand, he stared at the picture on top.

A barrel-chested Oriental man in his late teens had his arm around a pretty girl, also Oriental. A cigarette hung from his lips, a gun from the shoulder holster over his tight black T-shirt.

The next few pictures appeared to have been snapped at a Dragon party. In one, a half dozen men—two of them Bolan recognized from the duplex—stood in line, drinking beer and giving the camera the finger. In another, some of the same young men, and others, were clapping and cheering around a table on which a nude Oriental woman danced. Other photos showed couples engaged in various staged acts of lovemaking on couches, floors and one even in bed. In several, the Dragons lifted their girlfriends' T-shirts to expose their breasts to the camera.

The waitress appeared with a coffee cup. She glanced down at the pictures, shook her head in disgust and walked away.

Bolan shuffled on through the stack, seeing pictures of some of the Dragons practicing tae kwon do. More showed several kilos of cocaine wrapped in plastic and stacked on a table, and the last few were *Wild Bunch* pictures in which the Dragons mugged for the camera wearing sidearms and holding rifles.

The Executioner shuffled through the pictures twice more, finding nothing that might lead him to another Dragon den. When his breakfast arrived, he set the photographs to the side and picked up his fork.

Bolan took a bite of his bacon, a strange uneasiness creeping over him. He glanced back at the stack of pictures to the side of the table.

There had been something in one of them. Something out of the ordinary, and potentially important. Something that had registered in his subconscious. What was it?

The Executioner finished his breakfast and the waitress appeared with more coffee. After she laid down the check and took his plate away, he spread the pictures out across the table, and let his eyes travel loosely from one picture to the next.

They stopped suddenly on the *Wild Bunch* picture.

Bolan looked closely at the faces. Again, some of them had been at the duplex. The woods where Kim and his men were about to rape the girl had been too dark to be sure, but he suspected he'd seen some of the other faces there. All seven of the men in the picture wore the green satin Dragon jackets over black

T-shirts. Automatic pistols and revolvers were tucked into their belts. Three of them held AK-47s. There were two Uzis and the Winchester Trapper.

Bolan rubbed his eyelids. Young cops took these kinds of pictures after drug raids, soldiers did it after a battle and criminals had themselves immortalized, as well. At first glance, this photo appeared to be no more than another "brag" shot.

But what he was looking for was here. *Somewhere.*

Bolan opened his eyes, and his sight fell behind the young men this time. He felt his eyebrows lower and he leaned forward into the table. There, behind the boys, was a mirror. And in the mirror, partially obstructed by a camera, was a face.

Older than the Dragons in the picture, the man who had taken it was not Korean. Light blond hair, maybe even white, fell over his ears, and his skin had a chalky hue.

The Executioner lifted the picture from the table, holding it at different angles under the light. The man didn't look familiar.

Stuffing the photos back into the envelope, Bolan threw a ten-dollar bill on the table. The Dragons had chapters in every major city in the U.S., and he would be tied up for the next year if he kept trying to take them out one by one. What he needed was a "key"— something that could cut the head off the monster and cause it to die all at once.

The Executioner stood up. The white man who had taken the picture was that key—he could feel it. The Korean gangsters were among the most racist people in the world, and they wouldn't be hanging out with a white guy unless he was important to their operation in some way.

Bolan opened the envelope slightly as he walked to the door. The face of the man holding the camera stared back at him. Again, he couldn't tell who it was, and he wasn't sure if enough of the face was visible for anyone to identify it.

But if identification was possible, he knew just the man who could do it.

The Executioner opened the door and stepped out into the Philadelphia sunshine.

BEHIND THE WHEEL of the Plymouth, Jerry Wayne Waack pressed the cellular phone tighter against his ear. The interference over the airwaves was making Shim's voice sound like a hammer banging against a trash can.

"I have heard," Waack finally understood the Korean to say, "that this was once a peaceful and quaint little town."

The interference cleared from the line as Waack answered. "Yeah, nice little place, even just a few years ago. Just artists and writers and people like that. Then the friggin' yuppies decided to start dressing like designer cowboys and it turned into sort of an Old West Disneyland." He paused, glancing quickly to the sign across the street, then added, "But like Tennyson said, 'The old order changeth, yielding place to the new.' That's from *The Passing of Arthur*."

"You are across from the supermarket now?" Shim asked, using the code word they had agreed upon earlier: "supermarket" meant motel. With that as their key, they knew each other well enough to make up the rest of the code as they went. The cellular units might leak what they said to any CB or ham-radio operator in the area who happened to cross their frequency, and they were taking no chances.

Waack looked up at the sign again. Beneath the profile of a horse's head, he saw the words, Laughing Horse Inn. "I'm there," he said. "And you're outside the food broker's office?"

"Yes."

"Call me back when the delivery man leaves," Waack said. Then he disconnected the line and settled back behind the wheel.

Waack looked up and down Paseo del Pueblo, seeing few people out this early in the morning. He wasn't surprised. The inhabitants of this section of Taos fell into two categories: artists and tourists. Most artists worked late into the night and slept the mornings away, while the tourists found sleeping late a pleasurable break from their eight-to-five routines. There were exceptions, of course, and before long Waack expected to see the streets crowded with people. But for now what he saw before him was the colorful little town of Taos, New Mexico, which had not yet started its day.

Waack twisted, glancing over the seat to make sure the blanket covering the equipment in the back was still in place. The last thing he needed was some eager-beaver cop walking along his beat to glance inside and see a weapon. Satisfied, he returned his eyes to the Laughing Horse Inn.

The grounds outside the century-old hacienda looked like a run-down trailer park. Carpets were draped over clotheslines, worn-out bicycles were parked under a tin awning and a recent rain had left puddles in the gravel parking lot.

Thinking there had been a mistake in directions, Waack had checked out the hotel the day before and been surprised to find that the inside of the Laughing Horse had been transformed into a hybrid Old West-European pension. A communal kitchen sat in the center of the house, with a sitting room that boasted a television, VCR and thousands of movies on videotape.

The manager had gladly taken him on a tour of the vacant rooms, even knocking on the door of some that were occupied and asking if they minded Waack looking. No two rooms were the same. Some featured solid-wood bunk beds, others sleeping lofts and framed mattresses on the floor. Indian blankets served as bedspreads, and in one of the narrow winding hallways could be found a shrine to John Lennon.

Most of the floors were wood; a few were varnished dirt. All the rooms were small and cramped, yet a certain homey feel seemed to exude from them.

In any case, Waack thought, Senator William "Big Deal" Diel didn't need much space for what he had in mind during his brief stay today at the Laughing Horse. There would be plenty of room.

A middle-aged man wearing blue-and-gold designer sweats came jogging down the sidewalk. Waack lifted a map of New Mexico from the seat next to him and turned his face into it. The stiff paper touched his nose. He jerked at the pain it produced, and reminded himself that he needed to buy more sunburn lotion as soon as this was over. As the jogger passed, his mind drifted back to Shim, sitting outside a hotel much like himself. But the hotel the Korean watched was a Holiday Inn where Senator Diel should be just about to conclude his breakfast address to the Santa Fe Chamber of Commerce.

Waack was dropping the map back down beside him when the cellular phone rang.

"You are still at the supermarket?" Shim asked without preamble.

"No, I decided to drop down to Fort Sumner and visit Billy the Kid's grave," Waack said. He heard his friend chuckle as he watched two drunken tourists stagger along the sidewalk. "Of course I'm still here."

"The delivery man is just leaving," Shim said. "The meat is on its way."

"I'll get the freezer ready," Waack said, and hung up.

The tourists on the sidewalk weaved toward him wearing athletic shoes, shorts and newly purchased rough-cotton Mexican pullovers with hoods. Still drunk, they were on their way back to their rooms after a hard night of drinking. Waack watched them come without bothering to hide his face, knowing they were too drunk to notice anything. Still, he wanted them well past the car before he began uncovering the weapons in the back seat.

The man in the lead looked to be around thirty, with thick wavy hair and black wire-framed spectacles. He frowned into the Plymouth as he neared, then turned to his friend and said something Waack couldn't hear.

Both men laughed and continued to stare through the windshield as they approached.

The shorter man had a paunch that made the front of his pullover stick out like a bowling ball. As he reached the driver's side of the Plymouth, he leaned down and stuck his head in the window.

The fumes of stale alcohol assaulted Waack's sinuses as the man spoke. "Right you are, Benny!" he said. "A genuine albino!" He jerked his head from the Plymouth before Waack could speak and the two continued down the street.

Waack felt the malice shoot through his veins as if he'd injected it with a needle. He turned, looking over his shoulder, as the two men laughed again and continued on. Turning back to the front, he glanced at his watch.

Diel had just left Santa Fe. That should give him more than enough time to straighten this out.

Waack opened the door and stepped out onto the sidewalk. *I'll give them a chance,* he told himself. *Even though they've hurt my feelings, I won't hurt them. They just need to know. They need to understand.*

Turning up the sidewalk, Waack saw that the drunks had heard the car door close and turned around again. He started toward them.

The pudgy man staggered back a step, puffing his chest out and doing his best to suck in the huge gut. "You want somethin'?" he said in a surly voice.

"Yes," Waack said as he reached them. "I want to explain something to you. I know I look like an albino to some people. But if you'll look close, you'll see that I have a dark complexion. Brown eyes. Dark brown hair. Albino's have no pigmentation to their skin, and they have white hair and pink eyes." He paused and smiled. "Now do you see?"

The short man looked to his friend in sudden alarm. "He's crazy. Let's get out of here."

The tall man with the glasses ignored his partner, laughed and stepped forward. He squinted at Waack in mock seriousness, then said, "I'm looking close. No, looks to me like you got white hair, white skin and pink eyes." He stepped back again. "Yep, I was right the first time." He turned to his friend for approval and both men laughed.

Waack felt the prickling on the back of his neck. His ears buzzed as he looked up and down the street. Three blocks down, he saw a man wearing a chef's hat sweeping the sidewalk under the sign of a café. The streets were otherwise empty.

Behind the men, a short street led to a shopping area between the blocks. "Come with me," he said. "I want to show you something." He walked past the men and started for the recess.

"You a fag, too?" the tall man asked, and both men laughed again. The shorter man was starting to enjoy the game now. "An albino faggot," he said.

Waack heard their unsteady footsteps behind him as he ducked into the side street. He moved far enough back to be hidden from the street, then turned as the men followed him.

"So, you gonna suck our dicks or something, faggot?" the man with the glasses asked.

"No," Waack said simply, and drew the Beretta Minx from his right front pants pocket.

The first .22 short flew through the sound suppressor and entered the tall man's head just under the chin. Waack turned to the shorter man, aimed for the right eye and pulled the trigger again. He was on his way back toward the Plymouth before either man hit the ground.

Waack got quickly behind the wheel. After another quick look up and down the street, he threw the car into reverse and backed up Paseo del Pueblo and into the side street.

Thirty seconds later the two bodies were hidden in the Plymouth's trunk.

Waack glanced at his watch again as he drove down Paseo del Pueblo to a convenience store six blocks south of the Laughing Horse. Inside, he bought a tube of sunburn ointment, a can of Coke and a bag of Fritos. He asked the teenage girl behind the counter for some napkins.

The girl stuck the napkins in the sack and said, "Have a nice day."

"Why, thank you," Waack said, smiling pleasantly. "You, too."

Waack parked the Plymouth across from the Laughing Horse, spread the ointment over his face and arms, then dried his hands with the napkins. He popped the top off the Coke and opened the Fritos. As he dug in the plastic sack, he caught a quick glimpse of his face in the rearview mirror.

Jerry Wayne Waack smiled at what he saw. Dark brown skin with just a tinge of yellow. Dark brown hair. Brown eyes. The white of those eyes did look a little pink today, though, he thought. Must be allergies.

With a mouth full of Fritos and Coke, Waack settled back to wait on Senator William ''Big Deal'' Diel.

## CHAPTER FOUR

To the outsider, Stony Man Farm looked exactly like what its name implied—another working agribusiness set within the picturesque scenery of the Shenandoah Valley. Only a select group of covert agents and their masters knew of the tremendous importance of this facility to the U.S. intelligence establishment.

Mack Bolan dragged the wheels of a desk chair up the ramp to Aaron the "Bear" Kurtzman's bank of computers and took a seat behind the man's wheelchair. He watched the blur Kurtzman's fingers made as they flew across the keyboard. The horizontal crease in the computer genius's high forehead had deepened in concentration. Kurtzman suddenly sat back in his chair, put both hands in his lap, then leaned forward and tapped the Enter button on the keyboard.

The enlarged photo of the man holding the camera appeared on the screen. The Dragons had been trimmed out of the picture.

"Okay," Kurtzman breathed as he swiveled to face the Executioner. "It's been entered into my new program."

Bolan nodded. "So, what's it do, this new program of yours?"

Kurtzman smiled. "Sends out an image and searches files." He paused, and Bolan could see his mind working, choosing his words carefully. "You're familiar with the CompuSketch program?"

The Executioner nodded. "You enter a description of the suspect. Shape of the nose, ears, eyes. Things like that, right?"

"Basically, yes." Kurtzman nodded. "Ever heard of Detective Tool Kit?"

Bolan shook his head.

"It's fairly new," Stony Man's computer wizard said. "But it works off the picture itself rather than a description. It can scan files, magazine articles, whatever you want, but the kicker is you have to a have another lead—some relevant text—to go with it." He paused. "Which, of course, we don't have."

Bolan waited silently.

The computer beeped and Kurtzman turned briefly to the screen, then back. "What I've done is found a way to combine the two approaches, with a few changes of my own thrown in. In short, what I did was design a program that uses the measurement between the eyes, the size and shape of the ears, hair color, skin hue, things like that, as the relevant text to go with the picture you brought in."

"Sort of a high-tech Bertillon system," Bolan said, recalling the nineteenth-century police forensic expert who used body measurements for identification.

Kurtzman laughed. "Right. But old Alphonse Bertillon not only took facial measurements, he had the height, the spread from fingertip to fingertip, finger length—things like that to work with. We don't."

The computer beeped again.

"What's it doing?" Bolan asked.

"I linked all the agency files we're searching together," Kurtzman said. "So far the program's checked the BATF and DEA. It's now entering the FBI files, and from there it'll go to CIA."

Bolan heard footsteps behind him and turned as Barbara Price approached with three cups of coffee. The attractive Stony Man mission controller handed one to Kurtzman, another to Bolan, then took a sip from the third. "Having any luck?" she asked.

Kurtzman was about to answer when a curt series of buzzes suddenly sounded from the computer, and all three turned toward the monitor. The screen had divided in half, the left side still showing the picture of the light-skinned man holding the camera. On the right, an FBI file appeared. At the tip, the Executioner saw a mug shot that could easily have been the man who had taken the picture of the Dragons. Beneath it was a set of fingerprints, and below that, several case summaries.

"Hugo Eugene Lattimer," Kurtzman read. "Armed robbery, extortion. Could be—" he rolled the screen downward to reveal more of the file "—suspected in several other... Whoops. Nope, not our man." The computer genius leaned forward and tapped the final paragraph.

Bolan read the words. Lattimer had been stabbed to death while serving time in the state penitentiary at McAlester, Oklahoma.

"Still a few bugs to iron out in this thing," Kurtzman said as his fingers flew across the keyboard again.

The image of Lattimer disappeared and the mysterious blond man with the camera filled both sides of the screen once more. Then came another series of buzzes.

Bolan scanned the FBI file of another man who fit the profile, quickly learning that Richard Thomas Wade was currently incarcerated at San Quentin. Kurtzman reprogrammed the machine and turned to him, shrugging. "If this guy doesn't have a record, we may be up a creek."

Bolan, Kurtzman and Price waited in silence until they heard the beep telling them the FBI file probe was complete. "Let's try something," Kurtzman said. "I've got a hunch." His hands moved across the keyboard with the flow of a concert pianist. After a moment, more buzzes sounded.

Another face appeared on the screen, matching the unusually light blond hair, pale skin and facial measurements of their subject. Below the photo was a U.S. Army file. The name read Jerry Wayne Waack. Somewhere, in the back of Bolan's mind, a bell rang. He squinted at the young face, noting the bleached complexion and military-style short white hair. Light pink eyes stared back at him. The man was an albino.

The date below Waack's photo was December 6, 1968. The Executioner's eyes drifted to the longer-haired, older man on the other side of the screen, then he began reading as Kurtzman slowly rolled down the computer screen.

The profile read almost like a mirror image. Like Bolan himself, Waack had been a Special Forces sniper in Vietnam. A small-arms and unarmed-combat specialist, he had received cross-training in demolition.

Bolan sat back in his chair. He remembered Waack now. The man had been good, damn good, but had been the butt of thousands of pranks and jokes due to his condition. "Whitey Waack," Bolan said.

Kurtzman turned. "You know him?"

"I know of him. Good sniper in Nam, but the sun gave him problems. He never went anywhere without sunscreen and had to take special precautions to hide that hair. It stood out in the bush like a cottontail on a golf green." He paused. "Roll it on, Bear. Let's see if there's more."

After the U.S. withdrawal from Vietnam, Waack had been sent to Korea, where he worked behind enemy lines in the North. There was mention of his being MIA for several weeks, then he showed up again with a tale about capture and escape. His body had exhibited the scars of torture to prove the story. Shortly thereafter Waack had developed mental and emotional problems, been diagnosed with schizophrenia and given a medical discharge. His last known civilian address was in Eureka Springs, Arkansas.

Bolan turned to Kurtzman. "He's our man, Bear. He's the key to taking the Dragons out once and for all."

"How do you know?" Kurtzman asked.

"I don't know how I know, but I do. Any way for your magic machines to find out where he went after the army?"

"Not without more to go on than we have."

Bolan nodded and stood. "Thanks, Bear," he said. "Grimaldi got my transport ready?"

"He's warming her up now," Price said.

Bolan walked away. As always, Kurtzman's computers had gone above and beyond the call of duty.

Now it was time for the Executioner to do the same.

WAACK WATCHED the three-year-old Pontiac pull into the parking lot of the Laughing Horse and come to a halt. He smiled, looking at the dent in the car's front fender.

For what Big Deal Diel was about to do, the senator wanted a low profile.

Waack lifted the phone and tapped in Shim. "The delivery man's bringing the meat in now," he said, and hung up before the Korean could answer. He looked up and down the street. Men and women in tourist garb were showing themselves now, making their way toward the cafés along the street for breakfast. He had planned to use the scoped Ruger .22-caliber rifle in the back seat, taking Diel out as soon as the senator stepped out of the car. But the meeting in Santa Fe had lasted longer than he'd expected, and now there were too many potential witnesses.

"Ah, the best laid plans of mice and men…" he said under his breath, not bothering to finish the old Scottish adage. "Which, ladies and gentlemen, brings us now to Plan B."

Waack watched the senator get out of the Pontiac. He wore a navy blue suit and a burgundy-and-gray tie that went well with the shock of gray hair that fell over his forehead. Diel limped slightly as he walked around the car to open the passenger's door.

A pair of long slender legs in tight flesh-colored nylons swung out, and for a brief moment Waack caught a flash of the stocking tops and black garters. Then the top half of the young blond woman wearing the black skirt and matching leather motorcycle jacket followed the legs.

Waack looked at the woman's hair as Diel took her arm. "Rinse job." He grinned. "Eat your heart out, honey. Mine's natural."

The woman's figure swayed as Diel escorted her across the lot to the rear of the hotel. Waack pursed his lips and made several clicking sounds against the roof of his mouth. "Naughty, naughty, senator. Not a day over twenty, and I'd guess closer to eighteen." He laughed quietly. "Word of this could get back to the constituents."

Diel and the woman stepped through the rear door and turned to the right, and Waack had the answer to the question he'd been asking himself. Only two rooms stood on that side of the door. And the one closest to the entrance, he knew, was occupied by a couple from Texas.

Waack drummed his fingers against the steering wheel for five more minutes, giving the Senator ample time to get settled. Finally satisfied that Diel and the woman would be well into their first round of lovemaking, Waack left the car and walked across the street.

A man and woman in shorts and T-shirts on bicycles passed Waack in the parking lot. He returned their nods and smiles, then entered the Laughing Horse Inn and turned right.

Waack walked quickly to the senator's room and pressed his ear against the thick wooden door. Inside, he could hear heavy breathing and an occasional moan. He looked down at the lock and smiled. There would be no need to kick.

Pulling a credit card from his billfold, Waack slid it between the door and frame, and the lock clicked open. He grabbed the knob, drew the tiny Beretta and quietly opened the door.

The blonde lay on the bed facing the door, her back against the headboard and propped up with several pillows. Her eyes were closed, her lips slightly parted. The Indian-blanket bedspread covered her to the waist, and her small pink-nippled breasts were the first thing Waack saw as he entered the room.

Waack's eyes moved to the rhythmically moving lump under the blanket between the girl's legs. At the foot of the bed, he saw two gray-and-green-veined calves with blue socks covering the feet.

Waack grinned, then cleared his throat.

The girl's eyes shot open.

"You know, senator, what you're doing just might be illegal in this state," he said.

The senator's head shot up from under the blanket and twisted toward the door. "What...?" he sputtered, his eyes wide in shock and fear.

"Last time I vote for you," Waack said as he aimed the tiny .22 at the man's temple and pulled the trigger.

The Beretta coughed lightly and Diel's head jerked back. He rose to his knees, trying to get up, the blanket falling to the edge of the mattress. He made it off the bed and two steps toward Waack before the Beretta jumped again.

Senator William "Big Deal" Diel fell to his back on the floor.

Waack stood over him, looking curiously down at the senator's nude body. "Well," he said. "Big Deal didn't get his nickname *that* way, now did he." He turned his attention back to the bed.

The blonde had retrieved the blanket and covered herself to the chin. She sat shivering beneath it, her eyes wide with terror.

Waack smiled at her. "How old are you?" he asked.

"Twenty...two," she whispered.

"Hmm," Waack said, nodding. "You look younger. Now take the blanket off."

The girl hesitated.

Waack waved the gun back and forth.

Slowly the blanket began to come down the girl's smooth white body. Her breasts came into view, then she stopped the blanket at her waist.

"Come on, sweetheart," Waack said, waving the gun at the blanket. "I haven't got all day."

With a look of resignation, the pretty young woman threw the blanket to the foot of the bed.

Waack chuckled. "Yep," he said. "I knew it—a bleached blonde."

He pulled the trigger again.

EUREKA SPRINGS was the definitive retirement spot
and tourist stop of northwest Arkansas. Wedged between two old men driving mammoth recreational vehicles, Bolan caught brief glimpses of the village as he
drove the rented Ford LTD down the street at twenty
miles per hour.

On the sidewalks, carrying sacks that boasted the
names of the souvenir and craft shops he passed, he
saw more gray-haired men and women in Bermuda
shorts and walking shoes. Cameras hung from their
necks or were wrapped around their waists in fanny
packs. Empty tour buses filled the parking lots. Their
former occupants tapped canes behind guides who led
them down the street, pausing to listen to a short oration each time they reached some historical land-
mark.

A light mist began to fall over the Arkansas moun-
tain town as Bolan edged the Ford to the shoulder and
caught a flash of the sign a block down. German-
Czech Restaurant, it read, and he followed the RV
until he reached the parking lot, then turned in and
parked behind a Volkswagen camper-van.

Pulling a light windbreaker over his weapons, he got
out. His mind drifted to Jack Grimaldi, whom he'd
left at the small landing strip just outside town. Grimaldi would wait for him to return, or for orders to
pick up the warrior somewhere else. Bolan had a feeling all hell was about to break loose, and he had no
idea where the next stop would be.

He entered the restaurant to hear a fast polka blasting from the scratchy loudspeaker system. A middle-
aged woman in traditional Czech attire, who was

gathering dirty dishes from a table across the room, saw him and started his way. In her white blouse with white embroidery and colorful bodice, she smiled at Bolan and said in a deep Southern accent, "Party of one, sir?"

Bolan grinned at the contrast between her voice and costume. "I'm meeting someone," he said. Glancing over her head into the dining room, he saw a fortyish man with thinning brown hair stand up near the back wall. The man wore a khaki Caroll County Sheriff's Department uniform, a black belt and a shining silver badge.

The hostess escorted Bolan to a table and gave him a menu.

"Agent Belasko?" the man said.

Bolan nodded. "Deputy Gates?"

Gates nodded. "Just Harold."

Bolan took the man's extended hand. "How'd you know me?"

"Advanced police training," the deputy said, chuckling. He sat back down as Bolan took the seat across from him. "Actually, if you'll take a look around, you'll see that besides me and the waitress you're the only one in the place who's not going to qualify for the senior-citizen's discount when they pay the bill."

Bolan smiled as he opened the menu.

"If you like duck, I'd recommend it," Gates said. "My mother was Czech, and I hate to say it, but they roast it as well here as she did in her own kitchen."

A waitress wearing a colorful bodice, skirt and apron, and with flowers in her hair, appeared beside the table and both men ordered the duck and iced tea.

"They tell you why I'm here?" Bolan asked when she left.

Gates shrugged. "Kind of," he said. His voice grew serious. "The Justice Department guy—Brognola, wasn't it?—said you needed information on Jerry Wayne Waack." He paused. "By the way, Sheriff Landcaster said to tell you he was sorry he couldn't meet you himself. He's at a meeting in Fayetteville."

Bolan nodded. "So tell me about Waack."

Gates lifted his spoon and began toying with it. "I was a brand-new deputy when he came on years ago," he said. "In short, he was weird. I don't mean odd, or unusual, I mean downright weird." He looked up.

Bolan waited for him to go on.

"Maybe I should back up a little," the deputy resumed. "Waack and I grew up here in Eureka, and I knew him as a kid. Not real well—he was several years older than me, but this was a small town before the tourist invasion. He wasn't as bad when he was young, but he was different then, too."

"In what way?"

The waitress arrived and set a huge mason jar of ice tea in front of each man.

Gates tore open two envelopes of artificial sweetener and stirred them into his ice tea. "He was a loner. Not that that's so odd, really, but there was . . . just something about him. Something that gave you the willies when he got near, and it wasn't just that ghostlike skin and the pink eyes. You saw him around a lot, too. Eating at cafés by himself, just walking the streets—sometimes at maybe four in the morning. Sometimes you'd see him talking to himself, carrying on a conversation or even arguing with...with nobody." He lifted his tea and downed half of it. "People did their best to avoid him. He was spooky."

Bolan nodded. "What do you know about his Vietnam years?"

"Heard he was a good sniper," Gates said. "And trained in explosives and small arms and karate or some such shit. After the war, they say he went somewhere and did something with the CIA or somebody. That's about it, really."

The waitress arrived again and topped off Gates's jar before leaving.

"There were also rumors that Waack applied to a lot of the big police departments when he got back to the States. L.A., Dallas, even Little Rock. Their psychological tests knocked him out of the running. We aren't all that up-to-date around here, and I guess Waack took the deputy job 'cause he couldn't get anything better."

"How long was he a deputy?" Bolan asked.

"Eight months," Gates said as the waitress brought two salad bowls. "But I remember them. Those were a strange eight months."

Bolan waited until the waitress had left, then said, "Tell me about it. Why'd he last only eight months?"

"Well," Gates said, putting a forkful of lettuce and tomato into his mouth, "he didn't get fired. He quit. But it left a lot of questions unanswered. About the time Waack came on board, a series of tourist murders started. An old man would disappear here, an old woman there. Now I call them murders, but we never found any bodies. Technically they're still on the files as missing persons.'' He set his fork down, looking as if he'd lost his appetite. "Then there were his friends," he said.

"Tell me about them."

"Well, this is Arkansas, Mr. Belasko. And you won't find any finer people in the world. But like anywhere else, we've got our share of crazies, and around here they usually take the form of right-wing extremists."

"Which groups?" Bolan asked.

Gates waited as the waitress returned with two platters, each holding an entire duck, steam rising from the browned skin. She set them on the table along with side plates of potatoes and onions, then left.

"There's a little bit of everything scattered across this part of the state," Gates said as he tore off a drumstick. "The Klan is fairly strong, though not like they are along the Mississippi border. The guys Waack was hanging out with were with a group called the Right Arm of God."

Bolan lifted his knife and fork and cut a piece of duck. He had heard of the group. They weren't large, but they had connections to the Klan, the American Nazi Party and several other organizations that thought Anglo-Saxons were the only people worthy of inhabiting the U.S.

"Bear in mind," Gates said, "that it was only conjecture that these guys belonged to the Arm. It's like so much of police work, Belasko—you know it but you can't prove it in a court of law. But hell, I don't have to tell you that."

Bolan shook his head. "Anything else?"

Gates took a quick look around to make sure no one was listening. "Okay, I'm gonna tell you something the sheriff has told us not to talk about. So it's between you and me, right?"

Bolan nodded.

"The tourists disappearing wasn't the only strange thing that went on in this part of the country when Waack was here." Gates's voice had dropped to a whisper. "There were several other killings here in Arkansas and a couple in Mississippi. Two more in Louisiana. All black leaders, except a couple who were white civil-rights activists."

Bolan frowned. "You think Waack committed the murders?" he asked. He was skeptical. White supremacists didn't hang out with Koreans.

Gates looked around again, then said, "All of them were killed by methods in which Waack was trained. Some were shot from long distance with rifles. Cars blew up."

He set his drumstick down. "And I did a little checking into the duty roster. Waack was off duty every time one of the hits went down."

He stared at the Executioner. "Yeah, Belasko, I think he killed them. I think he did the tourists for kicks, or maybe they made fun of the way he looked—he never liked that. And I think he did the black leaders for fun and profit."

Bolan nodded. None of what Gates was saying meant Jerry Wayne Waack had pulled the trigger on the dead men. But it did mean he'd had the opportunity and the means to do so, which made him a suspect. Maybe Waack had bought into the white-supremacist doctrine during his deputy stint here, and maybe he had simply been making a little money on the side selling his skills to the Right Arm of God. If that were the case, another connection to the Anju Dragons didn't seem so unlikely. Waack certainly wouldn't have been the first hired killer to work for whichever side could pay his price.

"When was the last time you saw Waack?" Bolan asked.

"The day he resigned, years ago," Gates said. "He left town shortly after, and nobody knows where he went." He paused. "But the tourists stopped disappearing."

"Is the Right Arm of God still active around here?"

Gates nodded. "Oh, yeah. Stronger than ever."

"You know any of them?"

Gates's face reddened. He looked down at the table and nodded. "And now you're gonna ask me if there's anybody in the Arm who might talk to you, right?"

"That's right."

Gates looked back up. "Okay, Belasko, I want you to listen to me, and listen carefully. I don't like supremacist groups. White, black, red or whatever. Fact is, I hate the hell out of them. But you grow up in an area like this, you get used to them, and you realize several things about them. First, they've usually got some legitimate gripes regardless of what color they are. But second, they're going about correcting things the wrong way."

Gates set his fork down. "I don't make excuses for them, but I do try to understand their motives. And when you begin to do that, you realize that they're just as serious about what they do as you and I, and that anyone who gets in their way might just disappear into the lake or under six feet of ground."

Bolan studied the man's eyes. "Sounds like you're afraid of them," he said.

"I have a healthy respect for what they're capable of doing," Gates answered. "Even to a cop." He paused. "But don't confuse that healthy respect with an unwillingness to do my job."

Bolan nodded.

"Okay," Gates said. "I wanted you to know exactly where I stand personally before I answered your question. Do I know anybody in the Right Arm of God who'd willingly talk to you? No. Not willingly."

The waitress appeared again, tore a check from the top of her pad and set it on the table. When she'd left, Gates went on. "They might talk if I had a hammer on them and they were facing the penitentiary. But I don't."

"I have to try," Bolan said. "And I can be fairly persuasive."

Gates nodded, staring into the Executioner's eyes. When he spoke again, the words came out more statement than question.

"You aren't really a Justice agent, are you?"

"No."

"But you're with the U.S. government. At least somehow?"

"More or less."

Gates cracked a smile. "Okay, I'm gonna go on my gut instinct and trust you, whoever you are, Belasko. You look like a guy who's been around, and you look like a guy who could beat what he wanted to know out of someone but wouldn't do it for the wrong reasons. I hope so. Because a damn good beating is what it's gonna take to get anyone to lead you to Waack."

Bolan picked up the check. "Give me a name to go visit," he said. "Some place to start."

The grin on Gates's face widened into a full-fledged smile. "How about my brother-in-law?" he whispered. "He deserves a good ass whipping more than anyone I know."

## CHAPTER FIVE

Bolan slowed the LTD and turned down the gravel road. Through the dust clouds blowing from the rear tires of the 1965 El Camino, he could see the empty road ahead.

He had followed Harold Gates's patrol car from Eureka Springs to the deputy's mobile home in Berryville, then waited in the living room while Gates called in sick at the sheriff's department before changing into blue jeans, a black T-shirt, cowboy boots and a well-worn baseball cap. He'd now been trailing Gates's private vehicle up and down the hilly back roads of northern Arkansas for nearly an hour.

He chuckled as both vehicles slowed at a crossroads. Gates had a sort of Will Rogers-like country-wisdom delivery, and he was smart. So Bolan had been somewhat surprised at first to see how open the deputy had been after figuring out that the man with whom he spoke didn't really represent the Justice Department.

The answer to that seeming contradiction had been hinted at with Gates's suggestion that the Executioner go after the deputy's brother-in-law. Gates elaborated upon the idea as he changed clothes in the rear of the trailer. The deputy's clothes weren't the only thing that changed as Bolan sat waiting on the frayed couch. Harold Gates's accent seemed to become increasingly more Southern, and it became evident that the deputy had been working hard not to sound too "Arkansas" when they'd met for lunch.

"Son of a bitch grows marijuana up in the hills," Gates had shouted down the hall. "Then he comes out just to stick his nose into everything. *Everybody's* business—he just got to run it. He's a goddamn bully, is what he is. Got to have everything his way. And Jo Ann—that's my wife—damn, I don't know why, but she flat worships the fat bastard. Why, she'd believe a horned toad had wings if he told her so."

Bolan stepped harder on the accelerator as he followed the El Camino up a hill. Gates was in a sticky position. Taking an active part in an investigation that led to the arrest of his dope-cultivating brother-in-law might mean he ended up with a divorce, as well as a criminal case. But now the deputy saw an opportunity to get the man out of his hair by remote control, so to speak. In short, Gates's motive for busting his brother-in-law, Martin McCaslin, was a mixture of professional and personal.

But it would work out just fine for Bolan.

The El Camino pulled to the side of the road and stopped. Bolan parked behind it and waited. A moment later Gates's legs shot out of the driver's side. The deputy stood up, glanced nervously around, then hurried back to the LTD.

Bolan rolled the window down.

Gates crossed his arms and leaned on the door. "Okay," he said, casting his tense eyes up and down the road. "This is as far as I go. Those bastard dope fiends know the Camino and they'd know me in or out of uniform." He turned to look up the road again. "Go to the next corner and turn east. You'll come to a low section with a bridge. I wouldn't drive any farther—they got scouts." He tapped the hood of the LTD. "There's a little gully where you can hide this boat. Just the other side, you'll see a trail. Now, mind you, I wouldn't stay on that too long, either—word has it they got it booby-trapped."

"Anyway," Gates continued, "half a mile, maybe three-quarters of the way on in they got their field." He paused and his eyes stared through the window at Bolan. "Be careful, bud. Real careful. There's been a lawman or two just flat disappear around here. These guys play for keeps."

"Okay," Bolan said.

"Okay, then," Gates said. "Good luck, and thanks." He started back to the El Camino.

"Want me to tell him this is for you?" Bolan asked through the window.

"God, no," Gates said over his shoulder as he got into the El Camino.

Bolan waited until Gates had U-turned back up the road, then drove to the corner and made a right. The road dipped gradually lower, and a quarter mile later he saw the rickety wooden bridge the deputy had mentioned. A deep ravine could be seen to the side of the road. As he got closer Bolan saw that the shoulder sloped gradually down to it.

He guided the LTD to the bottom of the ditch, killed the engine, and got out. He opened the trunk and a moment later he'd changed from sport coat, slacks and tie into the skintight blacksuit, with the

Beretta and Desert Eagle under his arm and on his hip, respectively.

With the trunk still open, he twirled the wheel of a padlock that secured a hard black plastic case. Flipping the latches, he lifted the lid to expose a Calico M-960A with a threaded barrel.

Bolan pulled the submachine pistol from the cutout in the foam rubber. He inspected the sound suppressor first. Then, sliding a tubular drum magazine onto the Calico's top, he listened as the clips at the rear of the weapon snapped into place. Working the bolt, he chambered the first of the drum's one hundred 9 mm subsonic hollowpoints, flipped the safety on and slid the collapsible stock out into place.

The Executioner closed the trunk. He found the trail into the woods exactly where Gates had said it would be, then charted a parallel course, his practiced eyes skirting the thick branches and leaves for signs of life as he moved cautiously through the cover. The afternoon sun drifted down through the foliage in streaks and patches, and the humidity from nearby Beaver Lake soon brought a thin film of sweat to his brow. He pulled a black bandanna from one of the skinsuit's zipper pockets and donned it as a sweatband, then moved on.

The first of the booby traps had been set a hundred yards from where he'd parked the LTD.

Bolan heard a quiet swoosh on the dried leaves just beyond his boots. He froze. The noise stopped. He took another step and heard the sound again.

The Executioner's eyes lowered, scouring the dry leaves and twigs around his feet. He caught a quick glimpse of two shiny black circles. Six feet ahead, Bolan saw the dull eyes of a rattlesnake staring back at him.

Slowly he lifted the Calico and flipped the selector to semiauto. He let the sights fall into place, then gently squeezed the trigger. The Calico coughed quietly and skipped lightly in his hand.

The black eyes disappeared.

Bolan moved slowly forward, scanning the area around the bullet hole in the dirt. He stopped again as he neared the spot. Where there was one rattlesnake, there might be more.

Seeing no other immediate threat, he dropped to one knee. In the short grass he saw the headless rattlesnake's tail still uncoiling in death. The rattles that should have warned Bolan of the snake's presence had been surgically removed, and the altered but still venomous serpent had been tethered to a stake in the ground with a long cord.

Bolan stepped over the still-writhing body and deeper into the woods. Gates had warned that the men he was about to pursue were Nam vets, and leashing a snake to the trail was an old trick of the Vietcong. But Martin McCaslin and his white supremacist, marijuana-cultivating cohorts were even better than Gates had guessed. They had placed their snares to the sides of the trail, as well as on it, knowing that many law-enforcement officers had also witnessed the tricks of the VC firsthand.

Bolan took out two more of the snakes as he moved higher into the hilly Arkansas countryside. He came to a small clearing in the trees and stopped next to a green limestone rocks the size of his head. Ahead, directly in his path, thick leaves stretched from one side of the clearing to the other. Roughly six feet wide, the pile was too vast to step over.

The Executioner set the Calico carefully on the ground and pried the rock from the damp earth. He moved just outside the trees, then shoved it through the air like a shot-putter.

The stone landed in the center of the leaves.

The pile fell inward upon itself.

Bolan stepped up to the edge of the pit and looked down. Sharpened *punji* sticks had been driven into the ground six feet below the surface.

The Executioner retrieved the Calico, took a running leap and broad-jumped the pit. He had just entered the thick trees again when he felt something snap against his boot.

Bolan hit the ground face first. A whoosh of air sailed over his head as his nose struck the damp soil and leaves. A loud crunch sounded to his rear.

Slowly the Executioner rolled to his side. Where he had stood a split second before, he saw more of the razor-pointed *punji* sticks attached to a camouflaged frame. The frame in turn had been coupled to a pliant green branch that had been bent back and tied. The whole apparatus had been triggered by the unseen object his boot had struck along the ground. The *punji* points were now imbedded in the trunk of the tree to which the booby trap had been mounted.

Bolan moved on. By his calculations, he had travelled at least a half mile since entering the woods. He had to be close.

He was.

Seeing another clearing ahead, Bolan dropped to his belly and crawled forward. Through a break in the green foliage, he saw a small patch of dull yellow. As he watched, the yellow moved slightly.

He crawled farther and more things began to take shape through the perforations in the leaves and branches. The yellow patch became a battered straw cowboy hat. Beneath the hat, he saw the back of a neck.

Bolan lifted the Calico, sighted the neck at the nape, then slowly lowered the weapon. He could not see farther into the clearing, and for all he knew the clandestine marijuana field might be just the other side of the guard. At that range, even the hushed cough of the Calico would be heard, and if it wasn't, the man's tumbling body was sure to be noticed.

Crawling forward again, Bolan drew the Tanto. When he was directly behind the straw hat, he rose quickly to his feet. Standing a foot taller than the man who faced away from him, he had a brief second to recon both the sentry and the clearing beyond.

The man in the straw cowboy hat wore khaki shorts and a green T-shirt that helped camouflage him in the foliage. A 12-gauge pump-action shotgun was cradled in his arms. Over the top of the hat, Bolan saw the tall cannabis plants growing in the clearing. Several men—he had no time to count—were harvesting the plants.

The Executioner reached around and cupped his hand over the sentry's mouth. A muffled yell pressed into his fingers, and sharp teeth tried to bite into his hand as he jerked the guard back into the trees.

Bolan drove the Tanto's tip deep into the man's kidney and twisted the blade. The teeth relaxed. Jerking the blood-stained steel free, the Executioner brought it around to the side of the man's throat and stabbed it into the neck. The blade shot briefly out of sight, then reappeared through the skin on the other side. Bolan ripped the Tanto forward, and the man's carotid artery and jugular vein were severed in two.

The Executioner dropped the body to the ground and moved back to the edge of the trees. The marijuana field covered several acres and was hidden from view in a deep valley. To his left, Bolan saw another guard, perhaps fifty yards away, toting an Uzi. To his right, a man stood smoking a joint, a sawed-off double-barrel shotgun slung over his shoulder on a short sling. On the opposite side of the clearing, barely visible, the Executioner could see a fourth guard covering that side with an assault rifle of some sort.

Less than twenty yards from where Bolan crouched in the trees, four men were harvesting the crop. Two of the cultivators were busy with short-bladed sickles, chopping the plants near the base, while the other pair loaded them onto the back of a flatbed truck.

Bolan's eyes traveled to the cab of the truck. Behind the wheel, he saw a bearded face and brown hair. Fat cheeks puffed forward under the man's sunglasses, stretching the skin like an overinflated beach ball. As the Executioner watched, the man unwrapped a candy bar and crammed it past his bloated lips.

"Goddammit, Harvey!" the fat man shouted through the open window. "You guys get movin' before I get out and kick every one of your asses!" He unwrapped another candy bar.

Moving back slightly into the trees, Bolan began circling the clearing. He needed to take out the sentries first, then move inward to the harvesters, and leave at least one of them alive for interrogation.

Five minutes later Bolan came behind the man with the sawed-off shotgun. Within seconds the man lay dead on the ground.

The Executioner reached the far side of the clearing a few minutes later. The assault rifle in the dope guard's hands proved to be a Finnish Valmet. It fell to the leaves inside the forest as the Tanto did its job for the third time.

Bolan had watched the man with the Uzi chain-smoke four cigarettes as he'd made his way silently around the marijuana field. He was opening a new pack as the Executioner jerked him back into the trees and slid the blade into his throat.

The truck had been working its way westward as Bolan took out the guards. The workers were too busy to notice their friends' disappearance, and the fat man behind the wheel was too occupied with his candy bars. Bolan watched as they continued to chop and load, working their way close to where he hid. When they were twenty feet from the trees, he flipped the Calico to full-auto and stepped into the clearing.

Both of the men with the sickles were bent over when the submachine pistol coughed out the figure eight of subsonic hollowpoints. They fell to the carefully tilled soil, never knowing what had killed them.

The two men loading the marijuana onto the truck dropped the plants from their hands. The one nearest Bolan wore a Chicago Bulls cap and was shirtless. He fumbled for the grip of a large revolver stuffed into his blue jeans as Bolan swung the Calico his way.

The Calico chugged again, and a half dozen small red holes appeared on the man's naked chest. The other man loading the plants dived up and over the truck's side rail to disappear into the plants. Bolan saw a flash of blue steel, then the barrel of an M-16 shot out through the green leaves toward him.

The Executioner held the Calico's trigger back, saturating the cut marijuana with a steady stream of rounds. Shredded leaves and stems rose in the air above the truck. Sprinting forward, Bolan threw back the plants until he came to the man hiding in them.

Half of the marijuana cultivator's face was gone. Other rounds had exploded his heart and drenched his chest in crimson.

Bolan heard a voice call out from the cab. The words were muffled by the candy bar in the fat man's mouth. "What the hell?"

The Executioner turned to see the fat man staring into the truck's side mirror. He walked quickly to the window and shoved the Calico's barrel into the man's beard.

Martin McCaslin's mouth fell open. A thick brown mixture of chocolate and saliva dripped from his lips to mat the beard.

Bolan looked into the terrified eyes. "We need to talk," he said.

HAROLD GATES, Bolan suspected, would have given a year of his deputy sheriff's salary to see what happened next.

Bolan quickly glanced past the man, looking for weapons inside the truck. He saw only a near-empty plastic bag of Snickers candy bars, and a large watermelon.

Tears began to stream from McCaslin's thick-lidded eyes as Bolan opened the truck door, reached in and grabbed a flabby arm. "Mister, please—" McCaslin started, as the Executioner jerked him from the cab.

McCaslin hit the cultivated dirt of the marijuana field face first, and at least 350 pounds of blubber shimmied on the ground like an angry tidal wave. As the fat settled, Bolan stepped forward and put a foot in the middle of McCaslin's tight blue overalls.

"Mister, please—" he said again.

"Shut up," Bolan said. "I'll ask the questions, you give the answers. Do it well and you might live long enough to finish your candy." He slipped the toe of his boot under the mass of flesh on the ground and rolled it over.

Martin McCaslin looked like a beached whale as he stared up at the Executioner. His chest heaved for air. Dirt caked his beard and face, glued there by the sticky brown mess that still dripped from his mouth.

Bolan scowled down in disgust. The man was not only a bully, he was a coward and a glutton. Placing a boot on McCaslin's belly this time, the Executioner leaned on it. "I'm looking for a man named Waack," he said.

Air rushed from the lungs beneath the lard. McCaslin gasped for air.

"Maybe you didn't hear me," Bolan said, and added more weight to his boot.

"I...heard you!" McCaslin sputtered. "Don't... know any Waack."

Bolan lifted his rear foot, putting over two hundred pounds on the man's chest. He felt his foot sink down through the soft flesh as McCaslin let out a grunt, sounding like a pig on its way to slaughter. "Jerry Wayne Waack," the Executioner said. "You know him."

McCaslin's face had now turned from pale white to a bright fiery red. He tried to speak, couldn't find the words and nodded instead.

Bolan stepped off the man and stood to the side, aiming the Calico down at the dirty face. "Go on," he said.

Still fighting for air, McCaslin said, "I...haven't seen him in...years."

"He did some work for you and your Right Arm buddies, right? Several hits here and in Mississippi and Louisiana?"

McCaslin shook his head no.

Bolan lifted his boot.

"Yes!" McCaslin screamed. "Yes!"

Bolan fought the revulsion he had for this quivering excuse for a man. "Where's Waack now?" he demanded.

"I don't know!" McCaslin puffed. "He's moved on."

"Where?"

McCaslin gasped, then looked toward the truck. "I'm having trouble breathing," he almost whispered. "Could...could I have a chocolate bar?"

Bolan shook his head in revulsion, turned and strode back to the cab. He pulled the candy bars out, walked back to McCaslin, upended the plastic sack and dumped them over the man's fat belly.

McCaslin snatched up one of the candy bars and shoved it into his mouth, paper and all.

"Where is Waack?" Bolan repeated.

"I don't know," McCaslin grunted, paper hanging out of the corners of his mouth.

Bolan turned on his heel and opened the truck door again. He leaned in, lifted the watermelon, then set it on the ground an inch from the fat man's head. Reaching behind his back, he drew the mammoth Desert Eagle with his left hand, disconnected the safety with his trigger finger, then inserted the finger into the trigger guard.

The Executioner aimed down at the watermelon. McCaslin's eyes flickered to the side.

"I want you to watch this," the Executioner said softly. "I want you to see what this does to a watermelon." He paused to let his words sink in. "Then I want you to picture what you think it will do to your head." He pulled the trigger.

The Desert Eagle exploded, sending a volcanic eruption of pink pulp, seeds and liquid flying into the air. When it had settled, Bolan looked down to see

McCaslin's face, beard and entire upper body soaked in slime.

The obese man's fleshy lips parted. "I'm blind!" he screamed.

"You're not blind," Bolan said. "Wipe your eyes."

Ten pudgy fingers rose to McCaslin's face. A moment later he blinked up at the Executioner.

"I'm going to ask you one last time," Bolan said. "Then your head's going to look like the watermelon. Where is Jerry Wayne Waack?"

"I don't know," McCaslin whispered, then quickly held up his hands. His chest heaving an erratic rhythm, he said, "But last I heard, he was up in Missouri."

"Where in Missouri?"

"St. Louis," McCaslin panted. "There's a group there called the Missouri Fascist Party...they're...like us."

"Who's in charge of it?" Bolan asked.

McCaslin started to answer, but again the words wouldn't come. He grabbed another Snickers bar and jammed it into his mouth. A moment later he had calmed enough to breathe. "Becker. Dr. Lawrence Becker. He's a...surgeon."

Bolan holstered the Desert Eagle and shifted the Calico back to his right hand. He turned away from the corpulent form on the ground.

"You aren't...going to kill me?" he heard McCaslin grunt behind him.

"Why waste a bullet?" Bolan said. "Keep eating, McCaslin. You'll do the job for me within a year."

The Executioner was right about the certainty of McCaslin's death. But he had grossly overestimated the length of time the fat man had left.

Bolan heard a sudden "Uhh!" behind him and spun the Calico around to face McCaslin. His finger flipped the selector to full auto and entered the trigger guard, then stopped.

Martin McCaslin, compulsive overeater, marijuana cultivator and troublesome brother-in-law, had struggled to a sitting position and produced a small nickel-plated automatic from somewhere in his overalls. But as Bolan watched, McCaslin's entire body suddenly began to jerk. The gun fell from his fat fingers and both his hands clasped his chest. McCaslin's eyes opened wide, his lips forming a silent oh. He struggled for breath, his hands pushing harder against the fat over his heart.

Then, with one last high-pitched girlish shriek, Martin McCaslin fell back on the ground.

THE FOREST PARK Sports Medicine Clinic, Bolan had learned from Kurtzman via radio during the flight to St. Louis, was the clinic of choice for injured members of the St. Louis Cardinals baseball team, as well as athletes from the area's several universities and junior colleges.

The late-afternoon sun was dimming in the sky as Bolan, now in civilian clothes, pulled into the parking lot in another rented car—a Malibu he'd picked up at the airport. He parked between a Ford Thunderbird and a Yamaha motorcycle, then looked at the two buildings linked by a hallway. Both had been constructed of rugged building stone and rough cedar and had mansard roofs. A sign on left-hand building announced it as the orthopedic examination office; the physical therapy headquarters were to the right.

Bolan killed the Malibu, got out and locked the door. A moment later he found himself inside a large waiting room filled with men and women in casts, on crutches and wearing a variety of other restraints and supports. There was a window in the middle of the wall opposite the door. Bolan pulled the Justice Department credentials from his jacket as he reached the opening.

A pretty brunette in her early twenties looked up from the desk in front of her and smiled. She wore a burgundy golf-style shirt with the clinic's logo over her left breast, and Bolan noticed a sparkling wedding ring on her left hand. "May I help you?"

The Executioner returned the smile as he opened the credential case. "Special Agent Belasko to see Dr. Becker," he said.

"Did you have an appointment?"

"I'm not a patient," Bolan said. "I just have a few quick questions to ask the doctor regarding a man I'm looking for."

"Well," the woman said, her smile gradually fading. "He's awful busy."

"It'll take only a second," Bolan said.

"Well, okay. If you want to take a seat, I'll ask him."

Bolan dropped into a chair next to the window as the receptionist disappeared into another part of the building. He found himself between an overweight woman wearing a foot cast and a high school kid in cutoff jeans who was built like a football player.

A loud, angry, unintelligible voice erupted from the rear of the building, and everyone in the waiting room turned toward the receptionist's window.

"That's Becker," the stocky kid next to him informed the Executioner. "Man's got a temper."

Bolan nodded. He waited five minutes, then ten. When ten became fifteen, he looked at his watch.

He didn't have time to wait on tempers.

Moving back to the window, the Executioner looked through the glass to see the same woman seated in her chair, her eyes on the desk. A man of around forty-five, with long blond ringlets and a green scrub suit under his white lab jacket, stood behind her massaging her shoulders.

"Look, Marcy," the man was whispering in a soothing voice. "I'm sorry if I hurt your feelings. "You—" Suddenly sensing Bolan's presence, he looked up.

Marcy looked up, as well, and Bolan saw the smeared eye shadow.

"Who the hell are you?" Becker nearly shouted at the Executioner.

"Special Agent—" Bolan began.

"Yeah, yeah, yeah, she told me," Becker interrupted. "Look whatever it is you're selling, I'm not interested."

Bolan controlled the anger the man's condescending attitude produced in him. He forced a smile. "I'm not *selling* anything," he said. "I need to ask you a few questions about a former patient."

Becker shook his head. "A patient's medical record is privileged information."

"What I need to know has nothing to do with his medical record," Bolan said.

"I don't care. Get out of my office."

"I'd hate to have to subpoena you," Bolan said, dropping the smile.

"We have to do a lot of things in life we hate," Becker said, his face contorting into a nasty grin. "Now get out of here."

Before Bolan could reply, he turned away from the window and strode out of sight.

The woman looked up, dabbing her eyes with a tissue. "I'm sorry," she said. "He's under a lot of pressure."

Bolan smiled. "I understand."

The Executioner walked back to the glass door to the parking lot. As he opened it, he noted the clinic hours, then lifted his wrist to look at his watch.

He'd get the information he needed, whether Dr. Becker liked it or not. And without a subpoena.

In less than an hour.

"SO, WILL YOU be starting next year, Chip?" Becker asked as he rotated the patient's knee back and forth beneath the boy's cutoff jeans.

"I think so, Dr. Becker," the muscular high school football player said. "Coach thinks I've got a chance of making all state." The boy blushed. "A college scout called me this summer, too."

"Why, Chip," Becker said with mock surprise. "It's against NCAA rules to recruit this early."

The boy blushed even deeper. "He just said he wanted to say hello."

Becker chuckled and lightly slapped the boy's knee. "Well, in any case, we'd better get this knee back in shape." He looked up into the clear blue eyes above him. "You lifting weights with the team this summer?"

The boy nodded.

"Okay. No more full squats. No more—"

"But, Doctor," the boy protested. "If I don't—"

"You can substitute leg presses, knee extensions and leg curls. Half squats will be okay, too. But don't go any lower than halfway. You got that?"

The boy nodded again as Becker stood up from the examining chair and turned to his nurse. "Gwen, give Chip some of those Voltaren samples the salesman left this morning. No sense making a future college nose guard pay good money when we've got free ones rotting around here."

The boy's grin was wide.

Becker looked at him briefly. A good looking kid. Blue eyes. Blond hair. Big. Strong. Tough. He might make it at college ball. Then again, he might not. But in any case, he wasn't big enough for the NFL.

Which meant that even if he did play college ball, he'd be needing something to do, something to believe in, in four or five years. He'd remember Dr. Lawrence Becker as a man who'd helped him. He'd be ripe for recruitment, and that's where the Missouri Fascist Party would come in.

Becker left the examining room and entered the main business office, where his nurse was giving the boy a handful of small bottles that contained the anti-inflammatory pills. He moved up to the window that faced the waiting room, careful to stay out of sight through the glass. "Anyone left, Marcy?" he asked.

Marcy Hamilton—no, dammit, he kept forgetting it was Marcy Rogers now—turned to face him. She had wiped her eyes and redone her eye shadow since he'd yelled at her earlier, and Becker felt the thrill rush through him.

God, she was something. Twenty-two years old and breasts you could climb between and get lost in forever. When she wiggled across the room, or bent over the filing cabinet in one of those short skirts she always wore, he practically came in his pants.

"Just Mrs. Shaefer," Marcy said.

Becker leaned forward and snuck a glimpse of the waiting room. Empty except for the fat bitch in the foot cast. He moved back before the woman saw him. "Tell her I got called away to emergency surgery and work her in tomorrow," Becker whispered. He looked into the lovely green eyes that stared back at him guiltily, and felt the muscles in his lower abdomen tighten. "Then stick around a few minutes, Marcy. I need to talk to you."

Marcy turned back to the window.

Becker hurried back into the hall, then turned into his private office. He moved quickly into the rest room, hung his lab coat on a hook and pulled off his surgical greens. Standing nude in front of the full-length mirror, he took a quick survey of himself. Not bad for a guy in his late forties, although he could probably do with a few more sit-ups and abdominal crunches.

Becker lifted the can of deodorant and sprayed his armpits. A quick mouthful of Listerine, then he splashed some cologne on his neck and stared into the mirror.

He had been trying to get into Marcy's pants since she'd started working for him four months earlier. She'd been engaged at the time, and she'd brushed off all of his overtures. But she needed the job. Her brand-new, worthless blue-collar husband probably didn't make over twenty-five grand at the garage where he worked, and twenty-five grand didn't go far these days.

Becker tipped the bottle of cologne and rubbed several drops into his crotch. Goddammit, he'd have the little bitch. He'd have her tonight, too, or else she wouldn't have a job in the morning.

Becker pulled a white polo shirt over his head, then tucked it into a pair of kelly green golf slacks. He ruffled the long blond curls of his hair and reminded himself he had an appointment for another permanent tomorrow morning. He hung a gold chain around his neck.

The rest of the staff had gone home by the time Becker returned to the business office. He found Marcy still seated. She held her purse in her lap, both arms crossed in front of it protectively.

Becker dropped into a chair at the next desk, then rolled its wheels across the carpet until he sat directly in front of the young woman. She stared at him, her eyes frightened.

Becker smiled. He liked that. Fear. It added something to the whole process of seduction. The weak feared the powerful. No one was ever frightened of anyone else unless that person was powerful.

"You're lovely," Becker said in a deep husky voice.

"Doctor," Marcy said. "We've talked about this before. I love my husband. I don't want to do anything that might jeopardize—"

"You love your husband," Becker agreed, nodding his head. "That's nice. He's a nice boy."

"He's a man, Dr. Becker."

"Yes, a nice man," Becker said sarcastically. "So tell me, how is his mechanic job going?" He said the word *mechanic* as if it tasted bad.

Marcy's eyes fell to the floor. She didn't answer.

"Is there a problem?" Becker asked.

Marcy didn't look up. "He was . . . laid off."

Becker felt the adrenaline flood through his body as if he'd just injected it with a syringe. My, my. The mechanic had lost his job. An unexpected stroke of luck. "Well, how sad," he said in a fatherly tone of voice. "That must put quite a strain on the old pocketbook."

A lone tear began to roll down the young woman's smooth cheek. "I . . . love him," she whispered.

"Of course you do," Becker said quickly, his voice turning sarcastic. "So when the electric company comes by your house to turn off the power, just tell them you love your husband, and I'm sure they'll leave it on. When you run out of food, go to the grocery store, tell the manager about this deep devotion you feel, and I'm sure he'll let you fill your basket for free. When they come to repossess your car, Marcy, explain that you love your husband. They'll understand."

Becker leaned forward, reaching out and hooking a forefinger under the beautiful chin. He tilted Marcy's face up until he could look into those emerald green eyes again, and saw the fear had not left them. "Marcy, I want to help you," he whispered. "You've worked hard. You're a valuable member of my staff." He paused, luxuriating in the power he felt.

The fear in the young woman's eyes intensified.

Becker smiled, glancing down at the full round breasts that stretched the golf-shirt logo. *His* logo.

She knows what's about to happen, he thought. She's afraid. But she knows she'll do it. She has no other choice.

"How would you like me to double your salary?" Becker asked.

For a split second Marcy's eyes brightened. Then the fear returned tenfold.

Becker wheeled his chair even closer. "Of course, we'd have to add a few new duties to your job description."

Silence filled the room. Becker waited. Marcy looked down at the floor again. The lone tear became a silent flood streaming down her cheeks, ruining the new mascara job.

"Take off your shirt, Marcy," Becker said.

She didn't move.

"Go ahead."

Slowly the tears were joined by a soft gentle sob, and Marcy pulled the tail of her shirt out of her skirt.

She hesitated again, then pulled it over her head and dropped it on the floor.

Becker stifled a gasp. Goddammit, they were even bigger than he'd thought. "Now the bra," he managed to choke out.

Marcy leaned forward and reached behind her back with both hands. She still stared at the floor, sobbing quietly as the white brassiere fell free and joined her shirt on the floor.

This time Becker did gasp. Breathing hard now, he stood up. "Unzip my pants," he commanded, his voice hoarse. "And get on your knees."

Marcy was sobbing harder as she leaned forward and reached for his zipper.

It was then that Dr. Lawrence Becker heard the noise behind him.

## CHAPTER SIX

Jerry Wayne Waack watched the two heads in the front seat of the Cadillac as he pulled in behind them at the red light, and suddenly realized he was about to make history.

Waack didn't know for sure, but there might have been two U.S. senators killed on the same day before. But even if there had been, he was certain that there had never been two senators from the same state killed on the same day.

Waack straightened his tie in the rearview mirror as he waited for the light. A soft piano concerto was playing over the speakers in the back seat. He had kept the radio on during the drive from Taos to Santa Fe, waiting to see when the bodies in the rear room of the Laughing Horse Inn would be discovered. So far he had heard nothing.

The light turned green and Waack returned his hands to the steering wheel. He trailed the Cadillac on down Guadeloupe Avenue, then followed it into the corner parking lot of the Pontchartrain Restaurant. As he turned, the music on the radio ended and a news voice came on. "William Diel, veteran U.S. Senator from New Mexico, was found dead of gunshot wounds today in a Taos hotel." The radio station's news theme music came on, then the voice said, "More to come in a moment."

Waack saw Senator Randall T. Mitchell pull his Cadillac into one of two empty spaces in front of the restaurant, and guided his own car into the one next to it. He thought suddenly of the two dead bodies still in the trunk. He had not had time to dispose of them yet, and he grinned as an idea hit him as to how that might be done.

Senator Mitchell was rounding the car to open the door for his wife as Waack got out. He studied the man's face briefly; Mitchell evidently hadn't heard the news report. Good. The man would be less on guard if he didn't know Diel was dead.

"Why, Senator," Waack said in mock astonishment as he closed the car door behind him. "This *is* a pleasant surprise." He extended his hand.

Mitchell stopped in front of his wife's door. Although a rookie on the senate floor this year, Mitchell's smile was already that of the practiced politician. He took Waack's hand with his right and opened the car door with his left. "Thank you, Mr. . . . ."

"Hammerstein, John Hammerstein," Waack said, dropping the hand. "No reason you should remember me, Senator. I was but a small wheel in your campaign machine." He paused. "But I like to think I helped a little."

Verna Mitchell was out of the Cadillac now and took her place beside her husband. Waack glanced at her. With her long auburn hair and graceful build, and the senator's youthful good looks and charm, the only thing that kept them from passing as a set of Barbie and Ken dolls were the deep bags under Mrs. Mitchell's eyes.

"John, don't belittle yourself," Mitchell said, still beaming his vote-getter smile. "It takes all of the wheels working, and working hard, to make any machine run successfully. I appreciate your support. John, have you met my wife, Verna?"

Waack smiled at her. "The pleasure is mine." The three turned and started toward the door of the restaurant.

"We were just about to dine, John," Mitchell said. "Won't you join us?"

To the senator's side, Waack saw Verna Mitchell's face fall. "No, no. I wouldn't want to get in the way, Senator," he said. "I suspect an important man such as yourself has precious little time to spend alone with his wife."

"Nonsense, John. Please. Join us."

Waack shrugged. "All right."

They were met at the door by a host wearing black tails and tie, then escorted to a small candle-lit table near the corner. The host pulled the chair out for Verna as Waack and Mitchell took their seats.

The host was replaced by a dark sultry woman in a black evening dress who took their cocktail orders. Then a similarly dressed waitress arrived with menus.

"Have you eaten here before, John?" Mitchell asked as he frowned into the open menu.

"No, this is my first time."

Verna Mitchell, resigned to having what she thought would be a romantic evening with her husband ruined once again by politics, brightened slightly, and said, "Try the *boeuf aux champignon*. It's excellent."

"Why, thank you, I will," Waack said, as the waitress brought their drinks, then took their orders. "Would you like some wine, my dear?" Mitchell asked his wife. She nodded.

"Yes, I believe I would, as well," the senator said. He turned to Waack. "The house wine here is as good as any you can find in a bottle for under five hundred dollars. I'd recommend the Burgundy."

Waack smiled and nodded good-naturedly.

Mitchell waited until the waitress had left, then took a sip of his Scotch and soda and looked at Waack again. "I'm very sorry I can't remember you from the campaign, John," he said. "There were so many good, dedicated people helping me get elected. What exactly did you—"

"I was here, at the Santa Fe headquarters," Waack said. He lifted his glass of bourbon to his lips, then set it back down, noticing that the martini glass the waitress had brought Verna Mitchell was already empty. "Just did the usual. Answered phones, addressed brochures, that sort of thing. I met you one day when you stopped in, but really, Senator, I don't expect you to remember me."

Mitchell's face looked relieved. Waack smiled inwardly. Politicians, damn. Always looking for an out, and happy as hell to find one.

"So, tell me, John," Mitchell said. "What is it you do?" He laughed smoothly, easily, affectedly. "When you aren't helping me get elected, that is?"

"Oh, I dabble in this and that," Waack said, curling his fingers around his glass. "I own a pharmacy over on Galisteo. Got a half interest in a lumberyard here in Santa Fe, a little stock in another over in Albuquerque."

"An entrepreneur, eh?" Mitchell said. It was obvious he smelled wealth, which might be translated into big campaign contributions.

Waack forced an embarrassed smile. "I suppose," he said modestly.

"Well, that's fine, John, just fine."

The waitress reappeared with salads and a bottle of wine, which she poured for the dinner companions. Verna Mitchell stared at her glass for a moment, then slowly lifted it to her lips. She took a sip, which became a gulp, then suddenly the glass was empty.

Mitchell shot her a dirty look, then turned to Waack again. "So tell us about your family, John. Are you married?"

Verna was already pouring herself another glass of wine as Waack said, "No, not anymore. I'm afraid I'm a widower."

"I'm terribly sorry," Mitchell said quickly.

"Don't be," Waack said. "We had fourteen wonderful years together, and that's more than most people have in a lifetime."

Mitchell turned to his wife. "Do you see, my dear?" he said. "Do you see that what I always say is true? It is this kind of positive attitude, this kind of bravery in my constituents, that has made this state and this country great."

Verna nodded and set down her empty glass. "Yes, Mitch," she said, and now her voice was slightly slurred. "I think it's wonderful that his wife's dead and he takes it so well."

Mitchell lowered his voice and spoke softly between clenched teeth. "Please take it easy on the wine, dear."

Dinner arrived, and the conversation turned to the Mitchells' two sons and other family matters. They were almost finished eating when the host who had seated them arrived. "Senator," he said quietly, "I'm sorry to disturb you, but you have a telephone call."

Mitchell smiled to his wife, then Waack. "Duty calls," he said. He excused himself and walked through the dining room to the lobby with the man in the black tails.

Verna poured another glass of wine and the two sat silently.

When Mitchell returned, the blood had faded from his face. "Bill Diel was murdered in Taos this morning," he said.

Verna didn't change expressions.

"Good Lord, no," Waack said. "Do you know any more?"

Mitchell started to speak, then stopped, and Waack suspected the senator had just decided that John Hammerstein didn't need to know that Diel's body had been found with that of a young hooker. "No," he said. "I suppose we'll learn the details later."

Waack shook his head and looked down at the table. "What goes on these days," he said.

Waack and the Mitchells finished dinner in silence. When the waitress brought the check, Waack grabbed it out of her hand.

"But we invited you," Mitchell protested. "Please—"

"No, Senator," Waack said, pulling a hundred-dollar bill from his money clip and dropping it on the table with the check. "I insist. It's the least I can do." He paused. "I'm a fairly lonely man, you see, and to-night has been a pleasant diversion."

Verna Mitchell's drunken eyes clouded over, and Waack thought for a moment she was about to start crying.

"Yes, it has been nice," Mitchell said. "At least until we received the word about Bill's death. And that's no fault of the company here, of course."

Waack couldn't suppress a smile at the irony of the statement.

Mitchell took the smile to mean that Waack had enjoyed the compliment. "Give us your telephone number, John," he said. "Let's do this again. Soon. It'll be on us this time, and if we're lucky we won't have it spoiled by such rotten news."

Waack shook his head. "I'm afraid I can't give you my telephone number," he said.

"But why not?" Mitchell frowned.

"Well, I don't really have a permanent number anymore," Waack said as he unbuttoned his suit coat. "And even if I did, I'm afraid it wouldn't do you any good."

The senator's frown deepened. "I'm sorry, I'm afraid I don't understand," he said. "Why wouldn't it do me any good?"

"Because dead people do not make phone calls," Waack said as he stood up and swung the Ingram MAC-10 submachine gun to the end of the shoulder sling.

Mitchell's eyes opened wide in terror.

The dull clouds still covered Verna's eyes, and later Waack would wonder if her alcohol-soaked brain even realized she was about to be shot.

Holding the trigger back, Waack emptied the MAC-10's magazine into Senator and Mrs. Mitchell, dropped the untraceable gun on the floor of the restaurant and walked quickly past the shocked and frozen diners.

Back at the rented Plymouth, he opened the trunk, fished a tire tool from under the bodies of the two men and moved to the Cadillac next to him. Thirty seconds later the trunk of Senator Mitchell's car was open and the bodies were inside.

Waack got behind the wheel of the Plymouth as the first man brave enough to leave the Pontchartrain Restaurant stuck his nose out the door. Waack waved to him as he drove out of the parking lot.

"All's well that end's well, Senator," he said as he turned back down Guadeloupe. "That was Shakespeare, of course."

BEHIND THE WHEEL of the Malibu, Bolan watched as, one by one, the patients who had filled Dr. Lawrence Becker's waiting room left the clinic and began emptying the parking lot of cars. The Thunderbird at his side was driven away by an elderly man with one arm in a sling, then the athletic-looking boy who had warned Bolan about Becker's temper came through the glass door and got onto the motorcycle. A moment later the woman who had sat on the Executioner's other side struggled through the door on crutches and left in a ten-year-old Dodge.

Bolan saw two women wearing the clinic's golf shirts exit a side door and disappear to a parking area at the rear. They reappeared again in front of the clinic in a Volkswagen and drove away.

The Executioner waited ten minutes, then glanced to the brown Mercedes parked in Becker's reserved space next to the building.

Bolan had planned to catch the doctor on his way out of the building and take him to some secluded spot where they could have a little talk about Jerry Wayne Waack. But it was beginning to look like Becker would be staying late, and the Executioner knew that each second he wasted in the parking lot might mean the Anju Dragons raped another innocent girl, murdered another innocent man or sold another kilo of cocaine that would turn some unsuspecting kid into an addict.

After fifteen minutes, Bolan got out of the Malibu and crossed the parking lot to the building. He tried opening the door. It was unlocked.

A moment later he was in Becker's private office. As he moved silently across the carpet toward an open door in the opposite wall, he heard soft voices drifting down the hallway. He stopped at the door, listening.

"When they come to repossess your car, Marcy," Bolan heard Becker say sarcastically, "explain that you love your husband. They'll understand." There was a pause, then Becker said, "Marcy, I want to help you. You've worked hard. You're a valuable member of my staff.''

Bolan walked quietly toward the door through which the doctor's voice had come. He heard Becker say, "How would you like me to double your salary?" Then he ordered her to take off her shirt and bra.

"Unzip my pants," Becker said as Bolan reached the door.

The Executioner peered around the corner to see Becker standing behind a chair, facing away from him. Just beyond the doctor, the receptionist Bolan had spoken to earlier had knelt on the floor. Nude from the waist up, she was crying silently as she fumbled with Becker's zipper.

Bolan crossed the room quickly, grabbed a handful of Becker's long blond curls and jerked him backward. The chair rolled to the side as the doctor crashed to the floor, screaming.

The woman froze, then crossed her arms across her bare breasts and looked up at the Executioner.

Becker rolled to his side and came up on all fours to face the Executioner. "Goddammit!" he roared as he recognized Bolan. "Do you know who I am? I'll have your fuckin' badge for this! You can't—"

Bolan lifted a foot under the doctor's chin and Becker flipped backward onto the floor again.

The Executioner leaned over, grabbed the woman's shirt and bra from the floor and handed them to her. "Go back to one of the examining rooms and get dressed," he ordered.

She nodded. Keeping one hand over her breasts, she took her clothes with the other and hurried into the hall.

Becker shook his head to clear the cobwebs and started to stand up. Bolan reached down and grabbed him under the armpits, helping him.

"You've had it, you fucking pig," Becker said. "You're gonna be wearing a rent-a-cop uniform at some hospital when I get finished with you. I play golf every Wednesday with Congressman—"

Bolan drove a hard right into the doctor's belly. Becker doubled over and dropped to his knees as the air rushed from his lungs. He held his abdomen with both hands.

The Executioner stepped back, waiting angrily as the man caught his breath. When Becker looked up again, he said, "Is this what you have to do to get women to pay attention to you, Becker?"

As the air returned to his lungs, Becker's attitude returned with it. "She wanted it."

"It didn't look that way to me," Bolan said. He grabbed Becker again and dropped him into the chair. "I came to find out where a friend of yours is," he said. "Jerry Wayne Waack."

"I don't know any—"

Bolan backhanded the doctor. The chair tipped over and Becker landed on his back. Blood dripped from his swelling lower lip as he sat back up.

"Where is he?" the Executioner demanded.

The doctor didn't answer.

Bolan righted the chair, sat him in it again, then delivered another backhand. As he was lifting the chair once more, he said, "We can do this all night if you'd like."

Becker looked up from the floor. "I want a lawyer," he said. "And I want him now."

The Executioner chuckled. "Let's clear something up," he said. "You threatened to have my badge a minute ago. That's impossible. I don't have one."

Becker's eyes moved to the pocket where he'd seen Bolan stash the Justice Department credentials earlier.

Bolan answered the unasked question. "Phony," he said. "I'm on my own, and you're going to tell me what I want to know. One way or another, you're going to tell me."

Tears were forming in the doctor's eyes, and Bolan couldn't keep from comparing them to the ones he had seen on the receptionist's pretty face a few minutes before. Dr. Lawrence Becker was among the most detestable of men. He used his position to coerce sexual favors from women within his power structure, and Bolan had no sympathy for him.

Lifting the weeping man into the chair for the third time, the Executioner drew back his hand.

"Please," Becker whined. "Wait!"

Bolan's arm froze halfway to the doctor's face.

"I haven't seen Waack for some time," the doctor said. "Last I heard of him, he was in Tennessee with some of the Klan boys."

"How long ago was that?"

"Six, maybe seven months. Really. I don't know where he is."

In the corner of his eye, Bolan saw Marcy, now fully dressed, standing in the doorway to the hall.

Bolan turned to her. "Go on home," he said.

"And don't come back," Becker said. "You're fired."

The Executioner backhanded Becker again, then lifted him from the floor to his feet. Slamming him up against a tall gray filing cabinet, he stuck his nose an inch from the doctor's face. "No, she's not fired," he said. "She's coming back tomorrow to open the clinic, and as of this minute you've just doubled her salary like you promised." He paused. "And her job description *doesn't* change."

The woman moved forward, lightly taking Bolan's arm. "Thank you," she said. "But he won't do it. As soon as you're gone—"

Still staring at Becker, Bolan said, "He'll do it, all right. Because if he doesn't, I'll be back." He dropped Becker and the doctor slid to a seat on the floor.

Bolan turned to the woman. "Go on home," he said. "Open the clinic tomorrow morning and carry on as usual. Tell the patients that the doctor's going to be out of town for a few days."

Marcy nodded and hurried out of the room.

When he'd heard a door open and close, Bolan turned back to the sniveling man on the floor. "You have any clothes here?" he demanded to know.

"Just my golfing outfit," Becker said.

"Then I suggest you pack your little outfit," Bolan said.

Becker struggled to his feet. "You're *kidnapping* me?" he asked.

"Call it that if you like," the Executioner said. "But what it boils down to is you and I are going to Tennessee."

THE POWER of 260 horses generated a relaxing hum in the Executioner's ear as Jack Grimaldi guided the Beechcraft Bonanza through the darkening sky toward Memphis. In his other ear, Bolan listened to the ring of a telephone over the extension line hooked into the cellular phone in the hands of Becker.

Turned in his seat, Bolan could see Becker seated in the back of the plane as they waited for the line to be picked up. The doctor's eyes were wide with excitement.

Lawrence Becker was having fun.

The Executioner had seen the same phenomenon more times over the years than he could remember. A snitch who was frightened and belligerent at first often became enthralled with the "game" as he became part of it. He began to think of himself as a "secret agent" of sorts, and as the illusion grew in his brain, so did his enthusiasm.

Bolan heard the click as the phone was answered. "Hello," a voice with a deep Southern accent said.

"Hey, Crater," Becker said, his own cultured voice suddenly traveling several hundred miles below the Mason-Dixon line. "It's Becker."

"Hey, Doc," Crater Cargill replied. "Long time no see. Where you be?"

Becker cleared his throat, glanced at Bolan and winked. "On my way into town," he said. "Be at the airport in..."

"Fifteen minutes," Jack Grimaldi said behind the Bonanza's controls.

"Fifteen minutes, Crate," Becker repeated into the phone. "Why don't you meet us in the lounge and I'll buy you a drink."

"Like to, Doc," Cargill said. "But we're busier right now than a ring-tailed tooter. The tail of my coat ain't hit the seat of my pants for three days."

"What you got going?" Becker asked.

"This line safe?"

Becker looked up again to Bolan.

The Executioner shook his head. "Tell him to talk in generalities," he whispered. On the off chance that the cops had tapped into either of the lines, the Executioner didn't want them busting the man before he found out where Waack was.

"Don't be too definite," Becker said, then winked at Bolan again.

"Well, we got a deal . . . a business deal going down tonight. But we had some complications arise." He paused. "Our salesman got drunk last night and landed hisself in jail. Damn shame, too. This was one hell of a deal. Great opportunity, if you know what I mean."

"Not exactly," Becker said. "But I've got an idea. Maybe I can help."

A chuckle came over the line. "Thanks for the offer, Doc," Crater Cargill said. "But this ain't really your type of deal."

Becker's face reddened slightly. It was obvious that he was known to the Klansmen of Tennessee, but also that the "business deal" they had going down wasn't something they thought him capable of handling.

"I didn't mean me," the doctor said. "I've got an...associate along for the ride. And unless I miss my guess on what kind of deal you've got planned, I'd say he might be just the salesman you need."

There was a long pause on the line. Bolan listened to the static and waited.

Finally Cargill said, "Okay, Doc. We been battin' our heads against a brick wall all night tryin' to come up with a replacement. You bring this feller on in and I'll meet you at the bar at the airport. Can't hurt nothin'."

Becker brightened. "You got it, Crater. See you in a few."

The doctor killed the line and looked up at Bolan as the Executioner pulled the plug from his ear. "Hey, did I tell you I had connections?"

"We'll see," Bolan said. "What do you think they've got planned?"

"Can't be sure, but my guess is a hit. J. Patrick McGinney. They've been talking about him for a long time."

"Who is he?" Bolan asked.

"State representative," Becker said. "Liberal asshole who likes to agitate."

Bolan nodded. "You remember my story?" he asked.

Becker stiffened. "I don't have Alzheimer's," he said.

"Repeat it to me just the same," Bolan ordered. "I want to make sure you've got it right."

Becker looked him in the eye. "I haven't lived up to your expectations so far?" he said sarcastically.

The Executioner met the gaze and lowered his eyebrows. Becker was doing a good job, but Bolan hadn't forgotten that basically he was nothing but a scumbag who used his position to force innocent young women to have sex with him. "Do what I told you," he said.

Becker broke the stare and looked to the side of the plane. "Your name is Mike Belasko," he said. "We were fraternity brothers in undergraduate school at Louisiana Tech, and we've stayed in touch over the years." He paused and sighed, as if the whole speech was an effort far beneath him. "Hadn't seen you since college, then you showed up on my doorstep last week needing a place to hide."

"Go on," Bolan said.

Becker sighed again. "You'd always been obscure about what kind of work you did, and I'd always suspected it was something illegal, but never pried into it." He looked back at Bolan and his voice grew sarcastic. "Now, lo and behold, I find out you were a hit man for the mafia, and that you've recently fallen out of favor with the mob and needed not only a place to hide, but a way to make a living."

Bolan returned the sarcasm. "Very good," he said. "Now all you have to do is convince this Crater Cargill of all that."

Becker's eyes grew serious. "Cargill isn't the man we have to convince," he said. "He's the front man. It's Homer Shoemaker who'll have to buy this story."

"Who's he?"

"Shoemaker's the power and money behind the Klan in Tennessee. If things go well, you'll meet him."

The Executioner leaned between the seats and pushed his face close to Becker's as the lights of Memphis appeared and Grimaldi began their descent. "Make sure things go well, Becker," he said. "Make real sure. Your life depends on it."

THE AIRPORT LOUNGE looked like a thousand other airport lounges in thousands of other airports scattered across the United States. The easy-to-wipe glass tabletops were held in place by equally maintenance-free stainless-steel borders and table legs. The chairs were of the same glistening steel. The carpet had been woven into a soothing geometrical pattern that some psychologist believed would relax flight anxiety, and the entire rear wall was thick glass that afforded a view of the runways.

Becker and Bolan stopped just inside the door. "There he is," Becker said, nodding toward a corner next to the window. He led the way toward Crater Cargill's table.

Bolan would never know for sure how the fleshy man in the tight double-knit slacks, cowboy boots and cheap plaid sport coat got his nickname. There were two obvious possibilities. First, Crater Cargill had salt-and-pepper hair. But the "salt" in the oily black mess wasn't gray. It came from the huge rocklike chunks of white dandruff that were scattered across the top of his head and looked as if they had indeed left deep cavities in his scalp.

The other possibility, Bolan noticed as they neared the table, was the man's face. In his early fifties, Cargill still bore the scars of a grave case of teenage acne. The dips and curves in his jaws curled up as he smiled at the approaching men.

A red-haired waitress wearing a short green skirt and ruffled blouse had followed Bolan and Becker across the room. She waited for the three men to shake hands and exchange greetings, then took their orders.

The Executioner saw Becker staring at her legs. "Bourbon and Coke for me, precious," Becker said. "Crater?"

"The same," Cargill said.

The waitress turned to Bolan. "The same," he said. "But leave out the bourbon."

The woman smiled. "Just a Coke, then?"

The Executioner nodded, and she hurried away.

Bolan felt Cargill's eyes on him and turned to face the man. "You don't drink?"

"Not when it looks like I might be working."

Cargill's eyes swung to Becker. "This ol' boy just might do, after all," he said.

The men exchanged small talk as they waited for their drinks, beginning with football and ending with Becker's favorite subject when Cargill said, "So, Doc, you still gettin' all that office pussy?"

Becker gave him a warped grin. "All I can handle," he said.

Becker and Cargill laughed uproariously, Cargill's fat belly bouncing against the side of the table as he jerked.

The waitress returned and set the men's glasses before them, then skillfully dodged a pat on the rear from Becker and escaped to a table across the room.

"Okay, Crater," Becker said, lowering his voice to a whisper. "This deal you got going down what I think it is?" He looked to both sides. The tables next to them were empty. "McGinney?"

Cargill nodded, then crossed his arms in front of him and leaned in. "It was a sweet deal, Doc. The sweetest." He paused and glanced up at Bolan. "We can trust this guy, right?"

Becker nodded.

"McGinney's set to speak at the old Shiloh Theater tonight. Gonna give one of his nigger-agitatin' talks and get the porch monkeys up in an uproar again. But we got an inside man there at the theater. An usher." Now it was Cargill's turn to glance around and reassure himself they weren't being heard. "The rifle's already upstairs in the old projection room and there's a closed-off back staircase that ain't been used for twenty years." He paused and shook his head in disgust. "It was an in-and-out setup that couldn't have gone wrong."

"So what happened?" Becker asked.

"Jimmy Jack Warfield," Cargill said. "That's what happened."

"Jimmy Jack?" Becker said incredulously. "Don't tell me he was your shooter? He's a damn alcoholic, Crater."

Cargill shrugged. "This thing came up fast, Doc. He was all we could get. Besides, he can knock the eye out of a squirrel at five hundred yards, drunk or sober.'' He paused for another visual recon of the area. "Then he and his old lady got into it again last night. He's sittin' in the county lockup right now.''

Bolan saw Becker glance at him out of the corner of his eye. "What about J.W.?" he said. "Where's he?"

Cargill shrugged. "Waack?" he said. "Who the hell knows? But I'd give up two inches of my dick if that albino son of a bitch would walk through the door right now.''

Becker chuckled. "You'd might give up all of it if he heard you call him that," he said.

"That ain't no shit," Cargill agreed.

The waitress returned to check on their drinks, strategically taking up a position next to Bolan and away from Becker's groping hands. All three men shook their heads and she went away again.

Crater Cargill turned to Bolan but spoke to Becker. "This guy a shooter, you say?"

"The best," Becker said quickly.

"Tell me about him," Cargill said. He continued to look the Executioner up and down, nodding occasionally, as Becker went through his well-rehearsed story. When the doctor had finished, he said. "What got you on the outs with the greaseballs?"

Bolan remembered the laugh the other two men had enjoyed when the subject of Becker's female office staff came up. "It had to do with a girl," he said. "The daughter of one of the dons. I suspect I don't have to fill you in on the details for you to get the picture.''

Becker looked down at the table, shook his head and laughed. "It takes balls to bang the daughter of a guy like that," he said.

The waitress came back with the check and Crater Cargill reached into his pocket and pulled several bills off a large roll, then stood up. "Okay, then," he said. "What do you boys say we go meet old Homer?"

## CHAPTER SEVEN

The distant notes of "Beale Street Blues" drifted through the windows of the Chevy pickup as Cargill drove Bolan and Becker past a brightly lighted convenience store, then turned onto a private road leading up a hill. The waters of the Mississippi River appeared as they topped the incline and parked in front of a three-story antebellum mansion.

Bolan opened the door and got out, his eyes drifting down the slope as Cargill killed the engine. Cargill led Bolan and Becker up the steps to a porch that circled the house. A porch swing and other lounge furniture stood on the thin wooden slats, looking as if they should be occupied by beautiful women in floral cotton dresses and bonnets, drinking mint juleps as they fanned themselves against the heat.

Crater Cargill stopped in front of a double oak door between two sets of multipane windows and thumped the knocker against the wood. A moment later an elderly black man in tails and a bow tie ushered them in.

"Mr. Shoemaker waitin' in the den fo' you gentlemen," he said as he led them through an entryway and into an elaborately decorated living room with an eighteen-foot ceiling. "Can I fetch y'all somethin' to drink?"

"No thanks, Andrew," Cargill said. "We already had ours."

Another short hallway took them to the den. Andrew stuck his head through the open door and said, "Yo' guests is here, Mr. Shoemaker."

"Send them on in," a gruff unseen voice called out from inside the room.

Andrew stepped back and bowed. Cargill led the way into the room.

Bolan scanned the decor as he entered behind Becker. A few bookshelves had been built into the oak walls, but they held more knickknacks and odds and ends than books. Bolan saw several cast-iron sculptures of antique gin mills, and remembered that Cargill had mentioned that it had been Homer Shoemaker's great-grandfather who had started the family cotton empire.

Shoemaker sat in a high-backed leather chair, his legs covered by a multicolored afghan. He looked up from the open leather-bound book in his lap as the three men entered, but made no effort to rise.

Bolan took one of the chairs to which the old man pointed. This was a man who was used to giving orders and having them carried out. People stood when *he* entered a room, not the other way around.

"Good evening, Crater." Shoemaker smiled, smoothing out the wrinkles of his weathered face. "I see you brought some friends."

Cargill had taken the chair next to Bolan, with a small end table and lamp separating them. Becker sat on Cargill's other side. "Why, you've met Dr. Becker," he said, nodding to the man next to him.

"Yes, of course," Shoemaker said, though his eyes betrayed the fact that he didn't remember the man.

"He's with the Missouri Fascist Party," Cargill added.

A light went on behind Shoemaker's eyes. "Ah, yes, I remember the doctor now. Last year in Atlanta, am I correct?"

Becker nodded.

"And this is Mike Belasko, a college friend of Dr. Becker's," Cargill said, jerking his head toward Bolan. "But I got a damn good feeling he's about to become our friend, too."

Homer Shoemaker waited silently for him to go on.

"The McGinney deal is set up," Cargill said. "Everything's in place for tonight except the shooter, Mr. Shoemaker. And you already know what happened there."

Shoemaker glanced at Bolan, then cleared his throat dramatically. "Perhaps I should know a little more about Mr. Belasko before we go on, Crater," he said.

"Oh yeah, sure," Cargill said. He tried to cross his legs, but his chubby thigh slid off his leg. "Doc, you want to tell him about Mike?"

Becker went through the same story he'd given Cargill earlier, with Shoemaker looking back and forth between him and Bolan as the doctor spoke. When he'd finished, Shoemaker turned his attention back to the Executioner and smiled.

"That's an impressive résumé, Mr. Belasko," he said. He paused, furrowing his eyebrows, choosing his words carefully. "I have a few friends—no, let's say acquaintances—among the Sicilians." He chuckled slightly. "Occasionally we have found we had bilateral goals and have assisted each other—although it was a union both races would avoid were this a perfect world." He paused again. "I'd not like to insult you, Mr. Belasko, but surely you must realize that before we go further I must be certain you are not just some clever law-enforcement officer."

"Of course," Bolan said.

"Tell me who you've worked for that I might know."

Bolan hesitated. He could spout out the names of mafiosi for the rest of the night if that's what the old man wanted. He hadn't worked for them, but he'd worked against them, and he knew who they were. But if Shoemaker really did have contacts into the mob, and made a few calls...

No, the Executioner decided. The Klan leader would not have time—at least not before the hit tonight. McGinney's speech was set to begin in less than an hour, and Shoemaker would know that no cop masquerading as a hit man would actually kill an innocent Tennessee state representative just to authenticate his cover.

"I've worked several times for the DeLucas in Chicago," Bolan said. "Do you know them?"

Shoemaker shook his head. "No, I'm afraid our paths haven't crossed."

"How about Tony Fusco or Jack Lettieri in Miami?"

"I know of them, but we have not met."

Bolan blew air through his lips. "Okay, there's Salvatore Salerno in the Big Apple, Tush Toppacardi in

L.A. and Leo 'The Pussy' Turrin. And I've contracted to the Colombians on occasion, although the cartels usually take care of their own 'wet work.' Let's see, there's—"

"I'm rather proud to say I've met none of those cocaine animals, Mr. Belasko," Shoemaker interrupted. "Tush Toppacardi, however, and I were acquainted. I understand he was killed in a supermarket parking lot last year."

Bolan nodded. "Took a full cylinder from a .357 in the head," he said. "I had nothing to do with it. Word on the street was it was Jimmy Silver pulled the trigger." He paused, then said, "But we'll never know for sure. They found Jimmy floating in White Bear Lake north of Minneapolis three months ago."

Shoemaker nodded. "You mentioned Leo Turrin?" he said.

"Yeah. You know him?"

"I met him years ago during a trip to the North," Shoemaker said. "I've bumped into him a time or two since. They called him the Puss because he had the best stable of working girls in the country." The old man laughed. "I was younger then."

Bolan smiled, working hard to conceal his sudden excitement. He had thrown Leo Turrin's name out offhandedly, simply hoping that Shoemaker would have heard of the mob elder statesman. The fact that they'd met was almost too good to be true.

Leo Turrin was a well known mafioso. But he was also a career undercover specialist for the Justice Department's Orgcrime Division and an officer of Stony Man Farm.

"The Puss is a close personal friend of mine," Bolan said. "If you need verification, he'd be the man to call." He paused, letting his face turn serious. "I can trust him not to talk about it. You see, Mr. Shoemaker, like Dr. Becker told you, I've got a problem until this thing about the don's daughter dies down. I'd just as soon the Italians didn't know where I was."

Homer Shoemaker chuckled. "Yes, the don's daughter. I'm beginning to suspect you got to know the Puss the same way I did. Do you have a number where Leo can be reached?"

"Sure," the Executioner said. Stony Man Farm had several "hello" lines that were answered in a variety of ways for undercover operations. Any of them would reach Leo, and he'd know as soon as the name Belasko was mentioned that he needed to go along with the story. "But, Mr. Shoemaker, let's just say I was a cop. I could have another cop on the other end playing this Turrin's part, right?"

Shoemaker waved a hand in front of his face. "I'll ask Turrin enough questions that only he could answer to assure me it's him."

Bolan nodded. "You want to call him now?"

"No, no," Shoemaker said. "There won't be time. Besides, you're getting ready to kill a man for me, Mr. Belasko. That's pretty good evidence that you aren't a law-enforcement undercover man." His eyes narrowed slightly. "I'll call Mr. Turrin while you're gone. If everything goes smoothly, I'll have more work for you."

"Can you give me an idea what it'll be?" Bolan asked. "I like to kick these things around in my mind as long as possible."

Shoemaker hesitated, then shook his head. "We'll discuss it when you return." He turned to Cargill. "Crater, in the drawer of the table next to you you'll find an envelope. Please get it out and give it to Mr. Belasko."

Cargill opened the drawer, fished out a large brown envelope and handed it to Bolan.

The Executioner opened it to find several eight-by-ten color photographs of a thin man with fiery red hair and thick round, rimless eyeglasses. "McGinney?" he asked. "How recent are these pictures?"

"All within the last month," Shoemaker said. "But you shouldn't even need them. He'll be introduced onstage." He turned once again to Cargill. "Crater, take these gentlemen to the Shiloh Theater, then bring him back here when this is over."

Bolan and Becker stood up as Cargill started out of the room.

"Oh, Crater," Shoemaker said. "By the way."

Crater Cargill turned back to the old man in the chair.

"Take Holly and Olin with you, and stay close to Mr. Belasko and Dr. Becker. Just in case I'm wrong, and the shooting doesn't come off as planned..." Homer Shoemaker let his voice trail off for a moment as he raised his leather-bound book again. "Kill them both, won't you please?"

MEMPHIS'S BEALE STREET, had changed drastically since the days when W. C. Handy wrote his famous blues tunes named after St. Louis, Memphis and Beale Street itself. Where saloons had once operated twenty-four hours a day, and prostitutes of every size, shape, color and specialization could be found around the clock, as well, there now stood restaurants, cafés and shopping areas.

Beale Street was still colorful, just not as much so as it had been when the streetlights had been powered by gas.

Crater Cargill turned off Beale onto a narrow side street and pulled the pickup up to a parking meter along the curb. Bolan got out, watching the convertible carrying Shoemaker's hillbilly henchmen, Holly and Olin, pull in behind. Dressed almost identically in soiled blue overalls, work boots and dirty baseball caps, they got out and joined him, Becker and Cargill on the sidewalk.

Cargill looked to Bolan. "Okay, Belasko," he said, grinning. "Here's where you show us your stuff." He glanced down the street. "The Shiloh's two blocks on down and just to the right. Can't see it from here. But you go on past it and an ol' boy name of Skeeter'll meet you at the alley door. Just knock. He's an usher."

Bolan nodded. "And when it's over?"

"Skeeter'll show you how to get out. Just come on back here to the truck."

"Where are you guys going to be?" Bolan asked.

"Why, we're goin' in to watch that fucker talk sweet about the niggers." Cargill laughed. "Who knows?

We might all come out of there Yankees." He paused, then said, "Hey, no offense. Put one in the son of a bitch for me, huh?"

Bolan smiled. "You've got it."

The men walked the first block together, then Bolan dropped behind as they turned the corner. He continued on down the side street, watching them walk toward the front of the Shiloh Theater.

The Executioner watched Becker walking next to Cargill. Earlier, when they'd stopped for gas after leaving Shoemaker's house, he'd gotten the doctor alone long enough to explain what would happen to him if Becker took this opportunity to expose the Executioner's true objectives.

Becker had no trouble believing Bolan's first bullet would be for him. Still, with a guy like the doctor, it didn't pay to take anything for granted.

Bolan walked down the street, passing the two-story building and noting the ornate architecture of the gaslight era. According to Cargill, the Shiloh had once been a focal point of Tennessee entertainment, featuring burlesque performances, then adding silent films before finally turning to talkies. It had been shut down in the 1950s, then reopened a few years ago by a group of enterprising young businessmen intent on its restoration. They'd been renting it for concerts, stage plays and political rallies ever since.

The Executioner turned into the alley behind the building and walked to a modern steel door set in the ancient brown brick. He rapped the back of his hand lightly against the steel and the door opened immediately.

"Martin?" a voice said.

"No," Bolan said. "Belasko."

A soft but shrill giggle came through the opening and the door opened wider. Bolan ducked inside to see a grinning man in his early twenties. In the dim backstage lighting, the Executioner could barely see the broken, rotting teeth between the thin lips. The man wore a bright red usher's uniform, and long stringy hair fell from beneath his cap.

"Just checking, Belasko," Skeeter said. "Can't be too careful. Follow me." Turning on his heel, he led the Executioner along a curtain toward a framed ten-foot painting that leaned against the wall.

With a quick glance both ways, Skeeter shifted the picture to the side to reveal a doorway. "Steps back here ain't been used since they remodeled," he whispered. "They ain't secret or nothin', but it ain't everybody knows about them, neither."

Bolan followed the young man up the dusty stairs, wiping cobwebs from his face as he went. When they reached the second floor, they found themselves in what had once been the Shiloh's projection room. Now it was a storage area, with wooden crates and cardboard boxes stacked along the walls.

Through the projection window, the Executioner could see the balcony just below. Beyond that, the front seats on the ground floor were visible, and past them, the orchestra pit and then the stage. A podium stood center stage, and a row of chairs had been set up behind it amid rally signs and red, white and blue bunting.

Several dozen men and women had already taken their seats, and the low buzz of the crowd drifted up through the open window. Skeeter pointed toward the aperture. "You can shoot the nigger-lovin' faggot right through there," he whispered, then moved quickly and quietly to the stacked boxes. He returned a second later with a bolt-action rifle. "It ain't nothin' but a .22," he said. "But it ain't no long shot, neither. And I got it loaded with low-velocity .22 longs. Outta this long barrel, ought to be quieter than a silencer."

Bolan nodded and took the weapon. Not the ideal sniper rifle by any means, but like the man in the usher's uniform had said, it wasn't that difficult a shot. And the subsonic longs would keep the noise down.

The sound of brass instruments suddenly filled the theater as the band broke into "The Star Spangled Banner." "This is where I take off," Skeeter said. "Just drop that thing when you're through. Ain't nobody gonna trace it back to no one. And take the same steps you come up. You ought to be halfway back down the alley before anybody figures out what hit him." He grinned again, showing the Executioner his broken brown teeth, then turned and disappeared down the hidden stairs.

Bolan pulled a chair up to the projection window and leaned the rifle against the wall. People continued to crowd into the theater, and the buzz of excitement filled the air.

The Executioner reached inside his coat, pulled out the photographs of McGinney and set them in his lap. He looked down at the frail shoulders and gaunt face that seemed to contradict the strong fires of passion in the red-haired man's eyes.

Bolan stared out through the window. He was a half step away from acceptance by Homer Shoemaker. If he blew it now, even if he escaped the guns of Cargill and the other armed Klansmen below, he'd have lost what might well be his only chance of finding Jerry Wayne Waack.

The band increased its volume as the speakers began to mount the steps to the stage amid the excited applause of the audience. McGinney's hair was unmistakable. He came last, and spawned the loudest roar yet from the crowd.

Bolan leaned against the back of the chair. All he had to do now was wait.

And figure out how to keep from killing a Tennessee state representative without blowing the cover he'd set up with Homer Shoemaker.

BILL RHOADS, Tennessee's Democratic party chairman, took the podium. Smiling widely, he held his hands out palm down until the cheers, whistles and general pandemonium had quieted, then leaned forward into the microphone. "Good evening, and thank you all for coming," he said, then told an opening joke about Republicans that brought laughter and more applause. Finally he introduced Memphis City Councilman Mike Quayman.

Bolan turned to McGinney, who took a chair behind the podium. The Tennessee state representative had crossed his legs and was deliberating over several index cards in his lap. He wore a conservative blue suit, the coat unbuttoned. His multicolored tie had caught under the lapel and been pulled to the side, exposing the buttons on his white shirt.

The Executioner studied the man, an unexplained uneasiness creeping over his body. Something was different, and it wasn't the flaming red hair McGinney had gotten cut since the pictures in Bolan's lap had been taken. The round rimless eyeglasses were the same, as were McGinney's frail shoulders and long lanky legs. It was Patrick McGinney, all right.

But something was different.

Councilman Quayman took the podium and began discussing a recent outbreak of car-jackings in Memphis.

Bolan closed his eyes and rubbed his temples. What had changed about the man? Something subtle. But something important—he could feel it. Whatever it was, it had stirred the Executioner's intuition but was refusing to rise to his conscious mind, where it could be of use.

He opened his eyes again and tried to clear his mind of all extraneous thought. His vision fell on the open coat again, and the way the tie had been pulled off center. Careless. But the pictures he had seen also reflected a certain indifference for personal appearance.

Bolan lifted the rifle and raised the scope to his eye. He moved it up and down the representative's body, again trying to free his mind of anything irrelevant.

As if by its own accord, the scope moved to the open jacket and white shirt.

Whatever the difference was, it was here.

Quayman finished his speech and introduced Mayor Stephen T. Donaldson. The portly man rolled across the stage to the microphone and launched into a remarkable series of politically correct warm-up jokes before discussing the sewers of downtown Memphis.

Bolan moved the scope slowly from McGinney's neck down to where the man's right leg crossed over his left knee. A sudden rush of adrenaline shot though him as he realized what it was he had seen.

Patrick McGinney was no longer the slender man he had been in the photos. He had gained weight.

The adrenaline jolt intensified as Bolan lowered the scope and pulled the photos from his pocket, fanning them out in his hand. McGinney had gained at least twenty pounds since these pictures had been taken. But Shoemaker had said the photos were less than a month old. It didn't make sense. A man given to weight gain might put that much on, but McGinney had the physique of a true ectomorph, which meant adding either fat or muscle was difficult.

The grin started at the corner of the Executioner's lips and spread across his face as he realized what he was seeing. He lifted the scope to his eye once more and aimed it through the window.

The cross hairs fell on McGinney's face. It had the same gaunt look as in the photographs. He moved the optic sight to the shoulders. They were as frail as in the photos, although the man's coat had bunched slightly to the right of his neck.

The coat was too small. The ill fit had to come from the new bulk around McGinney's belly. And the Executioner suspected he knew why.

Patrick McGinney was either wearing body armor or he'd swallowed an entire drugstore's supply of anabolic steroids.

Bolan dropped the scope to the white shirt again and saw the buttons stretched tightly against the holes. The shirt had opened slightly at the chest, and a tiny spot of navy blue showed through the gap.

A navy blue undershirt? Bolan's grin became a chuckle. Not likely under a white dress shirt.

Bolan rested the rifle across his lap and stared out through the glass as Mayor Donaldson answered questions from the audience, then went into a long windy dissertation that practically covered Patrick McGinney's career from birth to the present. If the spot of blue he had seen was a ballistic nylon vest, and he was practically certain it was, it would stop the low-velocity .22 slugs.

Bolan rested the muzzle of the rifle on the window ledge and waited. The fly in the ointment was his very slight uncertainty. Could he risk the life of an innocent man?

No. He had to know for sure that McGinney was protected. He had to know beyond a shadow of a doubt. And under the circumstances, there was only one way to be certain.

McGinney took the podium and the crowd rose to its feet. He lifted the buttstock to his shoulder and centered the cross hairs over McGinney's heart. A "kill" shot at this distance, as Skeeter had pointed out, would be simple. But the Executioner was now planning a preliminary shot, one that would test all the marksmanship skills he had developed over the years.

McGinney didn't waste time. "There are three things we're going to talk about tonight," he yelled into the microphone as soon as the crowd had quieted. "Number one; the miserable condition of Tennessee's highways."

The audience roared its agreement as Bolan raised the cross hairs to the representative's left shoulder.

"Number two," McGinney shouted, waving his arms wildly, "the reprehensible way our Republican governor has handled the state lottery."

The Executioner tried to keep the cross hairs on the man's shoulder as McGinney nodded to more applause.

"And number three, the fact that four times more blacks in Tennessee are unemployed than whites!"

The crowd, a good many of them black, roared louder than ever. McGinney waved to them with both hands.

Bolan dropped the rifle and gazed over the top. He had planned to put a quick .22 across the top of McGinney's shoulder. If the representative was wearing a vest, the Executioner would see a small reaction to the force but little pain. And if the blue beneath McGinney's shirt was only an undershirt, the man would suffer no more than a scratch.

But Patrick McGinney was such an animated speaker, waving and moving with practically every word, that it was impossible to hold the cross hairs in place long enough to squeeze the trigger.

The Executioner returned the scope to his eye, again trying to follow the man's movements. Hopeless. The representative resembled a hyperactive five-year-old boy trying to sit through a boring church sermon. By the time he got through talking about Tennessee's highways and started on the governor, Bolan was about to abandon hope for the plan.

Then, suddenly, Patrick McGinney stopped shouting and froze. Slowly he reached to his throat and smiled. "I'm sorry," he whispered hoarsely as he leaned into the mike. "But you'll have to excuse me for a moment. As those of you who know me are aware, I sometimes get a little carried away."

The crowd laughed politely at the understatement.

McGinney reached down beneath the podium and came up with a water glass. The glass moved to his lips, his shoulder hunching slightly as his elbow bent upward.

The Executioner fired.

The .22 round flew across the theater and through the shoulder of McGinney's jacket. The man flinched slightly and a few drops of water spilled from the glass to roll down his chin. Then Bolan prepared to fire the second round. He worked the bolt and chambered it.

As McGinney lowered the water glass and wiped his chin, an expression of mild confusion on his face, the Executioner pulled the trigger once more.

This time the subsonic round hit the representative squarely over the heart. The water glass fell from McGinney's grip to shatter on the wooden stage. McGinney's eyes opened wide, his lower lip dropping in shock. He clutched his chest with both hands and leaned forward as if having a heart attack.

Bolan stared through the scope at the podium. He could see no blood. McGinney was simply reacting to the force of the round against the vest.

Without further ado, the Executioner dropped the rifle and hurried out of the room and down the stairs.

· HE REACHED CARGILL'S pickup a few minutes later and leaned against the fender to catch his breath. A minute later he saw two shadows turn the corner a block away and walk swiftly forward. Then two more men appeared across the street and headed his way.

Bolan recognized Crater Cargill's lumbering gait first, then Becker's golden ringlets appeared under a streetlight. The men reached the pickup as Holly and Olin crossed the street to join them.

"You got the son of a bitch!" Cargill whisper-shouted as he stuck the key in the driver's side. "Right flat square in his nigger-lovin' heart!" He slid across the seat and unlocked the far door. "Let's get the fuck out of here!"

Becker took the middle seat, his confused eyes never leaving the Executioner. He and Cargill must have rushed from the theater as soon as they'd seen McGinney bend over. They thought that he was either dead by now, or dying.

Bolan got in and shut the door behind him as Cargill started the engine. "I'm gonna drive by real quick," he said. "Keep quiet until we're past."

The Executioner saw Holly and Olin pull out behind them in the convertible. A moment later they turned the corner and saw the theater. Throngs of men and women stood outside, their heads bunched into groups, chattering endlessly. The pickup passed the theater as a fleet of black-and-white patrol cars came racing down the street from the opposite direction. Bolan turned in his seat as the cars squealed to a halt and uniformed officers jumped out, weapons drawn.

Cargill drove temperately on as if he'd just come from an evening on Beale Street. Two blocks later the chubby Klansman whooped with joy. "Son of a bitch!" he said again. "Where you been all our lives, Belasko? You killed that bastard as dead as my wife's Aunt Moline!"

Bolan gave him a small smile and turned back to the front.

"Switch on the radio, Doc," Cargill said. "Let's see what they got to say about it."

The radio was playing a new Garth Brooks tune. Suddenly the music was cut off. "This is Manny O'Daniel breaking into our normal programming to bring you this news flash. Sources say Tennessee State Representative Patrick McGinney was gunned down at a fund-raiser held at the Shiloh Theater less than ten minutes ago. I repeat, Patrick McGinney was shot by an unknown gunman at the Shiloh Theater tonight. More details as they come in." Then Garth Brooks was on the air again.

"Turn that Okie asshole off," Cargill said.

Becker leaned forward and punched the button again as Cargill guided the pickup toward the Memphis suburbs. "Son of a bitch!" he repeated several times as they neared the Mississippi River. His enthusiasm hadn't dimmed by the time they passed the convenience store and turned up the hill toward

Shoemaker's house. He was still breathing hard when he ran up the steps to the porch.

Bolan and Becker followed. Holly and Olin disappeared around the side of the house. The same elderly black man who had answered the door earlier now led them back to the den.

If he hadn't twisted his chair toward the television set, Bolan would have guessed Homer Shoemaker hadn't moved the whole evening. The Klansman still had the afghan over his legs, and the open leather-bound book rested over it in his lap as it had when they'd left for the theater.

The television was tuned to a local station. Bolan looked up at the screen to see what he guessed was a network movie. Shoemaker was watching it, expressionless.

"You heard it on the TV yet?" Cargill asked excitedly. "He got him! Got him square."

Shoemaker's eyes didn't move. "They announced it fifteen minutes ago," he said listlessly.

An uneasy silence fell over the room. Finally Cargill said, "Gee, Mr. Shoemaker. You don't seem too happy."

"I'm not," the old man said.

Shoemaker reached for the remote control and killed the picture. He turned to the three men. "Fifteen minutes ago they interrupted the movie to say that McGinney had been shot. I was happy *then*."

"Well, what—"

"Shut up!" Shoemaker suddenly screamed, leaping to his feet with the agility of a man forty years younger. The afghan fell to the side to reveal dark green pajama trousers. His face contorted into a mask of hatred and his shoulders began to quiver with rage. "Then they came back on two minutes after that and said the bastard was going to be fine. *Fine.*" He lifted the remote control over his head and slammed it into the floor. Pieces of plastic flew around his feet. "McGinney had on a vest, you blithering idiot!" he screamed at the top of his lungs. "A bullet-proof vest!"

Cargill opened his mouth to speak, then closed it again, exhibiting a wisdom Bolan hadn't yet suspected he possessed.

Shoemaker sat back down in his chair but his eyes stayed glued to Cargill. "What do you have to say for yourself, Crater?" he asked.

It was Cargill's turn to shake, but the quivers that now shook the fat of the overweight Klansman came from fear rather than anger. "I . . . I didn't know . . ." he stammered.

Shoemaker had regained control of himself and now spoke in the same quiet voice Bolan remembered. "Knowing things like that is your job, Crater," he nearly whispered. "You didn't do your job."

"Mr. Shoemaker—"

Shoemaker's gaze cut him off as surely as if the old man had slapped him across the face.

The Klan leader turned to Bolan. "They showed a video on the news break," he said. "Your bullet struck true, Mr. Belasko. And since you didn't arrive until this evening, and played no part in the planning stages of this operation, I can hardly blame you that it all turned out this way, now can I?"

Bolan remained silent.

Shoemaker turned back to Cargill and sighed. "Go home, Crater," he said. "Get a good night's sleep. We'll discuss this in the morning. Call me first thing."

Cargill's expression turned to one of relief. "Yes, sir, Mr. Shoemaker," he said. "Look... I'm sorry."

Shoemaker nodded. "Go home, Crater," he said wearily.

Cargill turned on his heel and hurried out of the room before the old man changed his mind.

"Dr. Becker," Shoemaker said. "My servants have prepared one of the guest rooms for you. I'm sure you're tired. If you'd like a nightcap or anything else, don't hesitate to tell Andrew. He'll show you to your room." He leaned over the side table and pushed a button on a small square box next to the telephone.

A moment later Andrew opened the door and ushered Becker out of the room.

Shoemaker turned to Bolan. "Sit down, please, Mr. Belasko," he said. "I have one more item to attend to, then I'd like to discuss something with you." He again leaned over the table, tapping a button on the telephone, and a dial tone came over the speakerphone. Shoemaker punched a number into the instrument and a gruff voice said, "Yes, sir?"

"Holly," Shoemaker said in the same easy tone the Executioner had heard all evening, with the exception of the one outburst. "We discussed Crater earlier, if you'll remember. He's just leaving. You and Olin make sure the body can't be found."

## CHAPTER EIGHT

Bolan dropped onto the floral cushion between the elaborately carved wooden arms of an old Victorian love seat across from Homer Shoemaker. The old man stood slowly, using his hands on his knees to help him rise, and exhibiting none of the spryness his earlier anger had fueled. He reached behind him, grasped his chair and angled it to face the Executioner.

Bolan watched each movement carefully. The old Klansman looked as if every movement taxed his patriarchal muscles to the limit. Was it an act for the Executioner's benefit? Did the bigotry and malice that coursed through his veins provide some perverse strength when it reached a climax?

Shoemaker sat down again, picked up the remote control and switched the television on. The movie was coming to an end and he hit the mute button, killing the sound. Turning back to Bolan, he said, "We'll talk until the news," then cleared his throat. "I reached our mutual friend, Mr. Turrin, while you were gone." He smiled. "Quite an impressive recommendation he gave you. And again, I want you to know that in no way do I hold you responsible for tonight's failure."

"That's nice to know," the Executioner said. "Particularly after what I just heard you tell Holly."

Shoemaker snickered. "I'm more tolerant than it would appear from what you have seen here tonight," he said. "Crater has become an increasing liability over the years, and this was simply the straw that broke the camel's back." He stopped and his eyebrows shot up. When he spoke again, his tone had lightened. "You informed me earlier that you never drink before you work. Your work is finished for this evening. Would you like something before we go on? A cognac, perhaps?"

"I could do with a beer," Bolan said.

Shoemaker smiled brightly. "Ah, a man who doesn't drink when he's working and only lightly when he isn't. I like that, Mr. Belasko. May I call you Mike?"

Bolan returned the smile. "Sure. Every time you say Mr. Belasko, I'm tempted to look over my shoulder to see if my father is standing behind me."

Shoemaker's laughter was genuine. He twisted to punch the intercom again. "Andrew," he said. "A cognac, please. And bring Mr. Belasko a..." He turned back to Bolan. "Is Beck's all right?"

"Perfect."

"Bring Mr. Belasko a Beck's beer," Shoemaker said, and turned on the television sound.

The movie had ended and a local used-car dealer was admonishing viewers not to trust their hard-earned dollars to any of his competitors. Shoemaker lowered the noise until it was barely audible, then said, "There's something I want to discuss with you, but we'll wait until Andrew has come and gone." He pulled himself to his feet again, limped across the room to a small alcove and stopped at a counter filled with pipe racks, tobacco jars and a large wooden humidor. The Executioner watched him open the lid and pull out an enormous cigar. Picking up a box of wooden kitchen matches, he returned to his chair as Andrew opened the door and entered with a silver tray.

"Now, Mr. Shoemaker," the black butler scolded as he set the tray down on the table. "Dr. Janson done tol' you not to smoke them things."

Shoemaker chuckled. "Yes, and I'll smoke one at Dr. Janson's funeral," he said.

Andrew shook his head and placed a brandy snifter on the table. "Your funeral be the one I worry about," he said, and moved toward Bolan.

Shoemaker chuckled again. "You can quit worrying, Andrew," he said. "I'll be around to torment you for years to come."

"I worry 'bout that, too," Andrew said as he poured Bolan's beer into a glass, then wrapped it in a paper towel. "You done been torturin' my poor soul since we was little boys, and Lord knows if there's a way to you be doin' it still in the Great Beyond."

Shoemaker threw back his head to laugh this time. "Andrew," he said, "get your old bones to bed."

"Yes, sir. I believe I do just that." With the tray under his arm, the old butler left the room.

Shoemaker was still smiling when he turned back to Bolan. "Andrew and I grew up together. His father held the same position for my father, and we spent many an hour together romping through the woods behind this house. He's a good man. And," he added, lifting his snifter to his nose and inhaling, "he knows his place."

Bolan held his tongue, wondering if Shoemaker could actually be as impervious as he appeared to the bigotry in what he had just said.

When he'd set his cognac back on the table next to him, the old man said, "There's something I'd like to discuss with you, Mr.—" He stopped suddenly as the commercials on the television ended and the scene switched to the local newsroom. The camera started with a wide-angle shot, then zeroed in on a carefully manicured man in a navy blue suit next to a woman with long blond hair. A stylized arrangement of "Dixie" served as the newscast's theme song.

"Two U.S. senators gunned down in New Mexico and an attempt on the life of a Tennessee state representative," the blond said seriously into the camera. "We'll be back in a moment."

Then another car salesman was on the air.

"We'll talk after the news," Shoemaker said, pulling three of the matches from the box on his lap. "I'd like to see the tape of you shooting McGinney again." He lifted the remote control, pushed a button and Bolan saw a red recording light flash on the VCR next to the television.

Shoemaker struck one of the matches and held it just below the tip of the cigar. "And I wish I knew who it was killing those senators," he said offhandedly. "He's picking the right ones. I'd like to congratulate him." The match went out and he lit another.

The newswoman returned and gave a capsule report of the two assassinations in Taos and Santa Fe, then she moved to the local attempt to kill Representative Patrick McGinney. The tape ran again, and Bolan watched carefully as Shoemaker finished his cigar-lighting ritual with a third match.

The video camera had been set up just below the stage to McGinney's left. The Executioner watched the man lift the water glass to his lips, then jerk slightly. He glanced toward Shoemaker. The old man hadn't noticed the odd movement.

A second later McGinney was dropping the glass and clutching his chest.

Shoemaker watched the screen silently as he puffed away at his cigar.

The newsroom returned and the screen showed both the man and woman shaking their heads. The man turned to face the woman. "You know, Jane," he said. "It's a sad commentary on society when the attempted murder of a local congressman isn't even the top story anymore."

The woman rolled her well-painted lips into her mouth and shook her head even more dramatically. Then, after a brief pause, she broke into a wide smile. "On a lighter note," she said. "Hundreds of people turned out for the annual Cotton Carnival today—"

Shoemaker lifted the remote and cut off the television. He turned to Bolan, puffed his cigar and said, "I mentioned earlier that there was another matter I'd like to discuss. Another job that needs attending to."

Bolan nodded. "Like I told you, I need work."

Shoemaker looked at the ash beginning to form on his cigar. "New Mexico's problems seem to have been taken care of," he said. "At least for a while. But we have a very troublesome senator in this state, as well."

Bolan knew Shoemaker meant Donald Loren, a senior senator and chairman of the Ways and Means Committee. Loren had started out as a conservative democrat, then became more liberal as the years passed. Many of Tennessee's conservatives felt betrayed.

"I want him dead," Shoemaker said bluntly.

Bolan let a small grin curl his lips as he nodded. "Whoever did the number in New Mexico also took out senators in New York and Georgia this week," he said. "Why not wait until he gets around to Loren?"

Shoemaker laughed. "Because I have no way of knowing for sure that will happen. Or even if Loren's on the list of whoever is behind the other killings." He stuck the cigar in his mouth again and then removed it. "Besides, by now Loren and every other U.S. senator will have employed bodyguards. This killer, or killers, is going to get caught or killed himself before long."

Bolan took a sip of his beer, then rested it in his lap. "But I heard on the news the other day that Loren is resigning his seat on the senate floor," he said. "Something about the president's job at the University of Tennessee, wasn't it?"

Shoemaker nodded and his eyes grew cold. "Exactly. But did you ever think of what harm the man could do there?" The cold eyes narrowed. "Our educational system is a shambles of permissive deviance already, Mr. Belasko. Drugs are available in every dormitory, fraternity and sorority house. Free sex is encouraged by handing out condoms. Homosexuality is rampant, and the goddamm queers are not only accepted, they're given preferential treatment." His face had reddened as he spoke, and his gestures become more fluid. "We are witnessing the destruction of the American way of life, Mr. Belasko. The end of morality. Everything good and decent is being replaced by things wicked and obscene. And Loren will add to that wickedness. He must not be allowed to do that."

Bolan listened as Homer Shoemaker spoke. As much as he disliked the man and all that he stood for, he had to agree with some of what he said. Morality in the United States was declining at a rate unheard of since the fall of the Roman Empire. Violent crime became more rampant every day as the criminal justice system crumbled under the assault. Light sentences— when jail time came at all—added to the general feeling that the murderer was as much a victim as the murdered, and that to hold people responsible for their actions was somehow inhumane.

The United States needed to get back on track— Bolan didn't disagree with that. But the assassination of U.S. senators or other officials, and the promotion of racism sponsored by Shoemaker's Ku Klux Klan and other such organizations wasn't the way to do it.

Bolan took a sip of his beer. He had a part to play, however, and as he crossed his legs he said, "So what do you want me to do?"

"Kill the son of a whore, of course," Shoemaker said. "Kill Donald Loren."

"Fine. Is he here or in Washington?"

"Here. But he's flying back late tomorrow morning to give his resignation speech."

Suddenly Bolan knew what he had to do, what direction to lead the conversation. But Shoemaker was smart—the old man would have to think it had all been his idea. "Then we'll have to take him out quick," Bolan said. "And it won't be easy. Like you said, he'll have bodyguards swarming around him like bees at the hive."

"You're a professional, Mike," he said. "I'm sure you'll find a way."

"Oh, it can be done," Bolan said. "Anybody can be taken out. That part's easy. It's doing it and then getting away that gets a little tricky sometimes." He closed his eyes as if searching his brain for an idea, although he'd known what he was about to say ever since Shoemaker had told him Loren would be flying to Washington the next day. "I'd say the airport would be the best place," he said, opening his eyes. "I'll work out the details tonight."

"I'll pay you well," Shoemaker said.

"I'm sure you will. And my partner."

"Your partner?" Shoemaker said, surprised. "I didn't know you had one."

Bolan shook his head. "I don't. But I'm going to need one on this." He paused. "He'll need to be a pro. A man who can act, as well as shoot." After another pause, he said, "And while I don't know exactly what approach I want to take yet, I'll probably need some other men. They don't have to be of my caliber—Holly and Olin and a few others like them could fill the bill—but they have to be reliable."

Shoemaker nodded knowingly. "Hollys and Olins I can furnish easily," he said. But the other man—the professional—do you have someone in mind?"

Bolan took a sip of his beer. "There are a couple of guys I've worked with before," he said. "But they're tied into the mob just like I was. They might just decide my head would bring a better price than Loren's, if you get my drift."

"Yes, of course," Shoemaker said. "That does present a problem." He frowned. "I know a man," he said slowly. "He's very good, and he's worked for us before. I even tried to get him on the McGinney operation, but he's been out of pocket recently. I could try again."

The Executioner nodded. He knew the answer to his next question before he asked it. "Do I know him?"

Shoemaker shook his head. "I doubt it," he said. "As far as I know, he has no ties to your Mafia people." He lifted his glass, drained what remained of the cognac, then said, "His name is Jerry Wayne Waack."

WAACK LIFTED HIS GIMLET and swiveled the tall stool to face the back of the open bar area. Across the lobby, he could see into the dining room, where Oklahoma's full-blooded Arapaho senator, Harvey Whitehead, sat with his wife and bodyguards.

Sipping the gimlet, Waack stared through the doorway to the third booth on the right. Yes, the surveillance environment in this Oklahoma City Harrigan's restaurant was good. But the fact that Whitehead had decided to pick up his new bodyguards here was not.

Waack twirled around on the stool and set the stemmed glass on the bar. The image of the dining room was still in his mind. Whitehead and his wife faced him, sitting with men who might as well have had Off-duty Oklahoma Highway Patrol stamped on the back of their sport coats. Four more men, all looking as if they'd come from the same cookie cutter, had taken the table next to the booth. Whitehead was talking to them as he ate a late-night platter of ribs.

"Last call," the bartender asked, and Waack looked up to see the man standing in front of him, drying a glass with a bar towel. "Want another one?"

Waack shook his head.

"We're getting ready to close, then," the bartender said, and moved on down the line.

Waack dropped a five-dollar bill next to his glass, stood up and descended the two steps to the lobby. A moment later he was crossing the parking lot to the black Nissan Maxima he had rented at Will Rogers Airport an hour earlier. The car faced the restaurant's entrance, and he slid behind the wheel and lifted the cellular phone to his ear.

Shim picked up his end after the first ring. "Yes?"

Waack listened to the sound of a large plane taking off in the background, remembering that the cellular phone was an easy "tap" and that it wouldn't do to get too specific. "Can't do it at the restaurant," he said. "Our man's invited too many friends for dinner."

A long pause. "Any ideas?" Shim said.

"Oh, yeah," Waack answered. He watched the door as he spoke. "I'm going to his room. I'll need a room number and key. You told me one of the local Dragons worked at the hotel?"

"Yes, but he's a busboy at the restaurant, Won Kwang. It's separate from the hotel, and he said he couldn't—"

"He's the one who knew where our man was staying tonight," Waack interrupted. "He can get access to the front desk if he wants. Why don't you... motivate him."

"The friends our man has with him will follow him to his room," Shim said.

"Yes, they will," Waack agreed. "But I doubt they'll sleep with him."

Shim laughed over the line, which made Waack smile. He liked it when he amused Shim.

"I'm heading that way right now," Waack said. "Tell your man to be in the main lobby." He paused. "You make that other call?"

"The answering service?" Shim said. "Yes. The same party that tried to reach you before called again."

"Okay. Tell the service I'll call back first chance I get."

Waack hung up and started the Maxima, pulling out of the parking lot onto Northwest Expressway. Ever since he'd discovered that he could make more money, and have more fun, on his own than he could as an Arkansas deputy sheriff, he had used an anonymous answering-and-mail service that operated out of Orlando. Repeat customers who wanted to contact him called the number, asked for "Mr. Ames" and left a code name he'd assigned them.

"Mr. Niles" had called for Ames three times that day, according to Shim. Which meant that old fart in the pointed hat and sheet in Memphis wanted somebody killed. Well, Shim came first—always had, always would. And Waack was too busy with his friend right now to take on anything else.

But that wouldn't always be the case, Waack realized as he passed a sign that told him Pennsylvania Avenue was the next intersecting street. And Homer Shoemaker and his backwoods hillbillies always paid well. He'd give the old man a call as soon as he finished Whitehead.

When he reached Pennsylvania, Waack stopped for the light, then turned. Penn took him to Waterford Boulevard, and that took him to the Waterford Hotel. He parked in the front parking lot.

In the lobby, Waack saw the registration counters manned by clerks in blue blazers featuring the hotel's crest. He turned to see a teenage Oriental in a white food-stained jacket walking casually toward him. The boy carried a rolled-up newspaper in his right hand. Waack walked down the hall on the boy's right, their eyes never meeting. Waack reached out and took the newspaper as he passed.

At the first hall, Waack turned again. Without breaking stride he unfolded the paper. The key inside read 2014, and he dropped it into the side pocket of his sport coat as he reached the elevators.

On the second floor, Waack followed the signs toward 2014. Turning a corner, he saw the big man with the receding flattop haircut, standing in front of a door, his hands folded in front of him.

Waack walked casually on. He didn't have to wonder which room he was guarding. The guard looked like the men who'd been with Whitehead at Harrigan's—another off-duty trooper clone.

Twenty feet away, Waack looked up as if he'd just seen the man for the first time. "Excuse me, you work here?" he asked, still moving forward.

The bodyguard uncrossed his arms.

"I'm lost," Waack said. He was now less than two steps away. "You suppose you could point me in the right—" As he reached the guard, he brought his knee up into the man's groin.

The guard bent forward. A sharp shriek shot from his lips.

Waack reached down, grabbed a handful of throat and squeezed. He felt his thumb meet his fingers behind the man's larynx, and a few seconds later the bodyguard lay dead on the floor.

The scream had not gone unnoticed. Four rooms down, a door cracked open and a nose poked out.

"Goddammit, Jesse, you know you can't drink," Waack muttered loud enough to be heard. "All right, let's get you to bed." He fished the key from his pocket, opened the door to Senator Whitehead's room and dragged the dead man inside.

Waack closed the door behind him and dropped his load just inside the door. Drawing the silenced Beretta .25, he hurried through the room, making sure it was empty. Returning to the entryway, he looked down at the dead man.

This guy presented a new problem. He had planned to hide in the room until the senator and his wife returned. But with the guard missing, the others were bound to come in and conduct a security check. He had no intention of taking on six well-trained highway patrolmen with a .25 caliber Beretta. Thus, he had to find a place to conceal himself, as well as the dead man.

Waack looked over his head and found the answer.

Sliding the chair out from beneath the desk, he lifted it to the desk top. The trooper was heavy, and getting him across the floor to the desk wasn't easy. Getting him on top of the desk was even harder, and lifting the man overhead and into the acoustical ceiling was almost impossible. But Jerry Wayne Waack got it done.

Sweat poured from his forehead by the time he had positioned the dead man across the supports along the ceiling. He dropped back down to the floor, hurrying now, knowing that the room would be the next stop on Whitehead's agenda, and remembering that the senator had been finishing his barbecued ribs as Waack left.

Waack jammed the chair back in place under the desk and jumped onto the desk. He was pulling himself up into the ceiling when he heard voices in the hall.

"I'm sorry, Senator," an embarrassed man said. "I...don't know where he could be."

The key entered the lock as Waack replaced the ceiling tile.

The voices became louder as the senator, his wife and the bodyguards entered the room. "I don't suppose it's any big deal, Jack," Whitehead said. "But it doesn't seem very professional of the man to disappear like that."

"It isn't, Senator," the other voice said. "And I'll have his ass for it, you can be sure." There was a short pause, then the voice said, "Pardon the language, ma'am."

Waack waited, squatting on top of a steel support beam as he heard the bodyguards open the bathroom and closet doors. Finally the man named Jack said, "It's all clear, Senator. I'll station another man in the hall tonight, and we'll be in the rooms on both sides if you need anything."

"I'm sure we'll be fine," Whitehead said. "You guys get some sleep."

"That's not what you're paying us for," Jack said. A moment later the hall door opened and shut again.

Waack waited while Senator and Mrs. Whitehead went about their nighttime rituals—undressing, brushing their teeth and rolling down the bed. They kept up a running conversation as they prepared for sleep, talking of the day, the bodyguards and family matters. Waack learned that Mrs. Whitehead's name was Nancy.

The springs squeaked as the two climbed onto the mattress. Waack quietly duck-walked along the beam until he was directly over the bed, then silently moved the ceiling tile a half inch to the side.

A lone beam of light from the side of the curtains bathed the room in a soft glow. Harvey Whitehead and his wife lay on their sides, facing each other. The blanket and bedspread were still rolled to the end of the bed. The senator wore the bottoms of a pair of brown paisley pajamas. Nancy wore the top, the gathered hem of her white cotton panties barely visible beneath the tail.

Not bad legs, Waack thought.

"I'm scared," Nancy whispered softly.

Whitehead scooted closer, kissed his wife, then moved his head back to look her in the eye. "Honey," he said. "The doors are locked, the hotel has security officers, the city police are patrolling the area and the highway patrolmen in the rooms next to us are all on the governor's pistol team." He chuckled and lifted a hand to stroke her face. "What more could you want?"

Waack pulled the sound-suppressed Beretta from his pocket.

"Just you," Nancy Whitehead said.

"Well, you've got me."

"I love you."

"I love you, too."

Waack only had to pull the trigger twice.

BOLAN TWISTED the shower knob, killed the water, opened the translucent glass door and stepped out onto the carpet. Pulling a long green bath towel from the wall rack, he looked around the guest bathroom as he dried himself. Two things were clear. Homer Shoemaker liked the color green. And the old bigot had money to burn. The light green solid-marble toilet and sink were trimmed in teak, and the towel racks were of shining copper.

Bolan wrapped the towel around his waist. What made a man like Homer Shoemaker, who had everything money could buy and more, hate so much that he murdered innocent people who didn't agree with him? Born into a million-dollar cotton empire, he had never known a hungry day in his life. It made more sense that he would have been grateful, that he would have thanked the Fates for smiling on him, and even would have wanted to share some of his good luck with those less fortunate.

Instead, Shoemaker had became Ku Klux Klan leader. Why? Was he really afraid that blacks, Jews and other minorities were planning to take it all away from him? Or was Shoemaker's hate based on something deeper?

Bolan walked into the bedroom. The Homer Shoemaker approach to life was something he had never understood. And he knew he never would.

The Executioner walked past the new shirt, socks and underwear Andrew had laid out on the bed. Shoemaker, the elderly black man had said, kept new clothing in various sizes on hand for times just like this—when his hired henchmen found themselves in the middle of an operation and in need of a change of clothes. That kind of foresight told Bolan that Shoemaker's acts of violence weren't rare.

Finding a coffeepot plugged into wall above the desk, the Executioner poured the hot brew into the mug that stood next to it. The paper and pencils he had requested had been placed on the desk, and he pulled out the chair and took a seat.

Bolan felt his eyes trying to close as he sat down. Sleep had been rare during this mission. He was used to that. But he reminded himself that no one, not even the Executioner, worked at peak efficiency when exhausted.

Bolan sipped some coffee. The caffeine opened his eyes a little. Okay, Plan A. If Waack arrived at Shoemaker's before the senator's flight, he'd take the man here. He needed Waack alive—needed to find out what strange connection he had with the Dragons. Then he'd devise a plan to put the Dragons out of business once and for all. And he needed to do so quickly—he had other plans when this was over.

With every dead senator the Executioner heard about on the news, it became increasingly clear that conventional law enforcement was powerless to catch the unknown assassins. It had become a job for the Executioner, and if he didn't get on the trail soon, the senate floor would soon be vacant.

The coffee had cooled a little and Bolan took a bigger gulp, finding that the caffeine increased his alertness. Waack might arrive at Shoemaker's before Loren's flight, in which case the Executioner would have to play it by ear as to how to take him. He needed Waack alive, needed to—

Bolan reached up, rubbing his face as he realized he was repeating things. He'd already gone over Plan A in his mind. He was more tired than he thought. He had hoped the shower would refresh him, and it had, but not completely. He took another drink of coffee, then refilled the mug.

Bolan had been to the Memphis airport before. A ramp led up to the departure-arrival area on the second level, and it was here that the senator's car would stop. He would get out with aids and bodyguards.

Okay, Plan B. Waack might take his instructions over the phone and only agree to meet them at the airport. Bolan frowned, putting himself in the hired killer's place. That's what he would do if he were to be working with a man he didn't know, and he suspected that's how Waack would handle it, too. Waack would devise his own plan, leaving an escape route, several escape routes, actually, in case the whole thing was a setup.

Bolan stood, took several deep breaths and rubbed his face. Sitting back down, he drew a quick sketch of the departure-arrival area outside the Memphis terminal. He drew in several bodyguards and aids as $X$'s, two airport security policemen as $O$'s, and used small rectangles for skycaps and other passengers. He would put himself in the role of the senator's triggerman, and use Waack to create a distraction. If Waack arrived early enough to argue about that, it would mean Plan A was still in effect. But if he refused over the phone, insisting that he be the man to take Loren out, that presented problems.

Bolan considered using pepper spray to incapacitate any innocent bystanders who might get hurt in the fray. The strong irritant was readily available for personal protection these days, and a shot to the eyes and nose caused almost instant incapacity. He wrote down the words *pepper spray*. The cops, guards and aids at the airport wouldn't die from it—they'd just think they were going to, and perhaps wish they could, for a half hour or so.

Bolan refilled his coffee. What distraction did he want Waack to perform? Or if the hit man insisted on pulling the trigger himself, what diversion could the Executioner create that would still leave him in a position to save the senator and take Waack alive for interrogation?

How about a heart attack? A man getting out of an automobile outside the terminal, carrying heavy luggage, might suddenly clutch his heart and fall to the ground. That might spawn an immediate desire to render assistance in both cops and bodyguards. The cops would move toward the diversion, their minds filled with CPR. The bodyguards' brains would be programmed to take care of the senator first, but they would be off-duty police officers of some type, the Executioner guessed, and years of that broader scope of public service would cause at least a momentary lapse of attention.

That was the moment when the men with the pepper spray had to move in.

Bolan sat back and stared at the paper, his vision blurring. If he took the role of triggerman, that would also be the moment he moved in, took Waack and commandeered the nearest vehicle to speed away during the confusion. But if Waack insisted on killing the senator himself, things would get trickier. He'd have to rise from the fake heart attack and somehow subdue Waack before the senator got his head blown off.

The Executioner felt his eyes grow even heavier. He rubbed the lids, then forced them open once more.

Okay, it was time to face reality. He was cutting it too close to pull this off alone. Especially as tired as he was. One small slip—one tiny unexpected change in what went down—could spell disaster for Senator Loren or some other innocent.

In short, he needed help, needed some men that he trusted in the background with high-powered rifles to take Waack out if necessary. He didn't want Waack dead, but if it came down to him, the senator or another blameless person who happened to be in the wrong place at the wrong time...

Bolan finished the coffee and set his pencil down. He'd have to contact Stony Man Farm, and the phone by the bed was too risky. Anybody could be listening in.

There was a pay phone outside the convenience store at the bottom of the hill. But that would mean slipping out of the house and taking the chance that Shoemaker, Andrew or another servant would notice his absence. He needed a reason to be gone—a good reason.

The Executioner closed his eyes and rubbed his temples. The problem was, there wasn't one. But the bottom line was that if he didn't get the help he needed, he was risking innocent lives. So if he couldn't come up with a good reason, he could at least come up with something.

Bolan stood and moved to the clothes on the bed. He reminded himself that Shoemaker had only met him that evening. The old man didn't know Mike Belasko well, didn't know his habits. So if they discovered he was gone, he would say he'd been for a walk along the river. Mike Belasko thought more clearly, planned better, when he walked.

Not an ideal solution, Bolan realized as he buttoned the new shirt, but the only one available.

He slipped into his slacks, then pulled the Desert Eagle and Beretta from under the bed where he'd stowed them. A moment later his sport coat hid the weapons and he opened the door to the hall, listening. The house was asleep.

Taking the back stairs, he went out the kitchen door and disappeared into the night.

# CHAPTER NINE

The old man lay on his back, facing the ceiling, his mouth open. Jerry Wayne Waack stopped in the dim light just inside the bedroom door and looked in. He could see black hairs growing from the old man's nostrils.

Old Homer didn't look peaceful in sleep, Waack thought. He looked more like a man sleeping under the burden of a heavy dose of guilt on his conscience. The old man hated anybody who wasn't white, and had centered his life around trying to wipe out all other races.

Waack chuckled quietly. Except the Koreans. Old Homer undoubtedly hated them, too, but he had the good common sense never to mention them when Waack was around.

Waack continued to study the troubled face, wondering what it might be like to fight a guilty conscience. He had never been troubled by such things. He did what he did because it was necessary to get what he wanted, whether it was money, sex or revenge. Mostly it was a dog-eat-dog world out there, Waack thought, and there damn sure wasn't going to be anybody looking out for you.

Except Shim, Waack reminded himself. Shim was different. Shim had looked out for him. Shim had saved him. He made an exception in Shim's case, and he'd be willing to die for the man.

Waack looked quickly about the bedroom, then back to the sleeping form of Homer Shoemaker. The army headshrinkers in Korea who had ended his military career had thought he was crazy. He'd even overheard the term sociopath being kicked around.

Well, maybe they were right. He was cold, he knew that. Waack smiled in the darkness. But if he was crazy, he was too crazy to care.

Waack's eyes moved up and down the bed, looking for signs of a weapon. No, old Homer wouldn't have anything. He wasn't the type. He'd rely on that scarfaced fool Crater Cargill and the other southern-fried Bubbas who infested this place to protect him. Well, too late for that, Homer. I've already slipped past all the Billy Bobs I saw.

Moving to the bed, Waack took a seat next to the old man. Shoemaker jerked. Under the lids, the old man's eyes fluttered back and forth. Rapid eye movement. Waack looked at his watch. Homer had had plenty of time to enter the sleep that brought on dreams while Kim flew him from Oklahoma City to Memphis.

Waack reached out, shaking the old man's shoulder. There was something about the old bastard he liked, though he could never put his finger on it. Maybe it was the fact that he even offed his own men when necessary. Whatever it was, it had caused Waack to make this stopover on his way to Louisville. Taking out Senator Donald Loren wouldn't take long, even though Loren wasn't on his and Shim's list.

A sharp snore shot out Shoemaker's nostrils but the old man didn't open his eyes. Waack shook his shoulder harder. "Come back to the world of the living, old man," he said.

Shoemaker's face came alive with a start. "What!" he said, trying to sit up. "Who—"

Waack held him down. "Relax," he whispered. "It's just me."

The old man's eyes finally focused. "What are you doing in . . . how did you get in here?"

Waack chuckled. "Sorry, Homer," he said. "But your boys aren't exactly the Secret Service." He moved slightly, allowing Shoemaker to sit up.

"Why?" Shoemaker said, then stuttered through a series of coughs that sent the odor of stale cigars through the room. "Why did you sneak in here like this?"

"Because I don't know this guy you hired," he said. "Never heard of any Mike Belasko."

"He was with the Mafia, like I told you. He got caught screwing the daughter—"

"Yeah, right, I heard all that over the phone. How'd you meet him?"

"Dr. Lawrence Becker introduced us. You know him?"

Waack nodded. "St. Louis. Who told you about this don's-daughter deal? Belasko, right?"

Shoemaker nodded. "Yes, he and Becker. But Belasko's all right, Jerry. I'm sure of it."

"How?"

"I called a mob guy. Leo Turrin. The Puss. You know him?"

"I know who he is," Waack said. Turrin was the real thing, all right. But was it really Turrin the old man had talked to? Or some elaborate cop scheme he'd fallen for?

"Lord, Jerry," Shoemaker said. "The guy shot McGinney for us. Right in the heart. It wasn't his fault McGinney was wearing a vest. I taped it from the news, and if you don't believe me, you can see for yourself."

"Oh, I'll watch it, all right." Waack said. "But first I want to meet this guy. He here?"

"Upstairs in one of the guest rooms. He's either still planning the hit on Loren or has gone to sleep. I can have Andrew bring him to the den."

Waack shook his head. "No, we'll go surprise him," he said. He stood up, lifted Shoemaker's bathrobe off the headboard and handed it to him.

A few minutes later Waack was standing next to a guest-room door, his hand on the Beretta in the side pocket of his coat, while Homer Shoemaker's bony knuckles rapped on the door. When there was no answer, Shoemaker said, "Mike?"

There was still no response.

"He must have gone to sleep," Shoemaker said.

Waack saw the light under the door and knew that wasn't true. But there was no reason to explain all that. He let Shoemaker crack the door and peek inside, knowing the old man would catch the first bullet if that was the game, and that he'd have ample time to return fire or get the hell out of there.

But the bullet didn't come, and a moment later Waack followed Shoemaker into the room. The bed hadn't been slept in. But there was evidence on the desk that the assassination plan was well under way. Waack glanced over the sketch and saw immediately what Belasko had planned. It would work, if everybody carried out their assignments, and the pepperspray angle was a damn nice touch. He assumed that Belasko wanted him either as the triggerman or the diversionary heart-attack victim marked on the drawing, but either way, that presented some problems.

If Belasko was an undercover cop he'd have several opportunities to take Waack out no matter which part he was playing. "You have any idea where he's gone?" Waack asked, still studying the sketch.

"No," Shoemaker said. "And I can't understand it. Maybe he got hungry and went to the kitchen."

"That's what you've got Andrew for," Waack said.

"He'll know Andrew's gone to bed. He may have gone on his own."

"I don't like it, Homer."

"I'm sure he'll explain when we find him. I suspect he's in the house somewhere."

"So let's find him," Waack said. He let the old man leave the room first, then followed him down the hall.

Ten minutes later they had been in every room of the house and checked the yard and outbuildings of the estate. Belasko was nowhere to be found.

"I'm sure he'll be back, and I'm sure there's a reason," Shoemaker repeated as they went back into the house.

"I'm sure he'll be back, too, and I know he'll have a reason," Waack said as they entered the den. "Whether or not that reason is pure pig shit is another question." He dropped down onto the couch, his hand on the .25 inside his pocket. "Let's see your videotape."

Homer Shoemaker pressed the appropriate buttons on the remote control and the television switched on. A second later Waack was watching Patrick McGinney speak from behind a podium, his arms waving with every word. Suddenly he stopped and lifted a water glass to his lips.

A split second later his shoulder jerked and a trickle of water ran down his chin.

Waack frowned. Even from an exuberant monkey like McGinney, who looked like somebody had overwound a key sticking out of his back, the movement didn't look natural.

The tape showed McGinney getting the water glass under control, then suddenly he dropped it completely. His hands went to his heart and he leaned over the podium.

"As you can see, Belasko's bullet hit him squarely," Shoemaker said.

"Run it back," Waack said. "Something's wrong."

Shoemaker ran the tape back to the beginning. Waack watched it all again. "Put it on slow motion," he said. "Then roll it through again."

Waack waited as Shoemaker rewound the tape slightly. What had caused McGinney's shoulder to jerk a second before the shot? A nervous tick? Muscle cramp? Some other kind of internal pain?

No. That was bullshit—fishing for an easy answer. Patrick McGinney was reacting to some outside stimulus. He looked like a man who'd just been jabbed with a pin.

As the tape rolled in slow motion, Waack focused on the shoulder. He watched McGinney lift the water glass, then suddenly a blur appeared on the left-hand side of the screen. The blur racing across the picture looked like the tail behind an airplane as it skimmed across the top of Patrick McGinney's shoulder.

For a split second a tiny patch of blue appeared inside the sliced fabric. Waack knew immediately what it had to be.

Another blur streaked across the screen, this time hitting McGinney in the chest.

"What was the first streak?" Shoemaker asked, confused.

"The first bullet," Waack said quietly.

"The *first* bullet?" Shoemaker said, even more confused now. "You mean Belasko missed the first time?"

Waack chuckled. "Hardly," he said. "I'd say he hit exactly what he was aiming at." He paused, then turned to the man. "Let's keep this little bit of information between the two of us, Homer. And you were right—the man's good. Real good."

He stood up and started for the door. "Tell your Mr. Belasko I'm sorry I missed him, but that I'll be at the airport at the appointed time. Tell him I'll be happy to fake the heart attack, and that I'll stand by as backup on the hit itself just in case anything goes wrong."

"Don't you want to wait and meet him?" Shoemaker said.

Waack shook his head as he left the room. "I'll meet him soon enough," he said.

And I'll be looking forward to it, he thought as he let himself out of the house. The shoulder shot he had just seen was the work of a true expert sniper. And other than himself, Waack knew of only one man who could pull it off.

Waack grinned as he walked toward his car. "Yes, I'm looking forward to it," he whispered under his breath. "I've wanted to meet Mack Bolan ever since Vietnam."

BOLAN HAD A CLEAR VIEW of the house as he jogged back up the road from the pay phone at the convenience store. Sometime during his absence, the den light had been turned on.

The Executioner slowed as he reached the grounds. It had appeared that everyone was asleep when he left. But that wasn't the case now, and it meant he had to make a decision.

Should he try to slip back in without being seen, or walk in boldly and go with his story of a walk along the Mississippi to clear his head and plan the hit? Whoever was awake might already know he was missing, and sneaking back in and acting like he'd never left would raise even more eyebrows than a flimsy story.

The morning sun began to peek over the horizon as Bolan reached the kitchen door and strode inside. Without breaking pace, he walked through the house to Shoemaker's den.

The old man was watching the early-morning news.

"Good morning," the Executioner said.

Shoemaker twisted in his chair, surprised. "Well, well," he said with a merriness that seemed a little forced. "You're up early, Mike."

"Up?" Bolan chuckled. "I haven't been *down* yet, Mr. Shoemaker." He took a chair across from the old man and leaned forward, resting his elbows on his knees. "No, I was up all night planning this thing," he said. "Got the basics down in the room, then took a walk along the river. I seem to think better when I'm moving." He smiled. "Particularly when I'm tired. Gets the oxygen flowing through the brain better, I guess."

As he spoke, Bolan had seen the old man's face gradually relax, and knew he'd been right. Shoemaker had known the man he called Belasko had left the house last night. And he'd wondered why.

Now Shoemaker smiled. "We had a visitor last night, Mike," he said.

"Not the mob or the cops, I hope," Bolan said.

"No, Waack arrived," Shoemaker said.

Bolan hid the effect of the adrenaline that suddenly shot through him. "Good," he said. "Is he awake? I can go over his part—"

The old man's shaking head stopped the Executioner in midsentence. "He had to leave again," Shoemaker said. "Said to tell you he'd meet you at the airport and that he'll be happy to fake the heart attack. We took the liberty of going over the drawing you left in your room."

Bolan shrugged. "I'd have liked to discuss it with him," he said. "Can you reach him before then?"

Shoemaker shook his head again. "I wouldn't know where to start."

Bolan nodded. "Well, it isn't all that important. He's a pro, and all he has to do is show up and grab his chest. Sort of like McGinney did last night." He watched Homer Shoemaker's reaction.

For a split second the old man's face hardened. Then Shoemaker forced another wide smile. "You look tired, Mike," he said. He looked to his watch. "You've got time to catch a little rest before you leave."

Bolan nodded. "Think I'll do just that." He looked at his own wrist. "Could you have Andrew wake me in an hour?"

Shoemaker nodded.

The Executioner turned, walked down the hall to the stairs and mounted them to his room. At the desk, he noticed that the sketch he'd drawn had been moved.

Shoemaker and Waack had been there, but he already knew that. Taking his jacket off, he draped it over the back of the desk chair, slid out of the Desert Eagle and Beretta rigs and stuffed the Beretta under the bed. The Desert Eagle went under the pillow as soon as he'd rolled back the covers.

Bolan kicked his shoes off and lay down in his clothes, staring at the ceiling. Something had happened while he was gone. He couldn't put his finger on what, but something. And whatever that something was, it had caused the new suspicion in Homer Shoemaker's eyes.

Bolan rolled to his side. He didn't know what had happened, but there was one thing of which he was suddenly certain. Waack had seen something here that tipped him off to the fact that there was more going on than the simple assassination of a senator. And that meant it would be Mack Bolan rather than Donald Loren that Jerry Wayne Waack would try to kill at the airport.

The Executioner slid his hand under the pillow and wrapped his fingers around the grips of the big .44 Magnum.

HOLLY TOOK THE steering wheel of the Chevy pickup as Bolan opened the passenger door and let Olin slide onto the seat in the middle.

"Awful nice a ol' Crater to let us use his truck," Olin said, grinning to exhibit a row of broken teeth and black gaps. A hand-held citizens-band walkie-talkie rested in his lap.

"He don't need it no more his own self," Holly said as he stuck the key in the ignition. He turned to Olin, trying to outdo his partner with missing teeth and gum disease. Bolan couldn't decide on the winner.

In the pickup's side mirror the Executioner watched six more Klansmen pile into a three-year-old Cadillac. They had arrived an hour earlier from Louisville. Along with Holly and Olin, they had been assigned to neutralizing Loren's bodyguards and any airport security cops or passengers who proved troublesome. Along with their instructions, Bolan had issued them each a can of pepper spray. The Executioner noticed that all of them had bulges distorting their overalls or the waistbands of their jeans.

Holly guided the pickup down the hill to the road, then turned toward the airport.

Bolan sat back against the seat and closed his eyes as the Klansman drove. The hour of sleep he'd gotten had helped—some. He had spent most of it in a half-awake state with his hand wrapped around the Desert Eagle.

Waack knew something was fishy, and he'd confided his suspicions to Shoemaker. Of that much, the Executioner was certain. But how did they find out, and how much did they know? That was impossible to tell. When it all hit the fan outside the terminal in a few minutes, would Waack try to kill him *and* the senator, or would he go simply for Bolan? Or Loren?

The Executioner didn't have a clue there, either. He would have to play it by ear.

Holly and Olin exchanged small talk, ignoring Bolan during most of the drive. It appeared that they, and probably the other Klansmen in the Caddy trailing them, hadn't been let in on the fact that Waack and Shoemaker smelled a rat.

Bolan wasn't surprised. Shoemaker still saw a chance to rid himself of Loren, and he had already proved that he considered his run-of-the-mill Klansmen expendable. A few of them might bite the dust during the hit, but that was all right.

Forty-five minutes after leaving Shoemaker's, the pickup pulled off the highway leading to the airport and onto a blacktop road. A green-and-white sign announced that a cargo landing strip and the U.S. Customs offices lay at the end of the road in the one-story building in the distance. Holly made a U-turn with the

Cadillac following, and both vehicles pulled off the road onto a gravel shoulder and killed their engines.

Bolan raised his wrist to his face. It was 0847. Loren's flight to D.C. took off at 0955—just more than an hour. His car should pass by them soon.

Olin flipped on the portable CB and adjusted the squelch. Bolan glanced down to see the radio was tuned to a little-used frequency. As they waited, a few words were exchanged between unseen men on other CBs, but for the most part the airwaves remained silent.

At 0906 the Executioner heard the voice with the deep Southern accent spit out of the instrument. "Breaker, breaker there, boys and girls. This is ol' Kentucky Rain comin' atcha. Got yer ears on, Memphis Blues?"

Olin lifted the radio and thumbed the button on the side. "We here ya there, Kane-tuck."

"Well, we's a leavin' the driveway and comin' yer way, Blue," the voice said. "'Bout ten minutes, I reckon."

"See you then, Rain Man," Olin said. He let up on the button and twisted to Bolan, grinning his semi-toothed smile. "They's a comin'."

Bolan repressed the desire to tell the man he'd figured that out on his own.

The Executioner focused his eyes on the patch of highway visible at the end of the blacktop. Eight minutes later the voice returned to the airwaves, but said only, "Gettin' close, Blue Boy." A minute after that Bolan saw a Mercedes go by, followed closely by a four-door Mercury.

Holly pulled out in a windstorm of gravel and dust, did a touch-and-go at the corner and turned after them. The Cadillac followed.

Bolan adjusted the Beretta under his arm and the Desert Eagle on his hip. When it started now, it would all go down fast, and he'd need every advantage he could get to figure out exactly what Waack had planned, then try to take the man alive.

The Mercedes and Mercury turned left onto the drive leading to the terminal. The pickup and Cadillac followed. They passed a hotel on the side of the road, then entered the airport proper, driving casually past several turns that led to parking areas. As they started up the ramp to the departure check-in doors, the Executioner drew the Desert Eagle.

"You ready?" Holly asked his partner. Sweat streaked his face.

"I was born ready," Olin said, pulling his can of pepper spray from behind the bib of his overalls.

The four-car convoy slowed as it neared the doors on the right. Bolan's eyes scanned the metered parallel parking spaces along the ramp, moved to the reserved taxi and limo area nearer the doors, then across the ramp to the eight-foot wall that separated the departure area from an upper-level parking garage.

Hidden somewhere in the area were Carl Lyons, Rosario Blancanales and Hermann Schwarz. The Executioner couldn't see the men of Stony Man Farm's Able Team. But he could feel their presence.

The Mercedes pulled to a halt under a Delta Airlines sign with the Mercury moving in close behind. The doors of the Mercury opened first, and four men in sport coats, ties and slacks got out, their eyes searching the area.

Holly pulled the pickup behind the Mercury as Bolan watched a Ford Fairmont arrive from the other direction and park along the garage wall. He looked to a revolving glass door that led into the ticket counters and saw two uniformed police officers standing to the side, smoking cigarettes.

The Executioner hid the Desert Eagle under his jacket as he opened the door of the pickup, and Holly and Olin slid out. The bodyguards gave the two men a quick once-over, then moved their eyes back to the Mercedes. One of the guards, tall and lanky and wearing a plaid sport coat, walked quickly to the rear door of the lead car and opened it.

Across the drive, Bolan saw a tall old man with white hair get painfully out of the Fairmont. The Executioner's eyebrows lowered, focusing on the white hair. His eyes dropped to the man's eyes as he rested momentarily at the side of the car. Blue. Medium blue. Waack could have disguised himself as an old man, and even could have worn tinted contact lenses. But he hadn't. This man was at least six inches taller than Waack's army records indicated, and even elevator shoes didn't add half a foot to a man.

Bolan watched the old man say something through the open door, close it, then move to the trunk. Holly and Olin casually made their way toward the cops by the revolving door. The six men from the Cadillac separated and began spreading out along the sidewalk in front of the terminal.

The old man on the other side of the drive pulled a suitcase from the trunk, slammed the lid and moved toward the passenger door. Through the windshield, Bolan glimpsed an elderly woman wearing spectacles and a pale blue scarf.

Where was Waack?

Far down the ramp, two men in business suits and carrying attaché cases came hurrying from the parking garage. Bolan moved to the back of the pickup, his eyes glued to the unfolding drama before him. He saw Senator Donald Loren helped out of the back of the Mercedes by a bodyguard in plaid as the elderly couple from the Fairmont moved across the ramp toward the doors, carrying suitcases.

Suddenly the old man with white hair dropped the suitcase in his hand, crossed his hands over his chest and groaned. The old woman at his side froze to his arm. As she began to scream, the Executioner saw the pepper-spray cans suddenly appear in the hands of the Klansmen.

And then all hell broke loose.

The two cops by the revolving door dropped to their knees screaming, rubbing their eyes as Holly and Olin delivered kicks to their ribs that drove them to the sidewalk.

Three of the senator's bodyguards shrieked as the Klansmen sprayed the strong pepper into their faces, then punched them.

The bodyguard in the plaid sport coat tackled Senator Loren, taking him to the ground as Bolan's eyes flew back and forth across the pandemonium.

*Where was Waack?* And who was the old man either faking the heart attack or having a real one? He was on his knees now, the old woman still clutching his arm and screaming for help. But he wasn't Waack. The Executioner was sure of it.

Bolan was about to turn away when the old woman suddenly dropped her husband's arm. A SIG-Sauer 9 mm appeared in her hand.

The first shot was hurried and sailed over the Executioner's head. By the time the old woman had pulled the trigger the second time, Bolan had dropped behind the bed of the pickup.

The gunshots drove the chaos outside the terminal to new heights now, with the Klansmen drawing pistols and the blinded bodyguards and cops fumbling for weapons, as well. Bolan heard a familiar voice yell, "Striker!" and turned behind him to see the two men in business suits sprinting up the ramp.

Their attaché cases had fallen open and they both held Calico submachine pistols. Nearer now, the Executioner recognized Carl "Ironman" Lyons and Hermann "Gadgets" Schwarz.

The old woman had moved from the middle of the drive to the Mercury, where she was systematically putting bullets into the heads of the blinded bodyguards while the Klansmen held them down. Bolan raised the Desert Eagle at her over the side of the truck, but she caught the movement and dropped behind the car before the Executioner could fire.

The Klansmen turned Bolan's way and a barrage of semiauto fire flew toward the Executioner. Bolan dropped the nearest Klansman with a lone .44 Magnum slug, then ducked down again behind the pickup. From behind him, he heard the steady burp of the Calicos and, rising once more, saw two more Klansmen fall to the rounds of Lyons and Schwarz. A second later the Able Team duo dropped down behind the pickup.

"Where's Blancanales?" Bolan shouted above the turmoil.

"On top of the parking garage," Lyons yelled back.

Bolan rose from cover again, swinging the Desert Eagle's sights up to fall on Holly, who had drawn a S&W automatic and was about to terminate one of the helpless airport cops. As if to confirm what Carl Lyons had just said, the roar of a high-powered rifle blasted through the confusion, and Holly dropped to the ground.

The Executioner swung to his side, putting the bullet he'd meant for Holly into Olin's chest, then dropping back to cover as return fire blasted his way. Lyons and Schwarz rose to take his place, tapping quick bursts of autofire into two more Klansmen as Bolan crab-walked to the front of the truck. He caught a quick glimpse of Loren, still on the ground by the open rear door of the Mercedes. The bodyguard in the plaid sport coat was frantically trying to shove the portly senator beneath the body of the automobile.

Bolan saw the old woman in front of the senator's car. Her scarf had come off in the bedlam that reigned outside the terminal, and for the first time the Executioner could see the pale skin of her face and neck. He recognized Waack immediately. Waack was making his way toward the right front fender, trying to get to the senator. Then suddenly he turned toward Bolan, his pink eyes squinting over the old woman's eyeglasses.

The Executioner dropped the sights on his chest and pulled the trigger.

The mammoth .44 Magnum round struck home, driving Waack two steps back. Then he dropped out of sight beneath the car. Bolan leaped to his feet, and had started down the side of the parked vehicles when another of the Klansmen stepped up and shoved a Colt Anaconda into his belly.

Bolan swept the gun away as the man pulled the trigger, but the muzzle-flash burned through his shirt to singe his ribs. Ignoring the pain, the Executioner returned the favor by shoving the Desert Eagle into the man's sternum.

The Klansman froze in place.

Bolan squeezed the trigger and the Eagle roared, sending blood, bone and tissue blasting out the back of the man's overalls. More of the crimson liquid splattered forward onto the Executioner's slacks, shirt and jacket. He cast the dying Klansman to the side and sprinted forward.

Bolan heard two more high-powered explosions, and a pair of Klansmen dropped in his peripheral vision. He looked up to see Rosario "Politician" Blancanales in the prone position on top of the parking garage. The Able Team man gave him a quick thumbs-up, then swung his rifle on.

The Executioner reached the front of the Mercedes and stopped. Gripping the Desert Eagle in both hands, he swung around the corner and aimed down at the spot where he'd seen Waack fall.

The pavement was vacant.

More Calico fire and the rounds from the Klansmen's various weapons exploded behind him as Bolan dropped to look under the car. Between the rear wheels, Loren's bodyguard in plaid had finally squeezed his overweight ward under the chassis, but Waack was nowhere to be seen.

Bolan rose, firing into the torso of a burly Klansman who wore jeans and a striped tank top over his sagging belly. He heard the sound of a car engine turning over, and looked across the drive to see Waack behind the wheel of the Fairmont.

Bolan cursed softly under his breath. Waack had taken a lesson from Patrick McGinney and worn a ballistic nylon vest beneath his disguise as an old woman. As he threw the Fairmont's transmission into drive, he stared back at the Executioner with recognition in his pink eyes.

Smiling, Jerry Wayne Waack mouthed two words through the window, then sped away.

Bolan turned the Desert Eagle toward the car, but before he could pull the trigger, the Fairmont was already down the ramp.

Sprinting back to the pickup, the Executioner dived through the open door and twisted the key in the ignition, knowing full well even before he threw the pickup into reverse that he was too late. The tires squealed in agony as Bolan backed away from the Mercury, made a sharp U-turn and took off after Waack.

Bolan raced to the end of the ramp, dodging cars and honking the horn as he threaded through the traffic coming into the terminal. Far ahead, he could see the Ford Fairmont. He floored the accelerator, trying valiantly to catch up in a game he knew he couldn't win.

Still a quarter mile ahead, Waack's vehicle disappeared beneath a dip in the road just before reaching the highway. The Executioner raced on past the hotel, then stood on the brake as he neared the end of the airport drive. He brought the pickup to a full stop when he reached the highway, his eyes searching the road, right and left.

Slowly, a hundred-pound weight slid from Bolan's throat down his chest to settle in his stomach. Waack was gone. He might have turned left, he might have turned right. And there was little hope in picking a direction and hoping the fifty-fifty chance came through.

Dozens of side roads, off ramps and intersecting streets stacked the odds further against the Executioner. Waack could have taken any one of them as he weaved to obscurity away from the airport.

Bolan turned the truck back to the terminal.

The gunfire had quieted by the time he returned. Holly, Olin and the other Klansmen lay dead on the drive and sidewalk outside the terminal. Two of the senator's bodyguards—victims of Waack's execution-style bullets—had joined them. Two airport cops and other bodyguards were washing their eyes in buckets of water brought by security policemen, and Bolan saw the man in the plaid jacket—the only bodyguard to have escaped the pepper spray—shove Senator Donald Loren back into his Mercedes and whisk him away.

Bolan emerged from the pickup to find that Blancanales had come down off the garage to join Lyons and Schwarz in front of the terminal. All three Able Team men had pinned phony Department of Justice credentials to their lapels.

Bolan walked toward them as several sedans filled with men in suits came up the ramp and screeched to a halt. Lyons looked up at him and said, "Unless you've got something else for us, Striker, I'd like to get the hell out of here." He tapped the ID card on his coat. "These things have worked great so far, but those are J. Edgar's children and they'll want to ask questions for the next three weeks."

The Executioner nodded. "Take off," he said, and turned back to the Fleetwood.

The FBI agents were just beginning to spread out through the chaos as he drove past and down the ramp the other way.

Bolan turned back toward Memphis, the two words Waack had mouthed through the window of the Ford Fairmont just before speeding away returning to his mind. They were words he hadn't heard for many years. Two words he had been known by in Vietnam.

"Sergeant Mercy," Jerry Wayne Waack had said.

## CHAPTER TEN

His chest felt like it had been struck by a twenty-pound sledgehammer, and Jerry Wayne Waack knew it would display every color in the rainbow tomorrow. But that didn't stop him from throwing his head back and cackling like a hyena in heat.

Waack pushed the Ford Fairmont along the highway, knowing that Bolan wouldn't bother chasing him. There were too many turns, too many paths he could take. And good old Sergeant Mercy—the eyes confirmed what Waack had already known in his heart, after seeing Shoemaker's video—had no idea that he was now less than a mile away from the terminal, doubling back to the small commercial landing strip where Shim waited.

Waack felt his heart still hammering. Damn, what an adrenaline rush it had been! All hits were fun and exciting, but this had been . . . well, special.

Waack slowed as he turned onto the blacktop road, steering the car with his knees as he unbuttoned the woman's blouse. He shrugged out of the vest. Thanks again, Mack Bolan, he thought as he ran his hand over his throbbing chest. I haven't worn a vest for a long time—didn't see the need. But your stunt with Mc-Ginney last night reminded me that this wasn't going to be your ordinary walk-up-and-shoot-em-up deal.

Finding that he couldn't remove the skirt as he drove, Waack pulled to the side of the road. Bolan would have gone back to the terminal, so the chances of him seeing the Fairmont were a million to one. Pulling the skirt the rest of the way off, he hurriedly worked a pair of blue jeans up his legs and threw a three-button polo shirt over his head before moving on.

The rush in his veins was ebbing now, and Waack replayed the gunfight in his mind. Damn, Bolan was carrying a fuckin' .44 Magnum these days. The excitement faded slightly and was replaced by a twinge of jealousy. Just like the show-off to carry a big piece like that, but even as he thought it, Jerry Wayne Waack recognized it for the lie that it was.

Waack drove on along the blacktop. No, Mack Bolan had never been a show-off. In fact, in Nam everybody said he was quiet, reserved. A loner. But when a Special Forces commander needed an enemy dead, it was Bolan they went to. If he was already busy, they'd come to Waack. But Waack had always been the second choice. That was why, even though he'd never met Mack Bolan, he hated the fucker's guts. Waack hadn't seen Bolan since those Nam pictures, and hadn't known what had become of him—but now, having seen him face-to-face, Waack wanted to kill him.

Waack looked up into the mirror and saw the pale skin of his face. That was why—his light complexion. They thought he was an albino, and that caused certain people to shy away from him. "But I am *not* an albino!'' Waack suddenly screamed, then saw his white face redden in embarrassment in the mirror.

Waack saw Shim standing outside the plane on the landing strip ahead. He pulled the Ford onto the grass, then up to the edge of the runway and got out.

Across several runways, he heard a shout and saw a man in coveralls jump into a golf cart and start his way. Waack ignored him, getting out of the Ford and walking swiftly to the plane. Shim had already boarded, and the engines were warm.

Waack pulled himself up into the passenger seat.

The exultation of battle faded in Waack's chest and was replaced by the anger he always felt when he thought of Mack Bolan. Why did they give him a name like Sergeant Mercy and tag Waack with an epithet like Whitey? He was every damn bit as good as Bolan. So... why?

Waack watched the golf cart near, saw the angry face through the windshield. The man wearing the coveralls was speaking, although he couldn't be heard through the glass.

Waack opened the door and said, ''What?''

''I asked who you thought you were!'' the man shouted, fire in his eyes. ''You think you can just drive out here like this and leave your fuckin' car in everybody else's way?''

Waack looked to Shim.

Shim shrugged.

''Yes, I do,'' Waack said. Lifting the SIG-Sauer, he centered the sights just above a pair of shocked, disbelieving eyes.

Jerry Wayne Waack knew the frightened eyes belonged to the man in the coveralls. But as he pulled the trigger and put a 9 mm hollowpoint squarely between them, it was Mack Bolan's face that he saw.

BOLAN SAW THE EXHAUST coughing out the tailpipe of the taxi as he pulled into the driveway in front of Shoemaker's house. He parked the pickup next to the waiting cab and killed the engine as Becker, suitcase in hand, came out to the cab.

The Fascist doctor saw the Executioner and froze.

Bolan pulled a fifty-dollar bill from his pocket as he circled the taxi. "We won't be needing you, after all," he told the driver as the man rolled down the window. "Sorry about the mistake."

The cabbie grabbed the bill. "At that price, make another one if you want," he said.

Bolan turned back to Becker as the cab backed away from the house. Walking swiftly up the drive, he shoved the man back against the garage door. "Where's Shoemaker?" he demanded.

Becker dropped his suitcase. "I...don't know," he sputtered.

The Executioner looked into the man's frightened blue eyes. Becker was lying. And Bolan didn't have time to screw around with him. Waack was gone, and the Executioner needed to know how Shoemaker had contacted him.

Raising his hand, Bolan started to backhand the doctor. The hand stopped halfway to its target when the terrified man screamed, "No, don't! I'll tell you!"

Bolan lowered his hand.

Becker started to speak, hesitated, and Bolan raised his hand again.

"He's in Oklahoma," the doctor said quickly.

"Where in Oklahoma?"

"A town called Seminole," Becker said quickly. "He got out of here as soon as he heard what happened at the airport. He's got friends there."

Bolan dropped his hand again. His first instinct told him to go after Shoemaker, find him and beat the information he needed out of the racist Klan leader. But there might be a faster way to find Waack.

Spinning Becker around by the shoulders, Bolan shoved him toward the house. "Who's inside?" he asked as the doctor opened the door.

"Just Andrew," Becker said.

Bolan bulldozed the doctor across a short rear entryway, past the back stairs and into the deserted kitchen. A phone hung on the wall to the side of the sink.

The Executioner shoved Becker into a chair at the kitchen table and moved to the phone. A few seconds later he had tapped the buttons that would eventually connect him to Stony Man Farm.

Barbara Price answered on the second ring.

Bolan kept his eyes on Becker as he said, "It's me. I'm 10-12."

Price knew that "10-12" meant "Officials or visitors present."

"Can they hear me?" she asked immediately.

"Just me," Bolan said.

"That ought to make it easy enough," the Stony Man mission controller said. "What do you need?"

"Patch me back to the Bear. I need the help of his magic machines." Bolan heard a click, and a moment later Kurtzman's line was lifted.

"Hey, big guy," the computer man said. "What can I do for you?"

Bolan watched Becker fidget nervously in his chair. In the background over the line, he could hear the hum of Kurtzman's computers in the Stony Man Computer Room. "Go back to the Dragon list," the Executioner said. "See if they've got a cell in or near Memphis."

"You got it," Kurtzman said, and Bolan heard keys being tapped. A moment later he said, "Looks like the closest thing is Little Rock."

Bolan hesitated. He had hoped there would be a Dragon chapter there in Memphis. Little Rock would require loading Becker up again for a flight. But at least the Arkansas capital was on the way back to Oklahoma, and even if he didn't find a link to Waack through the Dragons, he'd be halfway to Shoemaker again. "Okay, tell me about it."

Kurtzman tapped a few more keys, then began reading in a dry monotone, "Anju Dragons, Little Rock, Arkansas. Estimated strength—eight-seven members. Active area—docks along the Arkansas River. Leader—Rhee Chong."

"You have an address on Rhee?" Bolan asked.

"About three block from the river," Kurtzman said.

"Any idea how strong he is?" Bolan said. "In the overall Dragon setup, I mean?"

Kurtzman's hummed louder for a second. Then Kurtzman said, "Not sure. But I'd guess he's mid-level." He paused. "There's a top guy somewhere in the Dragons, Striker. Got to be. But we still haven't IDed him."

Bolan nodded silently. There was a chance that Rhee would have direct access to Waack. Even if he didn't, maybe he could put the Executioner onto someone who did. Bolan could either follow that up or simply move on to Seminole to collar Shoemaker.

"Thanks, Bear," Bolan said.

"Affirmative, Striker," Kurtzman said. "Hang on a second." Bolan heard the computer man's fingers drum the keys again, then Kurtzman said, "DEA files tell me there's a deserted landing strip just outside of town that drug runners used until a recent bust. Want me to radio the coordinates to Grimaldi?"

"Yeah," Bolan said. "It'll save us some time. And pass along that I'll need ground transport once we touch down. Something that doesn't look like a cop car."

"You've got it," Kurtzman said. He paused a second, then laughed softly over the line. "You take care of the Dragons in Little Rock, and I'm sure the President will want to thank you personally."

Bolan returned the chuckle. "Right now, that's not real high on my list of concerns, Bear." He hung up and turned back to Becker.

The doctor threw his head back nervously, swinging the long golden ringlets out of his eyes. "I've helped you all I can now," he said dubiously. "Could I...go home?"

Bolan looked at the racist doctor who liked to use his position to coerce sexual favors from his female staff, and couldn't contain another laugh.

"Not quite yet," the warrior said.

LITTLE ROCK LAY on the winding Arkansas River between the eastern alluvial plains and the foothills of the Ouachita Mountains to the west. Bolan had seen them both as the Beechcraft Bonanza dropped through the sky.

The wheels hit the dirt of the deserted landing strip and Jack Grimaldi taxied the plane toward two cars at the end of the strip. Bolan saw a dark blue sedan sporting several antennae and a well-modified Camaro. As they drew nearer, the forms of two men sitting on the hoods of the vehicles took shape. The man on the sedan wore a gray suit, white shirt and tie. The other man had dark skin and was dressed in baggy denim pants above high-topped black designer "combat" boots. In his early twenties, the man had pressed the jacket of a karate *gi* into service as a shirt. The back and sides of his hair had been cut to a long stubble, but the hair on top looked to be over a foot long.

Bolan grinned as the plane came to a halt. He could remember the days when young DEA undercover agents all wore long hair, beards and pirate earrings. Times had changed.

The Executioner turned to Grimaldi. "Thanks again, Jack."

Grimaldi shrugged as he cut the engine. "Another day, another dollar, Striker. I'll wait on you."

Bolan got out of the Beechcraft and pulled Becker down behind him. He turned to the two men who were walking toward the plane.

The man in gray was the first to speak. "Special Agent Belasko?" he said. Without waiting for an answer, he extended his hand and added, "I'm Donovan. And this worthless undercover maggot is Special Agent Robinson."

Bolan shook both hands, then turned to the cars waiting behind the men. Robinson led the way to the bright red Camaro and patted the hood. "You wanted something that didn't look like a cop car. You got it," he said proudly. "It's my baby, So try to bring it back in one piece, okay?"

Bolan smiled. "I'll do my best," he said. "How well is it known in the area?"

"Oh, it's known," the DEA agent said. "Especially downtown. These wheels belong to Taco John, crack dealer to the stars, baby." He turned away from the Executioner to show the back of his head. The word *TACO* had been shaved into the long stubble above the back of his neck and colored in with a green marking pen.

Bolan took the keys from him as he turned back. "How about along the river?" he asked.

The young agent smirked. "Not as much," he said. "But don't be surprised if somebody tries to score from you at a stoplight."

The Executioner nodded. The car would do. What he had planned was a simple "in and out" of Rhee's crash pad, and if the Camaro was recognized, he'd be gone before anyone had time to act.

Bolan looked at Becker, nodded toward the passenger door, then slid into the driver's seat. The big engine roared to life as the DEA men got into the sedan and drove away.

The Executioner pulled after them onto a dirt road that led through a short wooded area to the highway, then followed the directions Kurtzman had given him during the flight from Memphis, making several more turns on the back roads outside Little Rock before finally crossing a neglected bridge and entering the city limits.

Kurtzman's route took them through an amiable garden suburb along tree-lined streets before reaching the dock area.

Bolan watched the ships loading and unloading as he drove along the quayside. Before the coming of the railways, shallow-draft steamboats had toted their cargo back and forth between Little Rock and New Orleans. Now more modern ships did the same.

A few heads stared at the Camaro as it passed, all belonging to men or women who had the long, drawn look of drug addicts. Turning away from the wharf area, the Executioner entered a low-rent residential area, turned once more and drove past the address Kurtzman had given him.

Rhee Chong's house fit in well with the others on the block, and was in the same state of disrepair as the Dragon duplex Bolan had hit earlier in Philadelphia. Paint peeled from the outer walls. Shingles had blown off the roof during some recent storm and still lay covering the front yard. The front door was closed, the windows covered by blinds.

Bolan smiled. It was midafternoon, and the Dragons were no doubt still sleeping off a long night of drugs and terror along the riverside. Perfect for what he had in mind.

The Executioner circled the block, seeing the rear of the Dragon's lair between the houses on the other side. A rickety-looking wooden door sat in the middle of the frame, just beyond a clothesline that stretched across the backyard. Pulling to the curb, Bolan killed the Camaro's engine. "Let's go," he told Becker.

The doctor shook his head. "Forget it," he said. "I'm a doctor, Belasko, not some fucking commando."

Bolan turned to face him. "You may be a doctor," he said. "But you're also supposed to be a big tough racist warrior. Here's your chance to prove it. Besides, I don't intend to let you out of my sight until I'm sure you aren't any good to me anymore." He let daggers fly from his eyes and watched Becker cringe. "Now get out of the car before I have to pull you out."

Becker did as he was told.

Bolan led the way between the houses, across the first backyard and over a crumbling chicken-wire fence. They ducked under the clothesline and stopped at the back door.

Bolan pulled the Beretta 93-R from under his jacket and turned to Becker. "You stay next to me," he whispered. "*Right* next to me. If I lose sight of you, you'll get a bullet the next time I see you."

The curls around Becker's neck bounced up and down as he nodded anxiously.

Bolan twisted the knob and found it locked. The splinters around the door told him a strong shove would break the frame, but that would produce more noise than he wanted. The Dragons were asleep, he guessed, and he wanted to keep it that way.

Fishing into his pocket, Bolan produced the phony Justice Department credential case. He pulled the laminated ID card from the leather, slipped it between the door and frame and the lock popped open.

The Executioner led the way into the kitchen. He stepped to the side, waving Becker in behind him as his eyes took in the dirty dishes, pots and pans piled high in the sink and overflowing onto the filthy counters. The odors of stale marijuana smoke, beer and general decay filled his nostrils.

A short hallway led from the kitchen to the living room, and through the opening the Executioner could see a half dozen dirty mattresses and sleeping bags on the floor. Men and women in various states of undress lay snoring the sleep of the drugged.

Bolan turned to Becker. "Wait here," he whispered.

The doctor's eyes were wide with revulsion at the filth and depredation. "Don't worry," he said. "I'd rather you killed me than go in there."

"Try to get out the back and I will," Bolan said.

The nearest sleeping form lay in a stained red sleeping bag. Bolan approached the man silently, squatting next to the thick black hair. He patted the man on the shoulder and got no response. A rougher shake rolled the man to his back and opened one of the matted eyes.

The Executioner shoved the Beretta's sound suppressor under the man's nose. "Which one of you is Rhee?" he whispered.

The Dragon tried to sit up. Bolan pushed him back with the barrel of the Beretta. He flipped the safety off with a click that echoed through the house. "I don't intend to ask you again," he said softly.

The man's eyes opened wider in fear and understanding as he came to full consciousness. He nodded to the side. "On the mattress," he whispered. "With the two girls."

Bolan looked across the room. Just to the side of the front door, he saw a striped double mattress supporting two women and a man in the middle. The woman closest to him, an Oriental, wore a torn black bra and matching panties. The other, a flaxen blonde, was clad only in a pair of men's boxer shorts.

Between them, the Executioner saw a thin, wiry man in blue jeans and a black T-shirt. His long straight hair fell to his shoulders, and a diamond-stud earring showed through the thick oily mass. A thin wispy mustache and goatee grew from Rhee Chong's face and fluttered with each heavy breath from the sleeping Dragon leader's mouth.

Bolan looked back down at the Korean on the other end of the Beretta. "Thanks," he whispered. "Now go back to sleep." In one swift motion he raised the Beretta and brought it down along the side of the man's head.

Bolan moved silently over the sleeping bodies to the mattress where Rhee lay sandwiched between the two women. He jammed the Beretta's suppressor under the man's goatee and dug it into his throat.

Rhee's black eyes opened immediately.

Bolan held his free hand to his face, extending the index finger over his lips. "Shh," he said. "We wouldn't want to wake the girls. Now get up."

As he moved back to let the Dragon leader rise, the Executioner heard the back door in the kitchen open. He glanced that way, then reached down, grabbing the front of Rhee's T-shirt and hauling him to his feet.

The Executioner heard the sound of a brief scuffle in the kitchen.

Bolan shoved Rhee over the other sleeping Dragons and down the hall. When he reached the kitchen door, he saw a tall, heavily muscled man wearing a green Dragon jacket and squatting next to Becker, who lay still on the dirty tile.

The man was wiping the blade of a long lock-blade folding knife on the doctor's golf slacks. He looked up as Bolan and Rhee entered the room.

"Chong—" he got out of his mouth before Bolan drilled two 9 mm slugs into his thick chest.

The man in the green jacket fell over Becker as Bolan motioned Rhee to step to the side, then leaned over the doctor. He pressed a finger into the man's carotid artery, but even before he did, he knew it was useless. Lawrence Becker's dead eyes stared lifelessly at the ceiling as blood pumped from the knife wound in his chest.

Bolan stood and turned to Rhee. "Let's go," he whispered, jamming the Beretta into the Dragon leader's ribs. Rhee Chong didn't argue as they left the house.

BOLAN PULLED THE Camaro to a halt next to the humming engine of the Beechcraft Bonanza on the landing strip. He got out and dropped the keys behind the right front tire.

DEA Special Agent Robinson would be pleased. The Executioner had returned his wheels without a scratch.

Opening the passenger door, Bolan reached in and grasped the cuffs that joined Rhee Chong's hands in front of him. Another set secured the man's hands to his belt. The Executioner pulled forward and jerked Rhee from the car.

"Looks like your traveling companion has a new look," Jack Grimaldi said as Bolan climbed up into the Beechcraft's rear seat, then turned to pull Rhee into the front before closing the door.

The Executioner nodded. "I'm not sure if I traded up or down," he said.

Grimaldi shook his head. "The other one was cleaner," he said. "Where to?"

"We'll have to ask our new friend, Rhee," Bolan said.

The long-haired Oriental turned to face Bolan in the back seat. "Your new friend," he spit sarcastically, "will tell you nothing."

Bolan shrugged. "We'll see." Turning to Grimaldi, he said, "Take her up, Jack. We'll circle for a while while I talk to him."

Grimaldi let out a chuckle as he worked the controls and the Beechcraft started forward. "I've heard those talks before," he said.

Bolan waited until they were airborne, then reached up and grabbed a handful of Rhee's long greasy hair and twisted the Dragon to face him. "I need to contact a man named Jerry Wayne Waack," he said. "How do I do it?"

"I know no one by that name," Rhee said, his eyes filled with anger.

"I think you do," Bolan said. "At least you know who he is."

Rhee didn't answer.

Bolan lightened his grip on the Dragon leader's hair. "You know much about Vietnam?" he asked, knowing that Rhee didn't before he asked. He couldn't—at least not firsthand. The Dragon had still been in diapers when the U.S. pulled out of Southeast Asia.

"Only that America got her ass whipped," Rhee said, smiling.

Bolan shook his head. "No, I mean do you know anything about the way U.S. Special Forces sometimes interrogated captured Vietcong terrorists?" he said. "A simple technique. But very effective."

Rhee didn't speak. But the arrogance began to fade from his face.

Bolan tightened his grip on the Dragon leader's hair. "I'm going to ask you again, Rhee. How do I contact Jerry Wayne Waack?"

Rhee gritted his teeth as his hair was pulled. "I do not know any Waack," he said.

Bolan leaned forward around the seat and opened the door next to Rhee. Air rushed in, and he had to shout over it. "Have a nice flight, Rhee." He pushed the gangster toward the opening.

"Wait!" the Dragon screamed, his voice now high-pitched.

Bolan stopped with Rhee's head halfway out the door. "What?"

"I don't know Waack," Rhee said.

Bolan pushed again.

"But I know who he is!" the Dragon leader screamed.

Bolan relaxed his grip, closed the door and let Rhee sit back against his seat. The Dragon leader's breath came in short horrified pants as Bolan said, "Talk fast."

"I don't know if he'll be able to contact Waack," Rhee said between gasps. "He might not—"

Bolan opened the door again and grabbed Rhee with both hands. He shoved the gang-banger's head and shoulders out of the plane. The wind whipped Rhee's long greasy hair away from his head. "How far down do you think it is, Rhee?" the Executioner roared into the man's ear.

Grimaldi answered for the Dragon. "Seven thousand feet," he said. "Give or take a foot."

The Executioner nudged the man closer to death, but kept a firm grip on his hair and shoulder. Trying to brace himself, Rhee kicked his legs against the floorboard, hooked a foot under the dash. Grimaldi pulled a snub-nosed .357 Magnum revolver from under his shirt and rapped the heavy steel frame across Rhee's shin.

The Dragon leader screamed as pain shot down his leg. "No!" he pleaded. "I'm telling you the truth! Shim! You want a man named Shim! Shim will know how to contact Waack!"

"Who is he?" Bolan shouted.

"He's . . . he's our contact! He has something to do with the government in Pyongyang!"

"And where is this Shim?" Bolan shouted.

"Dallas!" Rhee shrieked. "Now, please! Close the door!"

"Where in Dallas?"

"Oh, God, please! I don't know where! A hotel or motel, I guess! But I don't know where!"

Grimaldi was already dipping a wing toward the southwest when Bolan pulled Rhee back inside the Beechcraft and slammed the door. As the horrified Dragon shivered and shook, the Executioner reached between the seats and pulled the radio mike from its brace. A moment later he had Kurtzman on the airwaves. "Get your machines tapped into all of the motel chains in Dallas, and any of the mom-and-pop outfits that are computerized. We want a man named Shim, but I doubt he'll be under that name. Look for any Korean name that checked in midafternoon. If you can't find one, start looking for Chinese, Japanese, any names an Oriental might be able to pass under."

Kurtzman chuckled over the airwaves. "You want that needle while I'm at it?" he asked.

"What needle?"

"The one in the haystack you're calling Dallas, Texas."

Bolan grinned. Kurtzman's grace under pressure was one of the things that made him so effective. And he knew when to lighten a situation. "It won't be the first one you've found for me," the Executioner said. "Cross-reference the check-in time with flight times from Memphis that began within thirty minutes or so of the airport incident, and then take into consideration a drive from one of the Dallas airports. That should narrow it down." He clipped the mike into the dash and sat back.

Grimaldi turned to glance at the Executioner and nodded toward Rhee, who was still shaking. "Well," the pilot said, "that little drama brought back some memories. But damn, Striker, I thought I was going to get to see a good aerial show."

The Executioner grabbed Rhee's greasy hair again and jerked back, then shoved his face an inch from Rhee's trembling lips. "You still might, Jack," he said. "And if we don't find Shim in Dallas, I promise you, you will."

## CHAPTER ELEVEN

Colonel Shim Sang glanced through the sliding glass door at the swimming pool as he pressed the phone to his ear, waiting for the line to connect.

A young bikini-clad woman with long black hair dived clumsily off the diving board, disappeared, then surfaced beside the ladder on the side of the pool. Slowly, methodically, she grabbed the rails and hauled her well-formed breasts into view. Shim watched her squeeze her elbows to her sides to accent the cleavage as she shook the water from her head, then pulled herself up onto the concrete deck.

The woman glanced at the two men in sunglasses reclining on towels a few feet away, then returned to the diving board to repeat her performance.

Shim felt a stirring in his groin and gripped the phone receiver tighter. The woman's brazen attempt to catch the attention of the two men would have landed her in jail in North Korea. Western decadence, he thought, and forced his eyes away.

A series of clicks came over the line as Shim turned to the open door to the adjoining room. Through it, he could see the sleeping man in the bed against the wall. "Western ignorance," he mouthed silently as he stared at the colorless skin and milk-white hair. Jerry Wayne Waack had been half-crazy when Shim had first met him, and the North Korean Special Purpose officer often wondered how he had slipped though U.S. psychological testing. Of course Waack had entered the Army during America's Vietnam fiasco, when anyone who could tell a cow from a pig passed the requirements. In any case, once Shim had found the "key" to the bleached-out, pink-eyed American sniper, brainwashing him had been like taking candy from a baby.

As the call to Pyongyang finally connected, Shim reminded himself that he was not on a secure line. Under the present circumstances, the CIA would almost certainly be monitoring all calls to North Korea. But that would not matter. The call had been answered at a small Pyongyang restaurant secretly run by the Central Committee's Research Department, the North Korean equivalent of the KGB, and the agency that worked hand in hand with Special Purpose forces when assassinations or abductions were expedient.

Shim immediately recognized the voice on the other end. Cho Kyu might currently be employed as a cook at the restaurant, but Shim doubted the man could even boil noodles. Cho did, however, have his talents. No one in the CCRD was a better demolition planner, and it had been Cho who had orchestrated the 1987 bombing of the Korean Airlines flight that made front pages all over the world.

"Good day, Brother," Shim said in Korean, keeping his voice low so as not to wake up Waack. "It is good to hear your voice." He smiled, awaiting a reply. Every call he had made back to Pyongyang since the assassinations of the American senators had begun followed a simple yet effective code. Shim and

Cho spoke to each other as the Shu brothers—Sik and Y.K. Anyone listening in would have believed that Sik, his wife Tae Yun and their two children had somehow escaped communist North Korea and made their way to the U.S. Y.K. and the rest of the Shu family had been left behind.

"Sik!" Cho said with the excitement of a man talking to a dear relative overseas. "You and Tae Yun are well?"

"Yes. She is sleeping."

"And my niece and nephew?"

"They are swimming in a motel swimming pool."

"And where are you?" Cho asked.

In the background, Shim could hear the clanking of pans in the restaurant's kitchen. "Dallas, Texas. Cowboys, Indians. Bang! Bang!"

Cho laughed. "Soon you will be riding a horse and wearing a big hat!"

"No, I don't believe so," Shim said, letting his voice grow more serious. "But I believe I am about to find a job." He took a deep breath. So far, everything both men had said was window dressing for the benefit of CIA eavesdroppers. Now it was time to get the report to Cho while still sounding like one big happy family.

"A job?" Cho said. "Good. That is good."

"Yes, Y.K. As you know, I found work in other parts of this country. But those jobs were temporary. They are finished, so I have come here."

"Will this job last?" Cho asked.

"Oh, yes," Shim said. "Work here will go well."

"Yes," Cho answered. "Did you have trouble getting the job?"

Shim knew that Cho was wondering if he and Waack had encountered any difficulties in setting up the assassinations of the two Texas senators, Shilling and Christianson. "No," he said. "It was practically waiting on me." He sat back in the chair, his mission accomplished. Cho now knew that they were ready to take out Shilling and Christianson, then move on to assassinate more of the American senators who were pushing for nuclear inspection in North Korea. A few more meaningless lines of family talk would end the transmission.

"Y.K.," Shim said, "I should go. Who knows who might be listening in on your end to find out where I am? They might take out their anger at me on you and your family."

"Yes, perhaps you are right," Cho said, his voice suddenly nervous. "The Central Committee has already visited our home and threatened us."

Shim found himself laughing silently.

"But Sik," Cho said, "call me back when you know for sure that the job will last. Someday my family and I will join you in America, and the hell with the committee."

"Your family has our love and prayers, Brother," Shim said.

"Goodbye," Cho said, and hung up.

Shim replaced the phone and twisted to look out the window. The woman who had so cleverly displayed her breasts to the two men now lay on a towel between them, laughing at something one of them had said. He turned his eyes back to Waack on the bed, then glanced at his watch.

It was time to wake the abominable quotation-parroting piece of white flesh. Shim studied him, wondering where, and why, Waack had picked up the habit of memorizing famous sayings. It was a habit the man had taken on before he'd been captured in North Korea, and with all the other intricate mind alterations Shim had needed to perform, it had been an aspect of Waack's personality that was not worth the effort of erasing.

But it was irritating, and when Waack started spouting out the words of Shakespeare or Thomas Jefferson or Oscar Wilde, Shim wished he had taken the time.

The North Korean shook his head as he continued to look at Waack, or Won Kwang, as he had convinced Waack his name had once been. Part of Shim would be relieved when this mission was over. Waack had outlived his usefulness, and he could eliminate the freakish abomination. The arcane thoughts of Western scholars would no longer ring in his ears. Yet part of Shim would mourn the loss.

In spite of his annoying citations and appalling appearance, Jerry Wayne Waack had been Colonel Shim Sang's greatest triumph, and Shim had to pat himself on the back. His "retraining" had instilled in Waack a loyalty to Shim which translated into a loyalty to North Korea. At the same time, it left the albino's previous homicidal tendencies intact.

Waack had returned home and behaved exactly as Shim expected, killing sometimes for profit but sometimes for his own perverse enjoyment. By the time North Korea finally needed him, the pale-skinned freak of nature had built up the perfect background to throw the Americans off his trail by working for the Ku Klux Klan and other right-wing organizations.

Shim watched Waack roll onto his side, still sleeping peacefully. When it had come time to stop a U.S. Senate pushing for nuclear inspection of North Korea, Shim had picked only those senators who also favored strict gun control, knowing that if Waack were caught, his links to the right would soon be discovered. It would appear that the senators had died for their stance on disarming their own country rather than his.

Shim smiled as he moved through the door to Waack's room. In a sense, he owed the albino the promotion to general he suspected would come as soon as the U.S. senators on the list had been eliminated and he returned to North Korea. So, he supposed, a small part of him would be sad to say goodbye to the symbol of his success.

Shim sat on the bed next to Waack. Gently he shook the albino's shoulder, fighting the revulsion he felt on the rare occasions when he was forced to touch the grotesquely white man. Only a few more times, he told himself. Do not spoil it now. Everyone this man has known since birth has spurned him for his appearance. It was your seeming absence of disgust, your acceptance, your willingness to be his friend, that created the bond this abomination feels to you.

Waack's eyelids opened. He looked up at Shim and smiled.

Shim patted his shoulder. "It is time to awaken, my brother," he said. "It is time."

BLACK STORM CLOUDS had covered the sun by the time the Beechcraft Bonanza began dropping through the sky over central Texas. Through the plane's windows, Bolan saw a flash of lightning to the west. A sharp crack of thunder roared as the first drops of rain tapped against the Bonanza's wings.

Aaron Kurtzman's voice suddenly cut through the static over the radio. "Stony Man, Birdman One. Stony Man...Birdman."

Bolan glanced at the control panel, made sure the scrambler light was flashing, then reached between the seats and pulled the microphone's twisted cord into the back seat. "You've got the Birdman, Stony. This is Striker. Go."

Kurtzman cleared his throat. "We may have a hit, Striker," he said. "A man named Shu Sik checked into one of the Dallas area La Quinta Inns a few hours ago." The computer man paused, then added, "The time element is consistent with Memphis. He had plenty of time to get there."

The Executioner thumbed the microphone's button. "Affirmative, Stony. But is that the only Korean name you got in the whole Dallas area?" He let up on the mike again.

"No," Kurtzman came back. "I've got a half dozen others that line up with the time factor." He stopped for a moment, then went on. "But Shu's the only one who checked in with a Caucasian and got adjoining rooms, 110 and 112." There was another pause, then Kurtzman said, "Barb called the front desk. The men arrived together in a taxi. The registration card says they represent an outfit called Korean Software in

Seoul. Before you ask, I already checked—there is no such company."

Bolan heard a click as another microphone key was pressed on, then Barbara Price's voice replaced Kurtzman's. "Don't worry, Striker," she said. "I told the girl working the desk I was with the company. We'd had some flight-scheduling problems and I wanted to make sure the two men had arrived for the meeting tomorrow. She said they were there, but looked tired when they checked in." Price cleared her throat. "Especially the one with white hair."

The Executioner felt the muscles in his abdomen contract. "Which La Quinta?" he asked.

"The West Airport Freeway, in Irving. Tell Jack to land at the Dallas-Fort Worth airport—it's less than a mile from the motel."

"Affirmative, Barb," Bolan said. He handed the mike to Grimaldi.

Fifteen minutes later they were on the ground. "Baby-sit our little friend while I get us some wheels, Jack," the Executioner said. "You have a bug and receivers on board?"

Grimaldi nodded toward the storage area behind Bolan.

"Then dress him out. I'll meet you in the rental parking lot." Bolan climbed out of the plane and jogged across the tarmac to the terminal. Taking possession of the keys and papers to a blue Oldsmobile, he hurried outside into the light rain that had begun to fall.

As they walked from the plane to the rental lot, Bolan saw that Grimaldi had cut the restraints from

Rhee's wrists to avoid drawing attention. But the Stony Man pilot carried a brown paper bag, his right hand out of sight inside. The expression on the Korean gang leader's face told Bolan he was well aware that Grimaldi's index finger rested on the trigger of his .357.

The rain increased, stalling traffic and stretching the five minute drive to the motel to ten minutes. Bolan pulled the Oldsmobile into the motel, circled the building and located the adjoining rooms. Cutting into the parking lot of a restaurant next door, he parked facing the swimming pool in the courtyard. The rain had driven the swimmers and sunbathers inside, but through the downpour Bolan could see the sliding glass doors to rooms 110 and 112.

The Executioner turned to Grimaldi in the passenger's seat. "You got him wired?"

Grimaldi nodded. He handed Bolan a small compact receiver. "I've got the other one," he said, patting the black plastic lump clipped to his belt.

The Executioner turned to the back seat. Rhee had calmed down since his near dive from the plane, but the fear was still poignant in his eyes. "We're going to call the room to make sure it's them and they're there," Bolan said. "Then you're going inside."

Rhee shook his head violently. "I can't!" he said. "I barely know the man! And what would I be doing in Dallas? How would I know where Shim was staying? He'll know something's—"

"Shut up," Bolan said. He got out of the Olds, opened the back door and jerked Rhee out into the rain. Marching the Dragon leader inside the front entrance of the restaurant, he stopped in front of a pay phone.

Bolan found the La Quinta's number in the phone book and dropped a quarter in the slot. A few seconds later a feminine voice said, "La Quinta, may I help you?"

"Room 110," Bolan said.

He listened to the ring as the line connected, then heard a thickly accented voice say, "Hello?"

The Executioner moved closer to Rhee, holding the receiver between his ear and that of the Dragon. "Hey, Charley," he said in a deep Texas drawl. "You got any ice down there? Damn machine on the second floor's busted all to hell."

"You have the wrong number," the voice said, irritated.

Bolan wanted Rhee to hear more of the voice. "Hey, you ain't Charley?" he said quickly.

"No, I am not Charley. I told you, you have called the wrong number."

"Listen, pal, I'm sorry to bother you. Maybe I can make it up. We're havin' a party up here. Why don't you come on up?"

"I am busy," the voice said, and hung up.

Bolan recradled the receiver and looked down into Rhee's frightened face.

"It's him," the Dragon said without enthusiasm.

Bolan guided Rhee back to the car, shoved him into the back seat and got in next to him. Grimaldi turned to face them.

"I'll go to the front, Jack," the Executioner said. "You stay here and watch the back." He turned to

Rhee, reached up and grabbed the man's collar. "You're going to knock on the door and go in, my friend," he growled. "Tell Shim that you have information for him about an American who's onto him."

"He will never believe—"

Bolan slapped the Dragon leader to silence him, then went on. "Tell him you wanted to get the information to him as quickly as possible. That's why you're here."

Rhee threw up his hands in bewilderment. "What do I say then?" he asked. "What is the information? Who is the American?"

Bolan looked him in the eye. "Me," he said.

"You mean—"

"Tell him all you know about me, except for the fact that I brought you here. Tell him I broke in the house in Little Rock and you overheard me and a man I was with mention the name Shim before you escaped."

"But how did I know Shim was here? At the La Quinta?"

Bolan gave him a hard smile. "You expect me to do *all* the work for you? Come up with something. You've got between now and the time you reach the room." The Executioner leaned past him, opened the door and shoved him out. "Remember," he said, looking down at the receiver on his belt. "We'll be listening."

The Executioner got out of the Olds and walked Rhee around the building, stopping at the corner as the Dragon moved on to room 110. He jammed an ear wire into the receiver and stuck the plug in his ear.

Bolan switched the unit on and heard Rhee's heavy breathing and footsteps on the concrete sidewalk. The rain fell with a new fury as Rhee raised his hand to knock on the door.

The Executioner ducked back around the corner as the downpour soaked him head to toe. The soft rapping of knuckles on wood filled his ear. Then he heard the bolt thrown back and the same voice he had heard over the phone at Denny's said, "Rhee?"

"I must come inside," Rhee said, out of breath. "I must talk to you."

The door closed again, and in the background Bolan could hear a television. "Why are you here?" Shim asked suspiciously. "And how did you know where to find me?"

"I called Baltimore," Rhee said, still struggling for breath. "Hwang said you would be here."

"I did not tell Hwang where I was," Shim said.

"But he knew!" Rhee said. "Somehow he knew."

There was a long silence, then Shim said. "Tell me what you came to tell me."

"Two Americans broke into our house in Little Rock," Rhee said. "They killed all but me. They were looking for you." He paused and Bolan heard him take a deep breath through the transmitter. "You must be careful."

Another long pause. Then Shim said, "You are lying."

"No!"

The Executioner heard the sound of a pistol slide racking back to chamber a round. No, he thought. Not yet, Rhee. Talk fast.

"Shim, you must believe me! I came to warn you. They are onto you."

"Sit down, Rhee," Shim said. "Do you know what we are doing?" Bolan heard the sound of one man dropping onto the bed.

"No," Rhee's voice said. "Only that you and an American would be traveling across the country doing something. And that all Anju Dragons should be ready to offer assistance should you need it."

Shim laughed. "We have not needed it."

"No, you have not. Shim, I—"

Bolan heard the sound of a slap. "Silence!" Shim screamed. "I am going to tell you something. Something no other Dragons at your level know." He paused. "Do you know a man named Waack?"

"I have heard of him."

"Waack and I are killing senators," Shim said simply.

Bolan felt all of the muscles in his body tighten at once. It was Waack behind the assassinations. The Executioner had considered pulling off his hunt for Waack to go after the killer. Now he found he had been chasing the assassin all along.

"But why?" Rhee asked, his voice trembling again. "What do the senators have to do with the Dragons? And why have you decided to tell me?"

Shim chuckled. "You are fools, all of you American-born Koreans. Did you think you were receiving weapons and aid from North Korea because of some sentimental attachment we had to you? It goes much deeper than that. The senators who have died, and will continue to die, are pushing for nuclear inspection of our country. If they cannot force the UN to take action, they will force the President to act independently. Someday we will be too strong to worry about such things. But at the moment we cannot confront the round-eyed bastards."

Bolan glanced away from the motel to an eighteen-wheeler passing on the highway, then tucked the earplug deeper into his ear against the noise. Suddenly everything was taking shape. Things that had made no sense before were now becoming crystal clear.

"And the reason I have decided to tell you all this," Shim said in the Executioner's ear, "is because I do not believe your story about the Americans or Hwang." He chuckled over the airwaves. "And you are about to die."

"No, Shim, please—"

A sudden screech from the transmitter threatened to burst the Executioner's eardrum. He looked to the highway again and saw the silhouette of the man behind the wheel of the passing truck. The man held the microphone of a citizens-band radio to his lips.

Bolan cursed softly under his breath as he sprinted through the puddles on the sidewalk toward the room. A freak accident—a combination of the rain-disrupted airwaves and the passing truck—had caused the CB to cross frequencies with the transmitter.

The Executioner slipped on the slick pavement, caught his balance and ran on. If he had heard the transmitter shriek on his end, Shim would have heard it on his.

"What was that?" Shim yelled as the Executioner neared the room. Bolan heard the sound of clothing tear, then Rhee screamed, "They forced me, Shim! They made—"

His words were cut off by the roar of a gunshot.

Bolan ripped the earplug from his head as he kicked the door. The Desert Eagle found its way to his hand as he charged through the opening to see Rhee lying on his back on the floor.

An older Korean stood over the Dragon holding a Chinese Tokarev pistol.

Shim tried to turn the weapon his way as Bolan raised the big .44 over his head and brought it down over the man's skull. Shim dropped like a pile of rocks. The Executioner crouched, scooped up the Tokarev, then swung the Desert Eagle in an arc to cover the room. Empty. He moved quickly to the open door to the adjoining room and went in low.

It was empty, as well. Bolan searched the bathroom and closet, then turned to the bed. The covers were turned back, the sheets wrinkled. It had been slept in.

But Jerry Wayne Waack was nowhere to be found.

"AH," SAID Jerry Wayne Waack as he stared across the street and down the block to Senator James Shilling's Spanish-style stucco house. " 'The Devil's children have the Devil's luck.' " The seventeenth-century English proverb brought a smile to his pale lips. For a moment his mind drifted from the house to the trunk of the Mercury Cougar he and Shim had rented at the airport. It had been empty when he opened it an hour earlier.

Now it contained the bodies of two police detectives from Grand Prairie, Texas.

The skies darkened with rain clouds as Waack watched the entrance of the senator's house. It had indeed been a stroke of luck that he'd seen the two men getting out of the multiantennaed vehicle at the McDonald's off Interstate 30 when he'd stopped for a couple of Big Macs. As he drove he'd been wondering how he would get past the rent-a-cops who guarded the entrance to the lavish Briarwood Estates housing addition, and debating on whether he should go over the wall to the south or just kill them and go on. Both methods had advantages and disadvantages.

Waack had found that the flash of a badge, and the story of a witness interview, had been better. It had worked wonders on the pimple-faced wannabe cop who even asked if he could be of assistance.

Waack lifted his eyes to the red clay tiles on the roof of the house as the rain began to fall. He had coaxed a free-running poodle into the car several blocks away, strapped his belt to the happy dog's collar to look like a leash, then parked on the other side of the block from the senator's house. A stroll through the neighborhood with the pooch in tow had brought no curious looks from a half dozen men and women working in their yards, and tossing a small piece of hamburger from one of the Big Macs into the senator's driveway, then releasing the leash, had given him the excuse he needed to chase the dog up to the garage door.

A quick rap of his fist had broken the digital opener on the stucco outside the door and rendered the door inoperable.

It had been a simple matter to walk the poodle on around the block, return to the Cougar, then park where he could see the house. The dog—who'd become a liability rather than an asset—now rested on top of the two cops in the trunk.

The rain came down in a steady sheet as Waack watched the front door open. He saw a middle-aged woman wearing a tennis skirt scurry out of the house, a nylon windbreaker held over her gray-streaked permanent. He grinned.

Mrs. Shilling—Marjorie, if he remembered right—must have tried the door from the inside and it hadn't worked. Waack watched her jog awkwardly from the porch through the rain to the garage door, lean down and tug on the handle, then scurry back into the house.

"Step into my parlor said the spider to the fly," Waack said, laughing. He started the Cougar's engine, circled the block and headed back toward the entrance to the addition wondering how long it would take for the repairman to arrive. Not long, probably. Senators and their wives wielded influence.

Twenty minutes later a lime green panel van bearing the logo of the Arlington Overhead Door Company pulled up to the guard shack at the entrance. Waack watched the pimply-faced kid in the blue uniform step out into the rain with a clipboard, lean down to speak with the man in the driver's seat, then wave the van through.

Waack let the van pass, then pulled in behind. He followed it two blocks, then pulled out as if to pass.

The van honked its annoyance at the violation of courtesy on such a narrow street, then honked again as Waack cut back in front of it a moment too soon, scraping the left front fender.

Both vehicles ground to a halt. Waack jumped out into the rain, feeling it beat against his face. He walked toward the driver as the man rolled down the window and said, "You stupid asshole."

"Why, what an ugly thing to say," Waack said as he brought the sound-suppressed Beretta .25 out of his pocket and fired a lone round into the man's open mouth.

Four minutes later the repairman was hidden beneath a tarp in the cargo area of the van, and Jerry Wayne Waack was driving the vehicle down the street to the home of Senator James Shilling.

Mrs. Shilling opened the door with a smile. "Come in, come in," she said, looking past Waack into the rain. "You'll catch your death out there."

Waack hauled the toolbox inside to a tiled entryway. "Thank you," he said. He looked down at the woman.

For an instant, Mrs. Shilling's eyes met his and the smile faded. It returned as fast as it had disappeared, but now it looked forced. "Well," she said stiffly, looking way from Waack, "just follow me. I'll take you to the garage." She turned, walking swiftly through the living room and into the kitchen, then opened a door to reveal a gray Mercedes in the two-car garage. Waack noted that she didn't look at him as she stepped back and said, "Just call me if you need anything."

Waack walked immediately to the garage door, disconnected the electronic opener and hauled the door up manually. Behind him, he heard the door to the kitchen close.

He worked swiftly, standing inside the garage and reaching out into the rain to rewire the digital opener. He noted the coded frequency that opened and closed the door, then replaced the broken plastic facing. As soon as he'd finished, he glanced to the kitchen door to make sure it was still closed, then pulled the top shelf out of his toolbox and began doing what he'd come to do.

Waack thought of the bitch inside the house as he applied the C-4 to the inside of the overhead door. "No different than all of the others," he whispered to himself as he pressed a detonator into the explosive, then wired it to a small electronic transmitter. He adjusted the frequency to match that of the door opener, then turned back to the kitchen door.

"She thinks I'm an albino," he said under his breath, then opened the door and stepped into the kitchen. A shower was running somewhere in another part of the house, and Waack knelt just inside the door next to the refrigerator. Opening his toolbox again, he crammed another charge of C-4 between the box and the wall, rigged it to the garage door frequency and moved into the living room.

Mrs. Shilling looked surprised as she entered the room in her robe, a towel wrapped around her head like a turban. "Well, that was fast," she said pleasantly, and now her smile seemed genuine again.

Too late, bitch, Waack thought. You already showed your true colors. He wrote out a quick bill, accepted her check, then started for the front door. As he opened it, he turned back. "I'm pretty sure it's fixed, Mrs. Shilling," he said. "But some of the wiring's almost worn out, and I didn't have any in the truck. I'll replace it tomorrow. Free of charge, of course. It's not your fault I ran out of wire."

Mrs. Shilling smiled again. "Oh, dear," she said. "Will it work tonight? With the delay and the rain, I've given up the idea of going to the store. But my husband will be home in a couple of hours."

"I think it'll work," Waack said. He glanced up at the ceiling, frowned, then said, "But just in case I'm wrong, you might want to wait in the kitchen where you can hear your husband's car." Waack chuckled. "We wouldn't want a wet senator on our hands now, would we?"

Mrs. James Shilling was giggling her thanks for the advice as Waack opened the door and jogged back out into the rain. He was still laughing quietly as he slid behind the wheel of the van.

The charge in the kitchen might take out the dingy bitch, and it might not. He had more C-4 in the toolbox and one more stop to make while he was in Arlington, but if he hurried, he had time to get back and watch.

Waack switched the windshield wipers on and pulled the van away from the curb. One more stop. One more bomb.

And this one was going to be the most fun of all.

## CHAPTER TWELVE

Jack Grimaldi could fly every aircraft known to man, from the forty-nine-cent balsa-wood glider, hanging on a rack in a drugstore's toy section, to the space shuttle. Flying made him happy, and flying for the men of Stony Man Farm—for Able Team and Phoenix Force—made him even happier.

But what most thrilled Jack Grimaldi, who was arguably the most skillful pilot in the world, was working with the man he called Striker.

Grimaldi was just getting used to the shocking revelation that North Korea was behind the assassinations of the senators when he heard the interference on the airwaves. A second later he realized that something had cut into the transmitter frequency, and a split second after that Shim let it be known that he was aware of the bug, too.

The gunshot came as Grimaldi emerged from the Oldsmobile.

Grimaldi drew the Smith & Wesson Model 66 from the clip-on holster inside his slacks and sprinted through the rain for the courtyard. He circled the pool, dashed through the open cast-iron gate and got to the sliding glass door as he heard Bolan kick the front. Finding the door locked, he hesitated briefly, wondering whether or not he should break the glass and take the chance of drawing the attention of the other motel guests.

No, Grimaldi decided as he turned toward the corner of the building. Bolan was already inside. If Striker was going to get shot, he'd already be down, and Grimaldi would have heard more gunfire from the transmitter. Bolan had things under control already.

Still, the thirty seconds it took Grimaldi to round the building to the front would go down in his memory as seeming like long endless days. He'd spent half his life lugging Mack Bolan to near-suicide missions around the globe, watching the man called the Executioner drift to earth beneath a parachute and silently praying that this time wouldn't be *the* time.

Always, Bolan returned. Sometimes battered, but never beaten. Still, Grimaldi knew it could happen, and the fact that the Executioner was the best warrior he'd ever met didn't totally erase his worry.

Grimaldi raced for the door. On the rare occasions he fought alongside Bolan on the ground, he found he worried about the big guy even more. Bolan had defied death too many times for his number not to eventually come up.

As he reached the open door, the pilot dropped his inside shoulder and pivoted into the room. Gripping the .357 Magnum in both hands, he saw two men on the floor—Rhee, and the man he assumed to be Shim. The rest of the room was deserted, but the door to number 112 stood open.

"Come on in, Jack," Bolan's voice called out from the next room. "And close the front door behind you."

Grimaldi turned and pulled the door toward him. The frame was splintered and one of the hinges had been driven half out of the wall. Finally he pushed the door closed enough that its damage wouldn't be noticeable from the outside, then entered the other room.

Bolan was going through a suitcase on the floor. "Shim starting to come around yet?" he asked. Before Grimaldi could answer, they heard a moan from the other room.

Bolan drew the Desert Eagle from his holster and moved to the doorway, where he could see the man in the other room. As he passed Grimaldi, he gave the pilot a handful of snipped wire scraps.

"You know what they are, Jack?" Bolan asked as he watched Shim come back to life.

Grimaldi nodded. "Waack's made a bomb."

Bolan continued to stare through the door. "Look for anything that might tell us where he's gone," he said. "I'm going to ask our buddy here a few questions." He disappeared through the doorway.

Grimaldi finished looking through the suitcase, finding nothing but the usual: clothes, shaving equipment, a paperback novel. He heard Bolan bringing Shim around as he looked through the desk, then the closet. A quick look under the bed turned up nothing but an aging copy of *Hustler*.

Grimaldi stuck his head through the door and saw that Bolan had tethered Shim to a straight-backed chair with plastic flex-cuffs, then turned back to his search. He examined the door from the top of the frame to the floor. The nails in the wood trim had been painted over, which meant it hadn't been pulled out.

He moved on along the wall, tapping lightly for a hollow sound, but finding none. His route brought him back to the desk, where he pulled all of the drawers completely out to inspect the bottoms and backs. Nothing.

Next, Grimaldi unscrewed the back panel on the television with the screwdriver on his Swiss Army knife, searched the underside of the stand for anything that might have been taped there, then dropped to the floor, scooted under the bed and looked up through the springs. The interior of a large easy chair and matching footstool proved no more promising.

Grimaldi entered the bathroom. The paneling around the bath came out quickly, but the dead space beyond it was empty. The toilet cistern proved to be the same, as was the floating ball cock when he cut it open. He tested the pipes beneath the sink and found they couldn't be budged, then pulled the shower curtain from the stall and held the rod up to the light to look down its length.

Nothing.

Grimaldi could hear Bolan questioning Shim in the other room. It didn't sound as if he were making much progress. He stepped out of the bathroom, closed his eyes and rubbed his close-cropped, curly hair.

Waack had made a bomb, they knew that. But where had he gone with it? Where was the clue that would tell them? Was there a clue in the room? Maybe not.

Grimaldi opened his eyes. No. There had to be. Somewhere, somehow, he had overlooked something. Somewhere in this room, or the one where the

Executioner now interrogated Shim, was more information, another lead. He knew it.

The Stony Man pilot took a deep breath. Okay, he'd searched the room from one point of view—his. Now it was time to try a different consciousness.

Grimaldi let his eyelids fall halfway shut. His eyes lost focus to the specific. He moved them slowly around the room, concentrating on nothing, yet seeing things his conscious mind had missed earlier. The fly on the wall took on the same importance as the desk as a potential hiding place. The brown stain on the ceiling where an overhead toilet had overflowed became as meaningful as the television had been. He moved from one wall to the next, seeing the shadow of the alarm clock's hanging electrical wire with the same intensity as he saw the short chest of drawers.

Suddenly the pilot's eyes stopped. He let his eyelids fall shut, then open fully again. His vision focused once more.

In front of him, Grimaldi saw a wall-mounted radio speaker.

The pilot smiled. The Swiss Army knife screwdriver came out again as he moved to the radio. Motels installed their radios so they were difficult to steal, yet so the inside of the unit could be reached for maintenance. This one was no exception, and a quick tug of the acoustic foam on the outside of the speaker revealed four screws in the unit.

A moment later Grimaldi had the cover off and was pulling out a large envelope.

The pilot took a seat on the bed and opened the envelope, dumping the contents out next to him. He found an installation-and-repair manual published by a garage-door company, a folded set of blueprints and a piece of scratch paper. On the paper, the name *Shilling,* an address and the words *Briarwood Estates, Arlington* had been scribbled in pencil.

The exultation Grimaldi felt at having found the stash was short-lived as he realized how simple the bomb would be to install. And how little time they would have to see that it didn't go off.

"Striker," he called through the door. "I've found something I think you'd better see."

ONE GLANCE at the envelope told Bolan all he needed to know about where Waack had gone and what he intended to do.

But little about how to stop it.

Bolan raced back into the adjoining room. "How long ago did he leave?" he asked Shim, knowing the Korean wouldn't tell him.

Shim just smiled.

The Executioner grabbed the phone book. He tried the Arlington residential pages first, then the blue government listings. Senator James Shilling had two campaign offices in the Greater Dallas-Fort Worth area. Bolan tried the one in Mesquite first and got a recording of office hours. The same voice greeted his call to Haltom City and he slammed the receiver down.

"He's already left for home," the Executioner said through gritted teeth as he jabbed in the number 411 with his index finger.

The information operator answered on the fourth ring. "Thank you for using Southwestern Bell, information for what city, please?"

"Arlington," Bolan said.

"I'm sorry, Arlington is in the 817 area code," she said in a high-pitched twang.

Bolan slammed the receiver down again, lifted it and dialed 817-555-1212. A man answered this time.

"I need a home listing for James Shilling," the Executioner said.

There was a pause, then a rude laugh. "I'm sorry," the man said. "Senator Shilling's number is unlisted at his request."

"This is an emergency," Bolan said. "I'm a special agent with the United States Department of Justice."

The voice laughed again. "Well, I don't know that, now do I?" Senator Shilling's number is unlisted at his—"

Bolan practically broke the phone this time, happy that the smart-aleck operator wasn't within arm's reach. He took a deep breath, got another dial tone and punched in another number.

Barbara Price answered with a simple, "Yes?"

"Get me back to the Bear, quick," Bolan said.

Price was too professional to waste time asking why. A moment later Kurtzman said, "Yeah Striker?"

"I need an unlisted number for Senator James Shilling, Arlington, Texas. Fast. Waack's planted a bomb on his garage door. I'll hold."

"Some things are easy," Kurtzman said, and Bolan could already hear him tapping into the confidential phone-company files. Ten seconds later he gave Bolan the number.

Bolan disconnected the line and dialed Shilling's number. A female answered on the second ring. "Hello?"

"Mrs. Shilling?" the Executioner said. "This is an emergency. I want you to listen very carefully and do exactly what I tell you to do."

"Who is this?" the skeptical voice asked.

"My name is Mike Belasko and I'm an agent of the Justice Department."

"You sound more like a crank who somehow got our number," the woman said, irritated. She sighed. "I suppose we'll just have to change it again."

"Mrs. Shilling, listen to me!" Bolan said. "Did anyone work on your garage door this afternoon?"

The voice that answered was suddenly unsure of itself. "Why...yes."

"He planted a bomb in the mechanism," Bolan said.

"That's ridiculous," Mrs. Shilling said. "I called the same company that's always serviced our door. My husband and I know him. He's a member of the country club and—"

"Did he fix it personally?"

"Of course not. He doesn't—"

"An albino fixed your door, didn't he, Mrs. Shilling?"

Bolan heard an intake of breath on the other end of the line. "Oh, my god," she said.

"Listen to me," Bolan said. "Stay away from the door and the opening devices. As soon as it starts to open, the bomb's going to go off."

"Oh, my God," Mrs. Shilling said. "I'm not good in crises. I can't—"

"You'll have to be," Bolan interrupted. "Does the Senator have bodyguards?"

"No," she replied. "I begged him to hire some with everything that's going on. But he refused."

"What kind of car does he drive?"

"It's a...a Jaguar," Mrs. Shilling said. "It's the pride and joy of his life. I tease him that an old man—"

Bolan didn't have time to hear about how Mrs. Shilling teased her husband. He broke in again. "How about a car phone?"

"He has one," Mrs. Shilling said, her voice beginning to shake. "But he hates the thing. He turns it off unless he wants to make a call."

Bolan gripped the receiver tighter. "Try him on it, anyway," he said. "But not from there. You've got to get out of the house in case we miss him."

"Oh, my God," Mrs. Shilling said again.

"Do you have a neighbor you could go to?" Bolan asked.

"Mayor Chambers and his wife live two doors down. Millie and I play bridge together."

"Go there as soon as we hang up," Bolan said. "But the man who did this may be watching. You've got to make it look natural. Something along the lines of borrowing a cup of sugar, Mrs. Shilling, but less hokey."

The Executioner heard her frightened breath over the phone again. Then she said, "Tomorrow night is our thirty-fourth anniversary, Mr. Belasko. Jimmy brought home a bottle of special single-malt Scotch to celebrate."

"Take a couple of glasses with you and make it look like you're just going to the neighbor's for a drink," Bolan instructed. "And I hope I don't have to tell you not to go out the garage door."

"If this man is watching," Mrs. Shilling said. "He won't..."

"No," Bolan said. "He won't. He's after your husband, Mrs. Shilling, and he won't take a chance of blowing that by coming after you first." He paused. "Now go. Try to reach the senator on the mobile phone. If he's not plugged in, call the police. Then go back to trying your husband. Have you got that?"

"Oh, Lord," she said, her voice trembling worse than ever. "I'm no good under pressure. I never have been. Jimmy always takes care of—"

"Mrs. Shilling!" Bolan cut in. "Repeat back to me what you have to do."

There was a pause, then the woman said, "Take the Scotch to the Chamberses. Try to call Jimmy, then call the police, then try Jimmy again."

"Good," Bolan said. "Keep repeating that to yourself. I'm on my way." He hung the phone up and turned to see Shim still grinning in the chair.

The Korean threw back his head and cackled. "You will never get there in time," he said.

"We'll see," the Executioner said, reaching into his pocket for more of the flexible plastic handcuffs. He secured Shim's arms and legs to the chair with several more of the strips, then ripped a section of bed sheet to fashion a gag.

Bolan and Grimaldi started for the door. Halfway there, Bolan turned around. "If you manage to free yourself before we get back," he said, staring the Korean in the eye, "I'd suggest you stay here, anyway. If you don't, I'll find you. No matter where you go, where you try to hide, I'll find you. And I'll promise you two things. First, I won't kill you." He paused, then said, "But you'll wish you were dead when I'm done."

As BOLAN AND GRIMALDI pulled out of the motel parking lot, the traffic had reached its pinnacle. Cars, vans, trucks and mobile homes crowded the streets and highways, and the five minute drive that had taken ten in the rain now looked as if it might last an hour in the rain and congestion.

"This won't cut it," the Executioner said after they'd sat for three minutes at an intersection. "It's only a mile. Let's go." Pulling the rental car into the parking lot of a gas station, he killed the engine and jumped out into the downpour.

Bolan took off running, paralleling the line of frozen vehicles as he headed toward the airport. Behind him, he could hear Grimaldi's footsteps as the pilot followed. Deep puddles and chuckholes in the asphalt shoulder soaked his shoes and socks in less than ten seconds. His sport coat, slacks and shirt lasted twenty in the rainstorm falling over his head.

The Executioner dodged a teenager on a motorcycle who tried to pull out of line, then vaulted up to the curb, racing along the grass in front of a shopping center. The airport appeared a quarter mile away, and he slowed to a jog for a moment, catching his breath and letting Grimaldi draw alongside. "You ready, Jack?" he asked.

The Stony Man pilot was too winded to answer. But he nodded.

"Then let's do it," the Executioner said, breaking into a sprint.

Bolan reached the airport less than a minute later. A ten-foot chain-link fence topped with concertina wire circled the grounds, and he sprinted along the side toward the parking area. He could climb it, of course, but that would draw the attention of the airport police.

The warrior smiled. Of course, the only other alternative he had would draw their attention, too. But by the time they reacted, he expected to be well past them.

Bolan bolted up a ramp past a line of parking meters to the front of the terminal, pushed through a revolving door, then sprinted past the ticket counters and down the first concourse he saw. Curious heads flipped his way, and as he neared the security checkpoint outside the gates, a tall black man in the uniform of an airport security officer looked up from the carryon bag he was digging through.

The Executioner didn't break stride. Like a tailback in open field, he took the man out with a straight-arm to the jaw, and burst through the metal detector. The alarm buzzed as he lowered his shoulder and drove through two more officers who were trying to draw their guns as they moved to block his path. A quick glance over his shoulder ten steps later told him that Grimaldi had followed his interference through the melee, and he continued on.

A door leading down the run to the plane was open at the third gate he came to, and the Executioner leaped over a small retaining wall, then cut through the rows of sitting passengers waiting to board. But as he reached the opening, the first of the deplaning flyers stepped out into the terminal, blocking his path.

Bolan shouldered the man to the side and heard a curse behind him as a suitcase hit the carpet. He continued on down the narrow tunnel, jostling people carrying luggage out of his way. Behind him, he heard a female voice scream, "What does he think he's doing?"

Grimaldi answered, "He left his umbrella on the plane, ma'am."

Shoving past a pair of surprised airline attendants, the Executioner burst onto the plane. Turning to his left, away from the passengers still deplaning, he jostled past a uniformed man wearing pilot wings and opened the door to the cockpit. A moment later he had leaped through the pilot's entrance and landed on the wet tarmac.

Bolan stopped, catching his breath until he saw Grimaldi leap from the opening to the ground. Then he took off toward a row of private hangars a quarter mile away. He ignored the whistles and orders to stop that came from somewhere behind him in the thundershower.

The Executioner listened to Grimaldi's labored breathing a few feet to his rear. Jack was holding his own and, like all of the warriors from Stony Man Farm, he kept in more than just respectable physical shape. But a good deal of the flyboy's time was spent seated behind the controls, which didn't help much when it came to a full-out race that would leave a decathlon champion winded.

Bolan finally slowed as they neared the hangars. Stopping at the first, he pried the padlocked double doors apart and peered through the crack. A small plane appeared as lightning flashed overhead.

Grimaldi arrived, and Bolan waved him on to check the next hangars. The pilot knew what they needed, and words were unnecessary.

Jimmying the fifth door he came to, the Executioner found what he'd been looking for: a small two-man helicopter. The rear of the skids rested on casters, enabling the light craft to be tilted, then easily towed in or out of the shelter. "Jack!" he yelled though the rain. "Over here!"

Bolan drew the Desert Eagle as Grimaldi raced his way. The .44 Magnum slug that drilled through the padlock not only opened the lock, it blew it from the door.

The Executioner turned to Grimaldi, at his side now. Across the tarmac, he could hear the shrill sound of several police sirens racing toward them. "Get her ready, Jack!" he yelled over a burst of thunder. "I'll stand guard."

Sticking the Desert Eagle under his coat, Bolan drew the Justice Department badge and held it in front of him. He watched the murky shadows of three airport police cars race through the falling rain, then began walking slowly forward as the one in the lead screeched to a halt.

He had shown the credentials, and was leaning into the open window giving the uniformed driver a cock-and-bull story about two men who had taken refuge in one of the hangars when the second police car ground to a halt.

"That's him! That's one of them!" a young officer shrieked through the thunder, lightning and rain. "I saw him!"

Bolan didn't hesitate. Before the other cops could react, he had opened the door in front of him and jerked the driver from the vehicle, spun the man around to face the other two cars and looped an arm around his throat. He jammed the barrel of the Desert Eagle into the cop's temple as the third car arrived.

Officers from all of the vehicles jumped out with revolvers and shotguns, taking cover behind doors, bumpers and engines.

Behind him, Bolan heard Grimaldi wheeling the chopper out of the hangar. "All right, listen!" he yelled, the rain falling into his mouth as he opened it. "We're taking this helicopter, that's all. No hostages, and I'll even let this man go before we leave if you'll back off."

Through the sheets of water between him and the other men, he could see five disbelieving faces.

"You decide!" Bolan yelled as Grimaldi started the chopper behind him. "Is this man's life worth more than a helicopter?"

An officer wearing sergeant's stripes rose slightly behind the bumper of the second car. He holstered his weapon, then screamed, "You son of a bitch, you let him go before you leave the ground! You hear me? You don't, and we'll fill that bubble full of lead in spite of him!"

"You've got a deal!" Bolan yelled back. "But here's how it goes down. All of you, except the sergeant, move back! You keep backing up until we're off the ground."

Behind him, Bolan heard Grimaldi yell, "Let's go!"

"When are you going to let him go?" the sergeant demanded.

"I'll hold on to him until I'm in the chopper, then let loose the second we start to rise."

"How can I be sure you'll do it?"

Bolan tightened his grip on the man in his arms. "How can *I* be sure you won't shoot after I've let go of him?"

Bolan got no answer. But a few seconds later the sergeant mumbled to his men and they threw the shotguns back in the cars, holstered their revolvers and started backing slowly away.

The Executioner kept his arm around the officer's throat as he backpedaled toward the helicopter, ducking instinctively as he drew beneath the twirling blades. He heard the passenger door open behind him, and caught it with his shoulder, still dragging the airport cop in front of him.

So far the man had not spoken. He had done little but tremble in fear and nearly go limp against the Executioner. Now he said, "You . . . really gonna let me go?" in a small terrified voice.

"You ready, Jack?" Bolan called over his shoulder.

"Ready," Grimaldi came back.

Bolan scooted up on the seat, then pushed the man away from the chopper with both hands. "There's your answer," he said as he closed the door and they rose quickly up through the air.

Through the bubble of what the Executioner could now see was a Schweizer 300C, Bolan saw one of the uniformed men on the ground draw his weapon from the holster.

"Uh-oh," Grimaldi said.

Then the sergeant who had cut the deal with the Executioner waved his arm to the side, knocking the man's gun hand off target. A small explosion penetrated the glass bubble of the Schweizer, but the shot went wide.

Bolan glanced at his watch. They had left the motel less than fifteen minutes earlier.

"I'm glad that's over," Grimaldi said as he leveled the chopper and started toward Arlington.

Bolan strapped himself into the seat. "It's just starting, Jack," he said. "It's just starting."

MARJORIE SHILLING was entirely, completely and totally drained emotionally. She felt like a robot as she walked to the cabinet over the refrigerator. She reached up, bobbed twice on the toes of her tennis shoes, but still couldn't reach the handle.

"Oh, my God," she said. Suddenly all of the fear, anxiety and dread she had felt during her phone conversation a moment before flooded back through her and she burst into tears. "Oh, God," she sobbed again. "Oh, dear precious Lord Jesus!"

Marjorie regained enough control to drag a chair from the kitchen table across the floor, stepped up and opened the cabinet. She took down the bottle of Scotch and had started back down to the floor when the chair slipped. She came down hard in a sitting position, her tennis skirt flying up to her waist. The bottle hit the floor and rolled against the kickboard beneath the sink, but didn't break. The sobs started again.

"Oh, God, please..."

Hauling herself to her feet, she smoothed her skirt, then reminded herself that she not only had to get out of the house, she was supposed to do it fast. Get the Scotch, go to the Chamberses'. Call the police...no, try to call Jimmy first, even though he won't have the phone plugged in. *Then* call the police. She dug through the cabinet over the sink until she found two highball glasses. But Jimmy *might* have his telephone plugged in this time. With all of the assassinations, he might.

"Get the Scotch, go to the Chamberses', call Jimmy, call the police." Marjorie repeated it over and over as she left the kitchen and started through the living room. A car raced by the house in the heavy rain as she passed the picture window, and she ducked behind the curtain.

Was it him? Coming back in another car to watch the explosion? To kill her? Her heart beat heavily and she dropped one of the glasses to the thick carpet.

Marjorie picked up the glass. The car hadn't stopped, and now she realized that it had been that Stevens boy from down the street in that hot rod of his. She'd tried to talk to his parents about his driving, but the chilly reception it had gotten her left no doubt as to why the boy behaved the way he did. His parents were just as self-centered as he was, and—

Marjorie, stop! she told herself as she realized she was still standing next to the window. Get your mind back on the business at hand. You've got to get out of here and warn Jimmy!

"Go to Millie and Frank's, call the police—no, call Jimmy first—then call the police, then try Jimmy again."

Marjorie got her raincoat from the closet in the front hall, then cracked open the front door and peeked outside. Rain blew through the opening, stinging her face, but the street was deserted. She wiped the tears from her eyes. That man on the phone—what had his name been? She couldn't remember. But she remembered what he had told her to do as she took a deep breath, then stepped out into the thunderstorm.

"Go to the Chamberses'," she whispered under her breath as she walked across the porch to the steps. "Call Frank. No! Frank is Millie's husband. Call Jimmy! Then call the police. Then call Jimmy again."

She walked stiffly across the grass of the front yard, not daring to look right or left. Ahead on the street, she saw a car turn the corner and her heart stopped. But her legs moved on, the repetition of the words she mouthed becoming a numbing force that motivated her. "Get the Scotch. Go to Millie and Frank's. Call Jimmy. Call the police. Call Jimmy."

The car—the Martins' new Rolls-Royce that they couldn't keep from showing off even in this hurricane—drove past. Marjorie walked on, the Chamberses' house now appearing through the rain as she crossed the next yard. The McKnights'. She wondered briefly if Bob had seen her through the window—he hated it, absolutely hated it, when anyone set foot on his precious manicured lawn. Suddenly she found herself walking up the steps to Frank and Millie's porch.

"Get the Scotch—go to Millie's—call Jimmy—call the police—call Jimmy again," she said as she rang the bell.

"Hi, Marj!"

Marjorie Shilling spun around in time to see the jogger running past her on the street raise a hand. She stifled a scream as the bottle and both glasses flew from her hands to the concrete porch. Frozen in place, she finally saw that it was Charlie Ogle from the next block over inside the rain hood. Nothing stopped Charlie's daily run—not rain, sleet, snow or tornados.

Charlie Ogle was gone by the time Marjorie realized she'd not only broken the glasses but the bottle of

Scotch, as well. Tears burst from her eyes, mixing with the rain as the door suddenly swung open.

"Marj!" Millie Chambers said. "For heaven's sake, what are you doing out in this?" Millie's eyes fell to the mess on the porch. "Is everything all right? Come in here!"

Marjorie Shilling began crying without restraint as her friend put an arm around her and guided her inside.

No, she told herself, she couldn't let down. Not now. She had things to do. Important things.

What were they?

Millie took her raincoat. "Marjorie, what's wrong, dear?" When she got no answer, she said, "Come on, I'll fix us a nice cup of tea."

"No!" Marjorie almost shouted. "No!" She paused, frowning, trying to remember what she had chanted all the way over. The frown became a trembling smile as she remembered.

Turning to her friend, she said, "I got the Scotch and the glasses. Now I'm here. I have to call Jimmy. Yes, that's it. I have to call Jimmy immediately." She stopped, relaxing slightly. "You go ahead and fix the tea, Millie. Lord knows I could use a cup, and I know where the phone is."

## CHAPTER THIRTEEN

The cellular phone on board the Schweizer 300C was the first stroke of luck the Executioner had fallen into since the mission began. The Dallas-Fort Worth area map he found in the glove compartment was a windfall, as well.

Radio traffic blathered news of the helicopter theft as Grimaldi guided the chopper away from the airport. Bolan switched the noise off. The police of every burg in the area would be aware of what had happened by now.

They'd be coming, sooner or later. The Executioner and Jack Grimaldi would have a front-row seat once the chase started, and it wouldn't do them any good to listen to the preparations now.

The map open in his lap, Bolan dialed Stony Man and connected the speaker attachment so Grimaldi could monitor the call. The seconds it took to route the call across the country seemed like an eternity. Finally Bolan heard a ring, then Price's voice.

"Get me the Bear again, *quick,*" the Executioner said.

The call was transferred to the Computer Room. "What you got?" Kurtzman said.

"Get me a fix on the Briarwood Estate housing addition in Arlington," Bolan said. "The address is

12316 MacInshire Chase East." He paused. "Shilling's place."

The sound of the computer digesting the information resounded over the line. Less than ten seconds later the Bear said, "Okay, I've got the map up on the screen. Where are you now?"

Bolan looked down and saw the tall buildings of the market area along I-35 below. "Close to downtown Dallas," he said.

"Head southwest," Kurtzman said. His voice lightened. "Does Jack think he can find Arlington?"

Grimaldi chuckled. "Kurtzman, you can kiss my—"

"We just need the specifics to the house," Bolan said. He glanced down at the map.

Kurtzman cleared his throat and his tone became serious. "Okay, look for Arlington Stadium on I-30. Stay southwest. You'll cross over Highway 80 and come to Lake Arlington. Briarwood is across the road that runs along the northeast shore. You'll see about a half mile of rolling hills, and pass a bait shop...hang on a minute. Let me tap into another file."

More computer keys, then, "Yeah...okay. The abstracts on file with the city show an eight-foot brick arch over the entrance to the addition. Probably to keep out trucks. From the front gate go four blocks along Greenleaf Lane, make a right on Shorehan, a left two blocks later and you'll be on MacInshire. The place you want will be to the right."

"We'll find it, Bear. Thanks." Bolan disconnected the line. He hoped he was right. He looked down through the pouring rain and saw that the lights of

Irving were barely visible as they crossed over the city limits.

Lightning flashed, then a massive roll of thunder shook the small chopper. Grimaldi fought the controls, and Bolan saw him looking in the mirror. "We've got company, big guy," the pilot said.

The Executioner twisted to see two blue-and-white police choppers bobbing toward them in the wind. He switched the radio back on.

Static from the electrified air crackled from the instrument. Faintly in the background, as if from miles away, a voice said, "Dallas PD chopper 901 to Schweizer. Land immediately! I repeat! Land immediately!"

Bolan unhooked the microphone and held it to his lips. "Unit calling Schweizer, 10-1. Sorry, you're breaking up." He reclipped the mike to the dash.

The blue-and-white choppers drew abreast of the Schweizer on both sides. Bolan saw men wearing flight suits with badges pinned to the breasts in both of the passenger seats. AR-15s were trained on the Schweizer's bubble.

All three helicopters bobbed up and down in the turbulent winds as the radio squawked again. "Chopper 901 to Schweizer. You will prepare to land immediately! We will escort you to the nearest site. Do not attempt to break formation or we will fire."

Bolan looked down. They were still above the suburb of Irving, and the cops weren't about to shoot down a chopper that could easily explode on the citizens below. But soon they'd be crossing the city limits into an open area where the risk of innocents being killed would be negligible.

The Executioner turned to Grimaldi. "We've got to lose them before we leave Irving," he said.

"We can't outrun them, big guy. They're bigger and faster."

"Then outmaneuver them."

Grimaldi grinned. "Hang on to your chewing gum."

Bolan felt the seat belt jerk tight around his waist as Grimaldi killed the engine. The Schweizer stopped in midair, then plummeted earthward. Silence reigned for a moment within the cabin, then the radio went berserk with unintelligible transmissions from the police choppers.

Bolan looked down to see the ground nearing. Thirty feet above a garage attached to a two-story brick house, Grimaldi breathed life back into the overhead blades and the chopper stabilized.

The Stony Man pilot moved the craft forward over the rooftops, the skids nearly skimming the shingles. The radio continued to scream. Above, barely visible through the steady downpour, the police choppers kept pace.

Even at the lower elevation, Bolan could see the rolling hills of the prairie land between Irving and Arlington ahead. He glanced back and forth from the map to the bubble. Suddenly, they had crossed Belt Line Road and were sailing across the open land.

"Land immediately or you will be shot down!" came over the airwaves.

"Whoops," Grimaldi said. "But not to worry." The chopper cut a hard about-face in the air and retraced its flight back into Irving.

Bolan watched the map again as Grimaldi steered the Schweizer along a thin line below them that the map called Shady Grove Road. When they reached MacArthur, Grimaldi cut south, bobbing the tiny chopper up and down, left and right, over a four-mile open stretch to Interstate 30.

Sporadic fire from the shooters in the police helicopters broke through the roaring storm. But the shots were few and far between. Grimaldi made good use of the rural houses dotting the landscape, zigzagging to take advantage of the protection they afforded. None of the rounds from the snipers' AR-15s found their mark.

When the lights of I-30 appeared, Grimaldi turned west again. "It'll take us straight on in," he said, breaking the silence he and Bolan had fallen into as they concentrated on the chase. "And there's enough traffic below that they won't keep shooting."

Bolan nodded. "Any ideas how to shake them for good."

Grimaldi turned toward him and smiled. "Oh, yeah," he said.

The chopper moved on down the highway, staying less than fifty feet over the traffic below. Threats of more gunfire still rushed from the radio, but the Executioner knew they were just that—threats. The Dallas PD wasn't about to sacrifice any of the men, women and children pounding through the rain below just to get back one Schweizer 300C.

Through the rain the Executioner saw the dark hole beneath the overpass a quarter mile away.

"When was the last time you had a haircut, Striker?" Grimaldi asked.

Before Bolan could ask what the strange question meant, the Schweizer dipped suddenly down through the air. Headlights from the vehicles across the median glowed through the formerly dark gaps in the piers supporting the bridge. Ghostly shadows danced across the concrete. Bolan saw Grimaldi's eyebrows suddenly rise, and a split second later the chopper dropped another few feet.

The chopper's skids skimmed the pavement beneath the overpass, sending red sparks shooting through the darkness. Bolan ducked instinctively, but by then they were through the opening, on the other side and rising again.

Grimaldi lifted the Schweizer just above the vehicles as they raced on toward Arlington. Horns honked their protest, and a new wave of threats and outrage sounded from the police choppers above. The Stony Man pilot pulled the same stunt two more times, the helicopter's blades narrowly missing the piers beneath a multispan beam bridge, then kindling more embers beneath the deck of a steel arch. Between the bridges, the buildings to the sides of the highway became more concentrated as they neared Arlington.

Bolan watched as the lights of a large shopping mall appeared to the north of another span-beam bridge.

"Now there's what we've been needing," Grimaldi said. "Say goodbye to the boys in blue." He turned to face Bolan as the smile crept back over his face. "They should be used to this duck-and-go-on act by now. So let's change the rules of the game a bit."

The Schweizer dropped beneath the overpass, narrowly missing a slow-moving pickup. But this time, as soon as they had cleared the bridge, Grimaldi twisted the controls and the chopper cut sharply up and to the right.

Bolan caught a flash of blue and white out of the corner of his eye as one of the pursuing helicopters narrowly missed them. He saw the larger, less maneuverable craft trying to change course as Grimaldi guided them over the shopping mall to the loading areas at the rear of the larger outlets.

Grimaldi's face was a mask of concentrated creases. "Okay... *there,*" he said out loud to himself.

The Executioner kept his eyes on the police helicopters as the Schweizer suddenly dropped behind the cover of a three-story store. Both of the blue-and-whites were still trying to twist back around in the air.

The Schweizer came to rest on the dock in front of the gaping mouth of an open loading door. Bolan leaped from the craft as Grimaldi killed the engine. As the blades slowed above his head, he grabbed the front of the skids, lifted them to his waist and rolled the chopper through the opening on the rear casters.

Two men stood inside the warehouse area next to a stack of cardboard boxes. One was in his midteens and wore jeans and a sleeveless shirt. The other was older and dressed in a dark green work shirt and matching pants.

Both of their mouths dropped open. The clipboard in the hands of the older man clattered to the floor.

The Executioner drew the Beretta and trained it on them. "Go close the door," he ordered.

The two men practically knocked each other down trying to beat each other to the opening. The door slid shut on its runners, and a second later the Executioner heard the flapping blades outside. He herded the men toward an inside door, locked it, then sat them down on the concrete, keeping the Beretta aimed in their direction.

Grimaldi got out of the Schweizer, stretched his arms over his head and yawned as if this was a standard layover in the middle of a long flight.

The police choppers buzzed the shopping center for five minutes, then Bolan heard their engines gradually fade in the distance as they broadened their search. He gave it two more minutes, then ordered the workmen to reopen the door.

Pulling the Schweizer back out into the opening, Grimaldi and the Executioner resumed their flight.

Bolan heard the distant police chopper pilots arguing over the radio as the Schweizer raced on toward Arlington.

EACH TIME IT APPEARED to be easing up, each time it looked as if it had moved on past the Schweizer 300C racing through the sky, the thunderstorm over the Dallas-Fort Worth area came back with a new fury.

"Kind of lonesome up here now, isn't it," Jack Grimaldi joked. They hadn't seen any sign of the police helicopters or any other air traffic since leaving the loading dock.

Bolan didn't answer. He was too busy trying to spot landmarks on the ground that he could reference on the map. Occasionally a gust of wind parted the falling sheets of water long enough to provide a glimpse of one of the tourist attractions just off the highway. But for the most part the headlights on the road were the only navigational base on which they could rely.

Bright lights penetrated through the foggy air below, and Bolan stared down. Grimaldi dropped the Schweizer lower over the highway, and they saw the rides and other attractions of Six Flags Over Texas. They also saw the dripping figures of park patrons huddled together under any available shelter as Grimaldi took them up again. Arlington Stadium, lay two or three miles farther off, just past a water park.

As soon as they spotted the stadium, Grimaldi fell back into the path Kurtzman had given them. Arlington Memorial Hospital passed beneath the Schweizer, then the rippling water of Lake Arlington.

Grimaldi cut the chopper to the northernmost point of the lake and they crossed Loop 303. The Stony Man pilot dropped low again, following the shoreline road and passing over several boat-slip areas, then a lighted sign that announced the Arlington Yacht Club. The bait shop Kurtzman had predicted was barely visible through the steady torrents of water still drumming against the Schweizer, but as soon as he spotted it, Bolan looked on to see the brick archway on the other side of the road a hundred yards away. "There it is, Jack."

Grimaldi cut back to the east, angling across the road to the Briarwood Housing addition. They passed over homes that cost more money than any ten normal men would make in twenty lifetimes.

A gnawing vexation gripped the Executioner's belly as they flew over the exclusive community. The houses were closed, there was no traffic on the streets. The only movement was the rain.

Where were the police cars that should have responded to Mrs. Shilling's call? There had been plenty of time for them to respond to a high-priority threat like a bomb—especially when it was called in by the wife of a U.S. senator.

As they neared the senator's house, Bolan knew the answer. He could feel it in his soul, suspected he had known it unconsciously even while talking to Mrs. Shilling on the phone.

The woman had been right about herself—she wasn't much use under stress. She might have remembered to get the bottle of Scotch, go to the neighbor's house and try to call her husband on his car phone. But she forgot the police.

Bolan activated the cellular phone again and tapped 911.

"Is this an emergency?" the answering voice asked.

"Only if you consider a bomb at Senator Shilling's house an emergency," the Executioner said. "It's set to go off when he uses the electronic garage-door opener—at 12316 MacInshire Chase East. Briarwood Estates. Mrs. Shilling has gone to the neighbor's—the mayor's house. But the senator's on his way home and he's driving his Jaguar."

"Who is th—" the voice started to ask as Bolan ended the call.

"There it is," Grimaldi said. He pointed down to a Spanish-style house with a clay-shingle roof. The garage door was still in one piece, and Bolan breathed a silent sigh of relief. Shilling hadn't been home.

The relief didn't last long. "Swing her around the neighborhood, Jack," Bolan said. "Look for an overhead-door repair truck or van, or any parked vehicle with anyone in it, or anything that looks out of place." He took a deep breath. "But keep an eye on the entrance, too. The senator's bound to come through the arch any second now."

Grimaldi lifted the Schweizer fifty feet and they began a sweep of Briarwood Estates. They didn't have to look long.

The green van was parked just around the corner, facing the Shilling residence. Bolan saw the logo on the side of the van at the same time his other eye picked up the headlights on the shoreline road outside the arch. The lettering on the logo was indecipherable from the chopper, and the car on the road was too far away to identify, as well.

But the Executioner's gut instincts told him who was in each vehicle.

"Take her down, Jack," Bolan said. "Quick."

Grimaldi dropped the chopper almost even with the van. The black-and-gold lettering on the side came into focus: Arlington Overhead Door Company—Installation and Repair.

"There he is!" Grimaldi suddenly yelled, and Bolan saw a white face staring at them through the driver's window. Grimaldi started to set the Schweizer down on the street.

"No!" Bolan said. "We don't have time. That was Shilling on the road."

"You sure?" Grimaldi said.

"No, but we can't take a chance."

The helicopter rocketed upward again and Grimaldi twisted it through the air toward the arch as the headlights turned into Briarwood. They swooped low over the bricks as the vehicle passed under them, and the Executioner saw the distinctive lines of a Jaguar.

"Buzz him, Jack," Bolan ordered Grimaldi. "He's got to be stopped before he gets inside the range of his opener."

Grimaldi twisted the chopper again and shot back over the car as it rolled through the water on Greenleaf Lane. The Schweizer twirled back to face the Jaguar, then practically nose-dived the oncoming car.

Bolan waved his arms in front of him as they bore down on the sports car. Senator Shilling looked up.

At the last second Grimaldi pulled up on the control and hopped the Schweizer over the roof of the Jaguar. They whirled again to see that instead of stopping, Shilling had floored the accelerator and was racing down the street.

"He thinks we're trying to kill him," Bolan said, shaking his head. "He'll never stop for us, Jack. We'll have to stop him."

Grimaldi guided them back over the Jaguar as it fishtailed onto Shorehan. Bolan rose to a kneeling position on the seat and strapped the restraint over the back of his right knee. Bracing his other leg on the floorboard, he opened the door with his left hand as his right drew the Desert Eagle.

The hard rain hit him in the face, soaking his head and shoulders as he squinted toward the oncoming Jaguar. Even with the seat belt binding him, the wind threatened to tear him from the chopper. Bolan raised the Desert Eagle, trying to steady it against the constant bobbing of the blustering little chopper, but by the time he had the sights on the right front tire, the Schweizer had flown past the senator again.

"I can take it down in his driveway, Striker," Grimaldi shouted as he swung them around. "If he doesn't stop for that, you can fire—"

"No way, Jack!" Bolan roared over the wind, rain and thunder. "He'll be inside the range of the opener. Take her back!"

The chopper slowed slightly as it neared the rear of the racing Jaguar. For a brief moment the wind died down and Bolan's front sight steadied on the right rear tire. But as he squeezed the trigger, a sudden gust swept the chopper to the side.

The exploding .44 Magnum slug drilled harmlessly into the car's trunk.

Grimaldi straightened the skids and took off again as Bolan wiped the rain from his eyes with his sleeve. He took another shot as the car turned off Shorehan onto MacInshire, but the Schweizer skipped again, this time jerking his aim over the car. The bullet sparked the pavement, then skidded harmlessly on.

The Executioner wiped his face again, then leaned back into the helicopter. "Take her past, all the way to the house," he told Grimaldi. "We'll come at him dead on. I'll have time for one, maybe two shots tops."

The pilot nodded and the Schweizer charged forward, cutting over the house on the corner and racing toward the senator's residence six blocks farther up the street. They revolved once more, then bore down on the headlights rushing toward them.

Bolan took a six-o'clock aim at the bottom of the tire this time, hoping if the chopper bounced again it wouldn't throw his round past the top of the tire. The Desert Eagle roared above a clap of thunder, but Shilling had seen it coming and swerved the Jaguar to the side.

"Hover!" the Executioner ordered.

The chopper stopped in midair.

There would be time for one more shot, and one more only before the senator passed under him and turned into his driveway. By now the Executioner suspected Shilling already had the electronic opener in his hand.

Bolan dropped the front sight on rubber again, started to squeeze the trigger, then stopped when the wind blew him off target again. He took a deep breath, returned the barrel to the tire and tried again.

Again, a sudden gust spoiled his aim.

Lightning flashed to his right as the Executioner set his jaw. The car was less than two houses away and coming fast. If he didn't stop the senator now, he never would.

Bolan didn't wait this time, snapping the trigger back as soon as it crossed the black of the tire. The explosion in front of his face drowned out the lesser eruption below, but the Jaguar skidding through the water along the curb told him the big slug had found its mark.

Grimaldi whirled the helicopter one final time, and the Executioner saw the Jaguar hit the curb of the house next to Shilling's and jerk to a stop. "Take her down!" he yelled, and a second later they were on the ground.

As the skids hit the street, the Jaguar's door opened. A tall, thin man with gray hair struggled painfully out of the sports car and started running toward his driveway.

In his right hand, he held a small black box.

Bolan vaulted from the Schweizer to the pavement. He didn't know what kind of range Shilling's garage door opener had. But the senator did. And already he was raising it in his hand.

Bolan realized he'd never catch Shilling before he pushed the button. Resting his arm against the glass bubble of the Schweizer, he looked down the barrel of the Desert Eagle and squeezed the trigger.

The door opener in the senator's hand disintegrated into a thousand pieces of plastic.

Shilling turned toward the Executioner, fell to his knees and screamed.

By now Grimaldi had dropped down from the helicopter. Bolan turned to him. "You talk to the senator," he yelled. "I'm going back to the van." He sprinted down the block and turned the corner.

The Arlington Overhead Door Company van hadn't moved since they'd dropped down to see Waack's ghostlike face staring out the window.

Bolan wasn't surprised.

But neither was he surprised that the only person he found in the van was the dead repairman.

The Executioner heard the sirens as he stepped back out of the van into the rain. He saw a man's shadow wearing a baseball cap jogging toward him, and recognized the gait even before Grimaldi's face appeared beneath a streetlight.

"The cops are here," the pilot said.

Bolan nodded. "The senator all right?"

Grimaldi nodded. "He's shaken up, but he'll live. I left him at the mayor's house with his wife."

Bolan looked down the street and saw the flashing red lights turn the corner and start toward the Schweizer in the middle of the street. "Let's get out of here," he said.

Both men turned and started jogging away.

And as they ran, as if to mock their efforts, the rain finally stopped.

BY THE TIME BOLAN and Grimaldi had cracked the steering column on the Chevy van two blocks from Shilling's house, gotten the vehicle started and returned to room 110 of the La Quinta, Shim had worked the plastic restraint so far into his left wrist that blood dripped steadily to a black puddle on the carpet.

A red fiery hatred filled the Korean's eyes and distorted his face as his captors walked through the door.

The Executioner moved forward and ripped the gag from Shim's mouth, then turned to Grimaldi. "Watch him," he said as he moved into the adjoining room and closed the door.

A moment later he had Kurtzman on the line.

"I was hoping you'd call back," the computer man said. "Got a present for you."

"What?"

Kurtzman cleared his throat. "I had a hunch and went snooping through the Army's medical records. Waack's name came up—flagged. He's in there, all right. But there's an access code that has to be entered before you hit the files."

"How long will it take to break it?" Bolan asked.

"I just did," Kurtzman said. "I was getting ready to call up the file when the phone rang." He paused, then added, "Merry Christmas."

"I'll hold," Bolan told him. For what seemed like the thousandth time in the past two days he listened while Kurtzman's fingers brought clicks to the keyboard. Then the noise stopped and all the Executioner could hear was the quiet sound of the computer genius breathing.

"Yep," Kurtzman said. "I just skimmed through the file, and what we've got are transcripts of sessions with several Army shrinks. Hang on and I'll read a little closer."

Bolan waited again.

Two minutes later Kurtzman said, "Okay, let me summarize Mr. Jerry Wayne Waack. Number one, he had problems before he supposedly got lost in North Korea, but they were worse when he got back. Two, the guy had one hell of a resentment of you."

"Me?" Bolan said, surprised. "I never even met him."

''That doesn't seem to matter,'' Kurtzman said. ''According to one doctor's summary here, 'Patient exhibits a deep-seated anger toward one Samuel Mack Bolan, who was also a Special Forces sniper in Vietnam. Patient believes Bolan received more than due credit and unfairly overshadowed patient's career, consequently limiting his chances of promotion.''' He stopped.

''Go on,'' Bolan said.

''Okay, here's an account of half a dozen sessions with a Dr. Kenneth Arnold in which the good doctor was trying to get Waack to come to terms with his albinoism. 'Patient suffers from severe case of denial except when directly confronted with his albinoism, at which time he becomes violent.''' Kurtzman paused. ''I guess Arnold directly confronted him, Striker, because there's a supplementary page here from the colonel in charge of the hospital. After this session Waack was transferred to another therapist and the doctor went to the emergency room with a broken jaw.''

''Anything else, Bear?'' Bolan said.

''More of the same, pretty much. Basically, Waack hates being an albino and he hates you. Which one he hates more is anybody's guess. But he just *loves* killing people. The various doctors couldn't agree on what caused all this—paranoia, schizophrenia, paranoid schizophrenia. They've all got a different diagnosis, but they all agree on that one point—Jerry Wayne Waack dearly loves to free the spirit from the confines of the body, so to speak. They never come right out and say it, but that's the general consensus if you read through the medical jargon.'' Kurtzman laughed. ''You want Dr. Kurtzman's professional diagnosis?''

''Sure.''

''Jerry Wayne Waack is totally fucked up.''

Bolan took a deep breath and let it out slowly. ''Can't argue there.'' He glanced at Shim. ''This deal about being MIA in North Korea, Bear,'' he said. ''Is that mentioned?''

Kurtzman cleared his throat. ''A couple of the shrinks thought he showed symptoms of brainwashing. Others didn't. He was in such a psychotic state by then, I imagine it would have been hard to tell for sure.''

The Executioner rubbed his forehead. Things were beginning to make sense. ''Bear,'' he said. ''Run me a profile on the politics of all the senators they've killed or tried to kill. Look for similarities. I want to know why Waack picked these guys.''

''You got it,'' Kurtzman said.

Bolan glanced toward the other room. ''And see what you can find out about a North Korean named Shim. He's an agent of some kind.''

''I'll tap into the spook files.''

''Thanks.'' Bolan hung up and walked into the other room. Grimaldi sat in the chair. The Executioner took a seat on the bed and looked at Shim. ''We need to have a little talk,'' he said.

Shim threw back his head and laughed. ''I told you nothing before, round eyes, and I will tell you nothing now.'' Looking back to the Executioner, he said, ''But tell me, is Senator Shilling dead?''

"Hardly."

A brief anger flowed across Shim's face, then disappeared. He shrugged his shoulders. "It is of little importance."

Bolan looked down at the man's wrist as he wondered what that meant. He needed to find out—learn why Shim and Waack were killing certain senators. But the Korean's self-inflicted wound meant that he didn't mind pain. Shim was well trained and tough. Torture had never been in the Executioner's arsenal of weapons. But even if it had, it was clear that suffering wasn't the way to get Shim to talk. The Executioner suspected he could beat Shim to death and still learn nothing.

No, he had to find another way.

The Executioner scooted down the bed to face the Korean directly. "You realize I'm going to kill Waack, don't you?" he said.

Shim gave him a lopsided smirk. "I realize you will try."

"You don't think I can?"

Shim shrugged his shoulders. "You are good. I have seen that. But Waack...he is better. He was good when I met him. I made him better. And he has fewer distractions."

Things were starting to fall into place, if only in an abstract way. Bolan suspected that what Shim had just said referred to the brainwashing that two of the Army shrinks had suspected.

The Executioner crossed the room, taking a few seconds to organize his thoughts, put into perspective exactly what was going on here. Shim would resist direct questioning, but he had just given up a vital piece of information by accident. Why? What had caused him to make the statement that Waack had been good but he had made him better? And how could the Executioner get him to make more unwitting revelations?

Bolan suddenly realized the answer, and it was simple and as old as mankind itself. Ego. Shim might be well trained, but at heart he was a conceited man fighting the battle between vanity and duty. Part of him knew that his mission of killing senators was the top priority. But another part wanted the world, or at least someone, to know what he was doing, how he was doing it and, most of all, how well he was getting it done.

Whirling around, Bolan stalked back to Shim. "You think Waack is better than me?" he demanded. In the corner of his eye, he saw a look of astonishment come over Grimaldi's face. He'd never seen jealousy as part of Bolan's character before.

"Answer me!" Bolan said before Shim could respond. "You think he's better than me?"

Shim stared him in the eye. "Very much so," he said.

Bolan walked to the wall and drove his fist through it. By the time he'd turned back, the surprised look had left Grimaldi's face. The pilot had figured out what Bolan was doing and was walking into the adjoining room to hide his smile.

The Executioner moved back to Shim, leaned down and spoke to the Korean nose to nose. "I can beat him any day of the week. Fists, knives, guns, any way you want." He paused. "You set it up. You'll see."

Shim shook his head. "It would interfere with our mission," he said.

"You think so?" Bolan said. He let the anger in his voice switch to a haughty tone. "Well, let me tell you this. I'm going to interfere with your mission one way or another. I've already proven I can beat your boy— I've stopped two of his kills already and I'll stop them all."

Shim's eyes told the Executioner he'd hit a sore spot. "Waack would kill you," he said under his breath. "His mind is not troubled by the thought of innocents dying in the wake of his deeds. Yours is. Waack eats, sleeps and kills. That is his only reason for existing." Shim paused, chuckled. "Unless, of course, you consider his penchant for memorizing meaningless quotations." He stopped suddenly, realizing he had admitted more than he'd intended.

Bolan knew he had to keep the man off-balance. "If you're so sure he can beat me, then set it up, you slant-eyed son of a bitch," he practically screamed. The racial slur went against the Executioner's grain, but it had the desired effect on Shim. Bolan watched the same eyes he had just insulted narrow in malice.

The Korean showed the same anger now that Bolan was feigning. The lapse of judgment the Executioner had hoped for was at hand. It was time to move in for the kill by giving Shim a way to combine duty and ego, and rationalize getting Bolan and Waack together for a showdown.

"Set it up if you think you've trained him that well," Bolan repeated. "I'll meet your windup monkey man to man. Then when he kills me, you'll be free to go on taking out senators to your heart's content." He laughed in Shim's face. "Do it," he said. "If you've got the guts."

The man in the chair looked as if his face might explode. "Cut me loose!" he screamed. "And give me the phone!"

# CHAPTER FOURTEEN

Waack parked the car in the Hertz parking lot and hurried inside the terminal. He stopped at the rental desk long enough to return the keys, sign the receipt and stuff it into his pocket. He fumed silently as he left the terminal and walked across the tarmac toward the plane. Mack-the-knife Bolan had fucked up another of his hits.

Waack was surprised not to find Shim waiting. He wondered what had delayed the man as he climbed on board the plane and took the passenger's seat. There had been more than enough time for Shim to pack their things, "sanitize" the room of incriminating evidence and meet him at the plane as they'd agreed. They were off to California.

So where was he?

Staring across the airport as a huge 747 took off in the distance, Waack pictured Shim in his mind. As always, the warm feelings of gratitude he felt when he thought of his friend came over him, washing away the hatred he had for Mack Bolan.

Shim. The only man who had ever understood him. The only man who had ever looked past the white skin and hair to see the Korean warrior who lived inside. Shim. His best and only friend.

Jerry Wayne Waack closed his eyes to wait on his friend. Before meeting Shim, he had given little thought to the theory of reincarnation. Actually, he had spent little time deliberating religion of any sort. But through his conversations with Shim, the recognition that the spirit lived on after the body died, and was then reborn into another body, had awakened in him.

But there was more to it than that. Far more to it, Shim had said. The body you turned up in each time around was determined by what you'd done in the last life. And obstacles not overcome in one existence were carried over from that time and place to the next.

Waack let his mind roam back over the centuries to the year 540 A.D. Shim had taught him the technique of calling up memories from his former lives, and he now saw the picture in his mind as clearly as if he was watching a movie.

Won Kwang, his name had been. It had been he who integrated the martial arts into his part of the Orient, as Bhodidharma had done in China. He had taught his skills to the sons of the nobles in the peninsula kingdom of Silla, later to be one of the three monarchies that became Korea. He had been the favorite of Silla's King Chin Hung, respected and honored, until a dalliance with the king's daughter had produced a bastard child.

Waack opened his eyes as he saw himself about to be beheaded. He had never actually heard the words the king had said the moment before the sword came down on his neck. Nor had he read of them in Korean historical accounts of the period. He hadn't needed to. Shim had told him what the king had said.

"You will return to this world without the blood that spills from your throat, Won Kwang," Chin Hung had predicted. "Except for the trace of it that will remain in your eyes, that you might always remember the betrayal which brought upon your death."

Waack let the vision in his mind fade, and shifted in his seat to look in the mirror. His pink eyes looked back at him, reminding him of that day so many centuries ago.

Waack looked down at his watch, surprised to see that the memory had taken him through the better part of an hour. Where the hell was Shim? Had something happened? For a second he considered renting another car and going back to the La Quinta to find out. But if there had been a problem there, the police would most certainly be waiting—a complication he didn't need. Not when there was a faster, safer and easier way to check things out.

Waack dropped down from the plane and returned to the terminal, stopping at a pay phone. He dialed the answering service in Orlando, waited for the connections.

If Shim's delay was of no consequence, he would have called to leave a message. If there was no message, Waack would have to go back to the motel to start looking for his friend.

A woman's voice answered. Waack gave her the numerical code that would gain entrance to his private recorder. He then tapped in the four-digit code that ensured the confidentiality of his messages from the service's employees, and waited for the computer to connect him.

Waack was prepared for either of two possibilities—a message from Shim, or a recorded voice that told him his tape was blank.

What he wasn't ready to hear was the deep, threatening voice that came over the tape and into his ear. "This is Sergeant Mercy," Mack Bolan said. "How are you, Whitey?"

EXCEPT FOR A LITTLE different decor, Bolan thought as he took a seat on the bed, the scene looked no different than it had two hours earlier at the La Quinta.

Shim's gunshot that had killed Rhee earlier in the day had evidently gone unnoticed during the thunderstorm. The door Bolan had kicked in was still splintered, and the Executioner worried that sooner or later a passing lodger would spot it and notify the management. So he had moved the operation down the road to the Holiday Inn.

Shim was again trussed to the straight-backed wooden desk chair, and Grimaldi dropped once more to a seat at the table next to the window.

The Executioner glanced over at the Korean and saw that his anger was now mixed with a hearty dose of uncertainty. Shim had cooled off during the transfer between motels, and had time to second-guess his decision to call Waack's answering service in Orlando.

Had he had enough time to regret the impulsive decision? Bolan didn't know. And he didn't care. He had obtained the information he needed to make contact with Waack, and it was too late for Shim to take it back now.

Bolan considered what direction to take when Waack called. An assault on the ego had worked on Shim, and unless the Executioner missed his guess, it would work equally well with Waack. If Waack was as jealous of Bolan as Kurtzman said, he would likely jump at the chance for a showdown.

The trick, as it had been with Shim, was to convince Waack that the showdown had to come before the assassination of any more senators. Bolan had a rabbit or two to pull out of his hat that he suspected would push the right buttons in the albino.

When the phone rang, Bolan stretched across the bed to reach it.

"Hello, Sarge," Jerry Wayne Waack said before Bolan could speak.

"Hello, Whitey."

The line went silent for a moment, then Waack said, "I never liked that name."

"So what? You ever look in the mirror? You'll have to admit it describes you pretty well."

"I look beyond the mirror," Waack said without hesitation. "*Inside* of it. I see things you could never see."

Bolan laughed. "You sound like a bad fortune cookie," he said. "You learn that kind of mystic mumbo jumbo from your little friend Shim here?"

"He's there?" Waack said.

"Big as life," Bolan said.

"Is Shim all right?" the assassin asked. "Let me talk to him."

"Sorry, he's tied up at the moment," Bolan said.

"You hurt him and I'll kill you, Bolan," Waack threatened. He waited a moment. "Why did you call me?"

"Oh, to see if you might want to take in a movie or a ball game," Bolan said. "Maybe go get a beer." He paused. "Why do you think I called you, Whitey? Because I think it's about time I killed you."

"Quit calling me Whitey," Waack said, his voice starting to sound edgy.

"What should I call you then?" Bolan asked. "Frosty the Snowman? Ivory Snow? How about Pinky Lee?"

"My name is Won Kwang," Waack blurted out angrily.

Bolan hesitated. Won Kwang? He had heard the name before somewhere—somewhere from Korean history. He forced a laugh as he tried to remember where. "Oh, Won Kwang, is it?" From the chair in the middle of the room, he saw Shim's expression suddenly change. "What's Won Kwang mean in Korean? White Ghost?"

"Shut up!" Shim suddenly shouted. "Shut up, Won Kwang!"

Bolan motioned for Grimaldi to gag the man, then said into the phone, "Don't you think it's about time for you and me to meet man on man, Whitey?"

"I intend to kill you, Bolan," Waack said. "But first I have more important matters to finish."

"Sure you do, Whitey," Bolan said. "But tell me, how you going to finish them without your little buddy here?"

There was a long silence while Waack contemplated the situation. The moment of truth was at hand. If Waack didn't take the bait the Executioner had thrown out now, he never would.

Bolan didn't want him to have too much time to consider the situation. "You recognized that voice a moment ago," he said. "How's a puppet like you going to carry on without Shim pulling your strings?"

After another long pause Waack said, "Killing you is going to give me tremendous pleasure, Sergeant Mercy."

Bolan looked across the room to Shim, who was violently shaking his head as he struggled to speak through the gag. "Quit bragging about killing me and come try it," Bolan said. "I'm in room 234 at the Holiday Inn down the street from the La Quinta."

Waack chuckled softly over the phone. "Right. Walk into what would probably turn out to be two hundred cops. You bet."

"It's just me, Shim and one of my men," Bolan said. "I'll send the other two away."

Waack laughed harder. "I'm supposed to believe that? I don't think so. Not there."

"Okay, then where?" Bolan asked.

"I'll have to think about it," Waack said.

It was the Executioner's turn to chuckle. "Sounds like you might be a little bit hesitant, Whitey," he said. "What's wrong? Got to change out of your Sunday school clothes so you don't get them dirty?"

"God, this is going to be fun," Waack growled. "How do I know that wherever I pick to meet you, you'll come alone?"

"I always worked alone in Nam," Bolan said.

"So did I," Waack said quickly.

Bolan didn't let up. "I heard that," he said. "But nobody seemed to think you did it as well as I did."

"After I kill you, I'm going to cut your nuts off and eat them, you motherfucker," Waack said, his voice finally rising to a controlled shout.

"I heard that about you in Nam, too," Bolan said. "But I heard you did it *before* they were dead."

"You bastard!" Waack yelled. Then the line went silent again, as if his outburst had shocked him, too. "You stay right where you are," he said, his voice lowering again. "I'll call you back in an hour."

And the line went dead.

THE EXECUTIONER TURNED the corner and pulled the van under a set of brick arches that looked vaguely like the ones outside the entrance to Shilling's neighborhood. But the lighted sign above this one read, Dallas's Historical West End.

Two blocks further, he made a left and drove past the remodeled warehouse that now quartered the Outback Pub and Dick's Last Resort. Pulling into a parking lot across the street, he passed another sign announcing that parking was two dollars an hour.

An elderly gray-haired black man reached the van as the Executioner parked by a steel post marked 118. He took the five Bolan gave him, handed back a receipt, then walked away.

Like the older warehouse areas of many large cities, the West End had been remodeled into a night-life hot spot with colorful theme bars, restaurants and specialty shops. Bolan left the parking lot and crossed the street through the crowd of Saturday-night partiers.

He climbed the wooden stairs to the long porch of the old warehouse. Couples and larger groups sat at the outdoor tables in front of Dick's Last Resort and loud Dixieland music blared from the band inside.

The Executioner walked though the doors of the Outback Pub. A waitress wearing a T-shirt that read, It's What's Down Under That Counts, came bouncing up to the Executioner as he stopped by the bar. "One for dinner?" she smiled.

"Just a beer," Bolan said. He nodded toward the bar, then took a stool. When the bartender came over, he ordered an Australian Stout, and a T-shirt with the Australian map on it, as Waack had told him to do.

"I've got a message for you," the bartender said in a thick Australian accent. "Your name Mercy?" His T-shirt featured a full-length shot of a kangaroo eating peanuts and said, Grab Your Nuts at the Outback.

The Executioner nodded.

"Pretty name. Your mate was in earlier but had to go. Said to meet him next door at Dick's. Still want the Stout?"

Bolan shook his head as he stood. "And I'll pick the shirt up later, too. But I'm curious. How'd you know who I was?"

The bartender shrugged. "Your mate described you," he said. "Said you were big, and you'd be wearing a tank top and shorts. You never order anything but Australian Stout. And you collect T-shirts."

Bolan nodded. "He knows me well." He turned toward the door.

"Hey," the bartender called out.

The Executioner turned back.

"He was wrong about one thing," the bartender said, smiling. "You aren't as ugly as your mate said. The fact is, you aren't ugly at all."

Bolan stepped back out on the wooden porch. A Dallas cop on horseback rode by as the Executioner passed the people at the outdoor tables and entered Dick's Last Resort. Inside, he saw couples, families and singles eating huge barbecued ribs from shiny steel buckets.

The Executioner scanned the room but saw no sign of Waack. Not that he'd expected the man to be here. He took a seat at the bar again, ordered another Australian and paid the bartender.

He had taken his first sip when the phone rang at the other end of the bar. The bartender answered it, set it down, then lifted a microphone to his lips. "Phone call for Sergeant Mercy," he said. "Is there a Sergeant Mercy here?"

Bolan moved to the other end of the bar, where the bartender handed him the receiver. "Mercy," he said into the instrument.

Waack chuckled on the other end of the line. "Pretty good so far," he said. "But you aren't dressed right."

"You gave me forty-five minutes to get here," Bolan said. "That included stopping to buy a red tank top and a pair of khaki shorts. Well, I'm sorry, Whitey, but Wal-Mart was fresh out of red tank tops and this was the best I could do." His fingers curled tighter around the phone. "Look, I'll play your game up to a point. But a black tank top tells you as well as red that I'm not armed."

"Red is easier to spot," Waack said. "Don't mess up again."

"Don't worry," Bolan told him. "You're the one who's messing up. Where are you?"

"Close. I saw you park and walk across the street. Then again when you left the Outback for there."

"Where do I meet you?" said Bolan.

"Not yet," Waack said. "I have to make sure you're alone."

"Get real, Whitey," the Executioner said. "You think that the waitresses next door are FBI? Or that the Dixieland band is really Delta Force?"

Waack ignored him. "Go to the corner, turn left and you'll find the West End Market Place a block and a half down. Fifth floor, second pay phone across from the open bar that's just off the escalator. I'll give you two minutes."

"I can't get there that fast," Bolan said. "Not with all the people on the street."

"I suggest you try." Waack snickered, obviously enjoying the power he was wielding. "I had you in my scope when you crossed the street from the parking lot. I'll have you there again. But don't worry, I won't kill you. If you're late I'll just pick out someone on the sidewalk and take them down."

"Waack—"

"I suggest you get started."

Bolan dropped the phone and sprinted past the surprised patrons of the pub. Dashing between the tables on the porch, he saw more startled eyes. When he reached the corner, he turned to see the cop on the horse standing at the intersection and was forced to slow to avoid the man's attention. He walked as quickly as possible past the man, saw him turn the other way, then broke into a sprint again.

The Executioner dropped from the sidewalk to the street to pass slow-moving strollers. He avoided some of those coming at him, but others who stepped into his path went sprawling to the pavement, shrieking and cursing. When he reached the West End Market Place, he jumped down the steps into a sunken outdoor sitting area, then raced up more steps to the front doors.

Inside, the Executioner found he was on the second floor. The escalators were in the center of the building and he dodged a thick support pillar next to a candy stand and leaped on board. The rolling staircase was packed with people, making further progress impossible without throwing them completely off.

His wristwatch told him that he had forty-three seconds left.

As soon as he reached the third floor, the Executioner raced around to the escalator moving up to the fourth. This time it was less crowded and he weaved his way in and out, ignoring the protests.

As he rounded the escalator toward the fifth floor, he glanced at his watch again.

Twenty-one seconds.

Bolan jumped onto the first step behind an elderly couple. "Excuse me," he said. "I need to get through."

The old man turned to face him. "Wait your turn," he said.

"Sir, it's an emergency," Bolan said. "Please."

The man didn't answer.

Faces of people he'd seen on the sidewalks of the West End flashed through the Executioner's mind. Waack would shoot one. He didn't doubt the man's threat. He looked to the sides of the escalator. If he bumped the old man or woman out of the way, they might go flying over the side. The fall could kill them.

Bolan looked at his watch again as the steps moved upward with agonizing slowness.

Nine seconds.

The Executioner leaned forward, lifted the old man from his feet and draped him over his shoulder. The woman screamed as the Executioner and her husband raced up the moving steps. The old man cut loose with a steady stream of curses, his bony fists pummeling Bolan's back like a windmill.

The phone began to ring as Bolan reached the top step. He set the old man down on his feet and tore the receiver from the hook. "Yes!"

His face livid with humiliation, the old man gathered himself together and took a swing at the Executioner as Waack said, "Congratulations. You just saved the life of the cop on the horse. I was about to pull the trigger."

Bolan caught the old man's arm in midflight and hung on. "Where do I meet you, Waack?" he demanded. "Stop playing games. Let's get down to business."

"Go back to the parking lot," Waack said. "There's a note on your windshield." He paused, chuckling again in a low, threatening voice. "You've got three minutes."

The line went dead.

Bolan dropped the old man's wrist. He turned back toward the escalator, then saw a sign marked Emergency Exit Only a few steps beyond. Bursting through the door beneath the sign, he heard an alarm go off. The screeching buzz followed him down each flight of steps and back out the front door.

Cutting down through the sunken sitting area again, the Executioner raced down the street toward the van. He could seen the white piece of paper under the windshield wiper, and was two cars away when the giant black form stepped out from where it had crouched between two other cars.

The man in the ragged khaki pants and equally threadbare white T-shirt could have been an offensive tackle for the Dallas Cowboys. Bulging biceps curled outward to intercept the Executioner as Bolan ran head on into his massive chest.

The force drove the man back a half step. He grinned, showing a ragged row of yellow-black teeth, then raised a hammerlike fist into the air. Bolan's arm shot up, blocking the blow as it came down, but at the same time he felt something slam into his kidney from the rear.

The blow dropped the Executioner to the asphalt parking lot. He looked up through clouded vision to see another man holding a baseball bat. Smaller than the first man, he could still have played next to his partner on the Cowboy's front wall.

"Easy money, Lenny," the second man said, raising the bat over his head.

Bolan rolled to his side and let the bat come down on the asphalt next to him. He raised his leg, driving a short, chopping roundhouse kick up into the batter's groin. The bat tumbled to the parking lot and rolled under the van. The man who had wielded it grasped his crotch with both hands, took two steps backward and fell to his back.

"Bastard," the first giant said under his breath. He raised a tree trunk of a leg to stomp, but Bolan rolled again and his high-topped basketball shoe skidded down across the asphalt, breaking his balance.

The Executioner shot one leg in front of the man's legs, the other behind, and scissored them together. The big black man went to the ground next to him, his forehead striking the asphalt. He moaned once, then was silent.

Bolan heard a whistle in the distance as he leaped back to his feet and ripped the sheet of paper from the windshield. He turned to see the mounted cop who'd been on the street earlier galloping his way. The man's hand was firmly planted on the Glock holstered at his side, and his head was tilted to speak into the microphone clipped to the top of his shirt.

Bolan unfolded the note and read it:

*If you're reading this, you've already met Lenny and Dexter, and I've got a better idea how you fight, asshole. Stay where you are. More orders coming.*

The note was signed Won Kwang.

Again the Executioner tried to remember where he had heard the name as he stuffed the note into his pocket. He watched the cop rein his horse in behind the cars and jump from the saddle, the Glock now drawn. "You okay, sir?" he asked Bolan.

The Executioner nodded. A cop witnessing the attack was something Waack couldn't have anticipated. And it complicated things immeasurably.

The officer dropped the reins and aimed his weapon at the two men on the ground as his well-trained mount froze in place. "Well, well, well," he said. "My old friends Lenny and Dexter. You guys been out of the county, what, now...almost a month? *Very* good."

Lenny moaned. Dexter, was still unconscious.

"Officer," the Executioner said quietly. "I'm not hurt, and I've got an important meeting—"

"Sorry, sir," the cop said. "I need a statement and other information from you. It's time these guys went back to making license tags."

Bolan glanced to the rear of the van. Waack's note had said more orders were coming. And when they came, he would have to move fast. But his van was blocked from escape in the opposite direction by the concrete post. He would have to drive out the front, past the officer and his horse.

A siren sounded suddenly as a black-and-white patrol car squealed into the parking lot, lights flashing. It ground to a halt directly in front of the van, terminating that possibility of escape, as well.

A pair of uniformed officers jumped out of the car and hurried to the two men on the ground, jerking handcuffs from their belts.

Bolan heard a swishing sound on the asphalt and turned to the side to see a young black kid of nine or ten ride up on a bicycle. "Your name Mercy?" he asked Bolan.

Bolan nodded as the mounted cop looked curiously on.

The kid pulled another note from his pocket, handed it to the Executioner and rode away.

Bolan unfolded the note: *Ditch the Heat. Centennial liquor store one mile west off Commerce Street. You've got five minutes.*

"What the hell—" the mounted cop said, starting toward the Executioner.

Bolan drove a hard right cross into his jaw, ending the sentence.

A second later he had grabbed the horse's reins, swung up into the saddle and was galloping off into the night across Dallas's West End.

THE EXECUTIONER dismounted a half block from the liquor store, dropped the reins and slapped the horse on the rump to send it on its way. He raced to the phone, which was already jingling at the front of the building.

Waack's voice had a near-maniacal ring to it as he chanted, "Ha ha ha, he he he, I can see you, but you can't see me." He laughed hysterically, and when Bolan didn't respond, said, "What's wrong, Sarge?

Don't you like games? Lighten up. As they say these days, get in touch with your inner child.''

"Spare me the self-help psychobabble, Waack," the Executioner said as he caught his breath. "And no, I don't like games. At least not when I'm playing them with a psychopath." He turned back to the parking lot. Empty, except for an old El Camino. Deciding suddenly to try a new approach, he said, "You're a coward, Waack. You're trying to wear me out. Get me so tired you can win. That'll defeat your purpose, Whitey. You'll never know if you were better than me.''

After a short silence, Waack said, "Nice try, but it didn't work. I've seen the kind of physical condition you're in, Bolan. What you've done so far hasn't even warmed you up."

The Executioner scanned the area outside the liquor store as he listened for any background noises over the line that might help him pinpoint Waack's location. If the lunatic really could see him right now, he had to be close.

"But just so you don't accuse me of cheating," Waack said, cackling, "we'll make the next lap an easy one. You know where DeSoto is?"

Bolan searched his memory of the area. "Suburb just south of Dallas," he finally said.

"Well, give Sergeant Mercy three gold stars," Waack said. "Now go inside the liquor store and tell the bitch with the big tits your name. I gave her a hundred-dollar bill to give you a present." The line clicked dead.

Bolan opened the glass door and entered the liquor store. A middle-aged woman with large breasts spilling out of her low-cut western blouse stood behind the counter in front of several rows of half-pint bottles. She smiled as Bolan walked up. "Help ya?"

"A friend said he left something for me here," Bolan told her.

The woman nodded. "He said to get your name to make sure it was you."

"Mercy," Bolan said.

"That's the magic word." The unwitting accomplice smiled, reached down under the counter and produced a battery-powered cellular phone in a black nylon case. "Have a nice day."

Bolan exited the store, opened the case and flipped the On switch. A moment later the line rang. "Long time no see, Sarge," Waack said. "Now start driving south on I-35."

"I'm on foot, Waack," Bolan said in disgust. "If you're really watching me, you'd know that." He was beginning to wonder just how close the assassin really was, and exactly what he could see from whatever vantage point he had chosen.

The answer came quickly as a two-year-old Ford Thunderbird pulled into the parking lot in front of the liquor store.

"There's your wheels, now," Waack said. "Now get moving."

Bolan walked toward the car as a young woman with blond hair opened the door. She looked up at him in alarm for a moment, then her eyes saw the phone receiver against his face and the sight somehow relaxed her. She swung her cowboy boots and tight jeans out of the Thunderbird and gave Bolan the keys.

"Thanks," Bolan said. He moved quickly past her, took the driver's seat, started the engine and backed out onto the street.

Since the cellular phone had no speaker, he was forced to drive with one hand, keeping the other on the receiver against his head. Waack was silent as the Thunderbird rolled up the access ramp to the highway, but his soft breathing echoed like thunder in Bolan's ear.

The Executioner had no doubt that the phone had been particularly well thought out by the crazed assassin. Waack had taken precautions not only to determine that the Executioner came unarmed and without backup, but also to make sure he had other advantages, as well.

The phone kept one of Bolan's hands busy. The steering wheel, the other.

"Take the Waco exit," Waack said.

"Where are you, Waack?" he said into the phone.

"A few miles ahead of you," the killer replied. "But don't bother trying to spot me. I'm disguised. You don't know my vehicle, and you'll never make it or me in all this traffic."

Bolan cut over two lanes and took the fork in the highway leading to Waco. "You a magician, or what?" he asked. "How is it you're ahead of me?"

Waack's demented laughter roared in the Executioner's ear. "I thought you'd never ask," he said. "The El Camino in the parking lot had a video camera in it. Impressed?"

"Only with the depths of your madness."

"Then how about this," Waack said, his voice irritated now. "Look in the back seat."

Bolan hit the brake as a Saturday-night drunk suddenly cut across the lane in front of him. He twisted the wheel, fighting the Thunderbird as it threatened to fishtail off the highway and onto the median.

"Wow! Excitement! Suspense!" Waack taunted as Bolan fought to regain control of the vehicle. "Chills! Thrills! Never a dull moment in the adventures of Sergeant Mercy, is there?"

Straightening the Thunderbird down the highway, Bolan glanced over his shoulder, but by now he'd figured out what he would see. Mounted in the back, and partially camouflaged by a child's car seat, he saw another video camera.

Bolan glanced over his shoulder again as the Thunderbird rolled on toward DeSoto. He squeezed the phone between his cheek and shoulder, switched hands on the steering wheel and reached into the back seat. "Let's even the odds a bit, Waack," he said as he reached for the camera.

"Naughty, naughty," Waack said. "Touch it, and the game's over. I'll take out a couple of drivers here on the highway, then go back to your precious little senators."

The Executioner pulled his arm back to the front. "Do that and you'll never see Shim again."

"Touché," Waack said. "So let's get on with this game. It's beginning to bore me, too. You'll see an exit to Wintergreen Street coming up in a few miles," he said. "Take it. I've got things to do right now, so I'm signing off. But you'll hear from me soon, so don't get lonely." The line clicked off.

Bolan disconnected his end and dropped the receiver on the seat next to him. He drove on, racing through the night, zigzagging in and out of the thinning traffic as he left Dallas proper and moved out into the less crowded suburbs.

Wintergreen appeared six miles later, as Waack had predicted, and Bolan took the off ramp. He turned in front of a Holiday Inn and started along the street, passing apartment complexes, gas stations and several cafés and restaurants still alive with Saturday-night diners.

The Thunderbird made it through the first intersection on a green light, then stopped at a red a mile farther down as the phone rang.

"Come on through the light when it changes and just keep driving," Waack instructed.

Bolan drove slowly past another area of apartments. A half mile later Waack said, "In a second you'll see a park on your right. There'll be wooden swings, slides, things for the little bastards to play on. Pull in and cut the engine."

A second later the Executioner saw the park. It looked deserted, the only movement being the wet leaves rustling in the wind as the overhead lights cast their eerie glow.

Bolan drove halfway down the block, pulled under a streetlight and parked. "Okay," he said into the phone. "I'm here. What do I do now?"

"Wait," Waack said, cackling over the line. "And think." Then the cackling stopped, and in a low, threatening voice, he said. "Think about what hell's going to be like, Sergeant Mercy."

The line went dead.

## CHAPTER FIFTEEN

Seconds became minutes. The minutes turned to hours.

Bolan sat behind the wheel, staring out through the windshield. Somewhere nearby, Waack was waiting on him. Probably putting the finishing touches on whatever trap he had planned, but more than that, hoping the hours alone and waiting would cause the Executioner to lose his nerve.

The dark horizon had begun to lighten when the cellular phone finally rang.

"Get out of the car and walk toward the wooden castle in the center of the park," Waack said. "Just leave the phone in the car. You won't need it anymore. I'll pick it up after I kill you."

"Where are you, Waack?" Bolan asked for what seemed like the millionth time that night.

"I'm close, Sarge. Real close. You'll see me in a minute. Now do what I told you." The line went dead.

Bolan got out of the car. It would be face-to-face now. One-on-one. Man-to-man.

His eyes darting back and forth across the park, through the swings and slides and other wooden playground toys, the Executioner walked slowly toward the two-story castle. The structure was child size. The front door—the only door—was no taller than his waist.

The Executioner scanned the thick grove of trees between the playground and a still-darkened softball diamond to the west. Wherever Waack was, he wasn't in the castle. The man was far too smart to trap himself in a building that small with only one escape. Yet he was close, Bolan knew, as he neared the tiny walls just beyond the miniature drawbridge. Waack was somewhere nearby, watching, waiting. Reveling in the fact that the moment he had waited for since the Vietnam war was finally at hand.

The Executioner stopped in front of the concrete moat circling the castle and looked down at the leaves drifting in the current. Waack was watching. Behind him. He could feel the man's eyes on his back. Would the crazed, brainwashed assassin just shoot him now?

The Executioner knew that was a possibility. But his gut instinct told him that wasn't in the cards Waack had dealt. Waack wanted Shim back, but beyond that he had been jealous of Bolan for too many years— years during which he believed he'd been given a raw deal, playing second fiddle to him in Vietnam. Jerry Wayne Waack truly wanted to prove, once and for all, if only to himself, that he was the better man.

"That's far enough," the voice behind the Executioner called out. "Freeze."

Bolan stopped in his tracks.

"Like they say in the cowboy movies," Waack snorted. "Throw up your hands and turn around *slow.*"

The Executioner raised his hands over his head and turned. In front of him, he saw the white hair and almost transparent skin glowing in the early light of day.

Waack wore a black shirt and slacks, enunciating his paleness even more. In his hand, he held a SIG-Sauer semiautomatic 9 mm.

"*You're* Waack?" Bolan asked, again wanting to fuel the man's anger.

"I'm Won Kwang," Waack said in a calm voice.

"Well, whoever you are, this is sort of an anticlimax," Bolan said. "I was expecting somebody who at least *looked* tough."

Waack didn't let the insult get to him. He smiled, showing two perfect rows of white teeth that matched his skin and hair. "You're about to find out," he said.

"Why don't you cut the melodramatics and let's get this started," Bolan said. "Or do you plan to just shoot me from there and then tell yourself that proves you're the better man?"

Waack laughed now, a high-pitched laugh of excitement, his dream on the verge of fulfillment. He was about to show both Bolan and himself that it was Jerry Wayne Waack who should have been renowned as a war hero in the jungles of Southeast Asia.

Waack took a step closer and squinted through the dim light. "You look different than you used to," he said. "I noticed that earlier."

"How would you know?" Bolan asked. "We never met before."

"Oh, but I saw pictures. Everybody saw pictures. And in every one of them you were looking right at me, your eyes mocking me." His face screwed into an ugly scowl. "The great Mack Bolan setting up in the jungle to take out an enemy at a thousand yards. The mighty Bolan going after POWs alone behind enemy lines." He turned and spit into the dirt. "Or that picture that showed you letting a wounded gook kid drink out of your helmet, *Sergeant Mercy*. That kid was probably VC."

"Maybe," Bolan agreed. "But we had no way of knowing. And he was dying. Giving him a drink of water didn't hurt anything."

"Shit," Waack said, shaking his head in disgust. The head stopped, and he said, "You haven't answered my question."

"What question?"

"Your face, Bolan. It's not the same."

"The miracles of modern medicine, Waack," Bolan said. "Cosmetic surgery. It came in handy a couple of times over the years."

Waack nodded. "Yeah, well, you must have stepped on some big toes after the war. You must have really thought you could do anything, and get away with it scot-free. Like ruin people's careers."

"I did what I had to do," Bolan said simply.

Waack took another step forward. "Yeah?" he suddenly screamed in rage. "Well, why you? Huh? Why you?" The barrel of the SIG-Sauer waved wildly back and forth. "I was as good as you, you bastard! I was better! So how come you got the glory? How come you got the names, Sergeant Mercy? Can you tell me that?"

"Because I never killed anyone who didn't deserve it," Bolan said.

Waack's chest heaved in and out with fury. "Okay," he said. "Okay. It's almost time." His voice calmed again and a tiny smile started at the corners of his lips. "Just two more things we have to clear up first. First, there's something I want you to think about while I'm cutting you into little strips."

Bolan waited silently.

"You saved James Shilling," Waack went on. "But does the name Peter Christianson ring a bell?"

"He's the other Texas senator."

"And did you know he lives in Arlington, too?"

Bolan didn't answer.

Waack's grin began to spread. "Maybe you did, maybe you didn't. But I'll bet you didn't know he was a member of the First Baptist Church in Arlington, now did you?"

Bolan watched the demented smile grow as he wondered where Waack was leading.

"And I'm certain you didn't know until now that there's going to be a little explosion at the church at 11:55 tomorrow. Right about the time the Baptists start what they call the 'invitation' and the poor souls who feel guilty about cheating their business partners and screwing around on their wives start running down the aisle to rededicate their lives."

He paused, and now the evil grin encompassed his face entirely. "Why, who knows, Sergeant Mercy? Maybe there'll even be a few new Christians who get saved tomorrow, too. They can shake the preacher's hand, turn around to be introduced to the congregation and then...boom! Straight to the pearly gates." Waack threw back his head and howled like Satan himself. "Talk about making it to heaven by the skin of your teeth," he roared.

Bolan started to move slowly forward but Waack caught the movement and levelled the 9 mm. "Getting anxious?" he asked. "Okay, me too. But there's one other thing. Where's Shim?"

Bolan didn't answer.

"Where's Shim, dammit!" Waack screamed. "Did you kill him?"

Bolan shook his head. "I considered it," he said. "Him and Homer Shoemaker, both. But at least right now they're both worth more alive than dead."

"I don't care about Shoemaker!" Waack shouted at the top of his lungs. "I want my friend Shim Sang!"

Bolan raised his wrist and looked at his watch. "Right about now some friends of mine should be handing him over to the CIA. When they're through pumping him for information, who knows? Maybe *they'll* kill him." He paused.

Waack's chest heaved in and out. "You bastard," he growled. "I'll find him after I kill you. And maybe just to spite you, Shoemaker, too."

"You won't get the chance to find either one of them," Bolan said. "But in case I'm wrong, try the FBI for the old man. They picked him up in Oklahoma and I hear they're learning all kinds of interesting things about the KKK."

Waack's eyes narrowed into tiny pink slits. The white skin of his cheeks became a deep crimson. Without further ado, he pulled the magazine from the SIG-Sauer and threw it as far as he could into the trees. Working the slide sent the chambered round flying off into the dawn. He grabbed the barrel of the weapon and sent it sailing into the trees after the magazine.

Jerry Wayne Waack strode forward and stopped two feet from Bolan. "I'm unarmed now, too," he said. "So let's rock and roll." As the last word left his mouth, he lashed out with a short jab.

The blow caught Bolan on the chin, jerking his head back. As he fought to keep his senses, he felt a sharp pain in his knee and looked down to see Waack's foot retreating after the kick.

The Executioner backpedaled, watching through blurred vision as Waack spun and slammed the heel of his foot against the side of the Executioner's head.

The kick sent Bolan reeling back. He felt the water soak into his feet and ankles as he stumbled into the shallow moat around the castle. Waack splashed after him, spinning again and launching a follow-up backfist. The Executioner ducked and the fist whizzed harmlessly over his head.

Bolan felt the splintered wood of the castle wall against his back as the crazed albino cut loose with a flurry of rights and lefts. "Sergeant Mercy!" Waack screamed. "No mercy from me!"

Bolan caught his balance, cleared his eyes and raised both arms like a boxer pinned against the ropes. He caught the force of Waack's blows on his forearms and shoulders, waited for an opening, then lashed out with a vicious front kick to the assassin's knee.

Waack squawked like a wounded bird and staggered back. Bolan threw a right cross that caught the man's chin but slipped across the sweaty face, losing most of its force. Still, it was enough to throw Waack off-balance, and the assassin fell to his back in the moat, water splashing around him.

The Executioner shoved off from the castle, but by the time he moved forward, Waack had spun out of the moat.

Waack's pink eyes glowed like fiery embers in the light of early morning. He gyrated into a deranged dance on the grass just beyond the moat. "Come on, Sergeant Mercy!" he squealed. "When we're finished maybe I'll give you a drink from my helmet!"

Bolan stepped out of the moat and moved carefully toward the performing madman. Waack shifted into a fighting stance and began to circle to his right. Bolan moved with him, keeping his guard up, his knees slightly bent, ready either to block or to attack. He felt his knee beginning to stiffen from Waack's earlier kick, but other than that, he had survived the barrage of fists and feet with nothing more than scrapes and bruises.

Waack suddenly dropped into a horse stance, lashing his front leg forward toward the Executioner's leg. Bolan lifted the limb and the sweep kick sailed under it. "Nice, real nice," Bolan said. "And you still think you're the best?"

The miss angered Waack, and more blood rushed to his chalky face. He stormed forward with a brutal front kick, which the Executioner parried to the side. Waack twisted out of the block and threw a side-thrust kick at Bolan's head.

Bolan caught his foot for a second, but Waack snapped it back, even more enraged.

The Executioner watched the man regain his balance and take a step back, steam practically rising from his ears. So far, Waack's anger had been the Executioner's ally. Whenever the madman lost his temper, his ferocity increased but his judgment faltered.

Bolan decided to play it for all it was worth.

"Hey, Whitey," he said as they began circling each other. "You ought to do this more often. It puts some color in your face."

The shrill sound that shot from Waack's throat came from low in the bowels of his hopeless soul. He streaked forward with a series of kicks and punches— all of them strong, yet none having the controlled focus necessary to penetrate the Executioner's defenses. Winded, his outrage tempered, Waack stepped back to catch his breath.

Bolan took advantage of the moment, leading with a low roundhouse kick and following with a punch to Waack's throat. But the killer had not yet lost complete control, and he blocked both blows with ease.

The Executioner circled again as he studied Waack's eyes. The man had been a walking time bomb for twenty years, always on the edge, always about to explode into complete and total madness.

It was time to ignite the bomb once and for all and rid the world of the well-trained assassin who killed for both profit and fun. But how? What was the final match that would light the fuse?

Bolan continued to circle, blocking an occasional kick or punch, then returning them in kind, reacting instinctively to the attacks as he searched his brain for the answer. What technique had Shim used to take control of Waack's mind? What was the key? He suspected it had something to do with Waack's hatred of his albinoism, and the inexplicable fact that the madman seemed to think he was Korean.

As if to confirm the Executioner's suspicion, Waack launched an arching crescent kick and mumbled under his breath, "I am Won Kwang."

Bolan stepped out of the way of the attack, and the words seemed to come on their own. "That's not what Shim told me."

Waack froze in place. He didn't speak.

Bolan stopped but kept his guard up, his feet ready to move at the slightest sign that Waack was about to attack again. He had somehow hit a sore spot. But how? He didn't know. The best thing he could do now was stay with it, keeping his comments as general as necessary and narrowing them down only after Waack revealed more.

"No, that's not what Shim said at all," Bolan repeated.

Waack started to move again, but slower now. "You're lying," he muttered.

"No," Bolan said, mirroring the man's movements. "Shim was laughing about it, in fact—you thinking you were Korean."

"I am Won Kwang," Waack said.

"Shim told you that?" Bolan laughed, blocking a halfhearted reverse punch. "Shim told me you were just a stupid albino who memorized quotations trying to sound smart. He said all you knew how to do was eat, sleep and kill." He paused. "And he said you weren't all that good at any of them." Suddenly Bolan knew how to put the icing on the cake. And considering Waack's jealousy, he knew he had the right detonator for the bomb in his brain.

"And guess what, Whitey?" the Executioner said. "Shim knew I'd kill you. So he's offered me *your job* when I'm through."

The noise that escaped the assassin's mouth was inhuman. His fists suddenly lashed through the air at some imaginary opponent. Then he streaked forward, arms and legs cutting through the air like pistons.

Bolan blocked an overhead blow and drove an uppercut into Waack's sternum. Air rushed from the madman's lungs but he still moved in. The Executioner sidestepped a knee thrust to the groin and countered with a roundhouse right nearly that snapped Waack's head off his neck. But still, the madman came.

Waack threw a series of kicks—front, side, then back. The Executioner blocked each with a slap of his hand, then lifted his leg and sent his own front kick moving forward at half-speed.

And the crazed man took the bait.

Waack saw the kick coming and grabbed the Executioner's ankle with both hands.

Bolan hopped forward on one leg, his right hand crashing into Waack's jaw. He felt the bone splinter beneath his knuckles as Waack's hands dropped away from his foot.

The Executioner drove a left and then a right into Waack's belly. More air rushed from the assassin's lips. He fell to his knees, his eyes staring blankly ahead.

Bolan took a half step back, crouched low and sent a right cross into the broken jaw.

Jerry Wayne Waack shot to his back on the grass.

Bolan fell over him, his knees on the madman's shoulders, and lifted his fist.

Waack's unhinged, hate-filled eyes stared up at him. "I am Won Kwang," he sputtered through his shattered jaw.

Bolan finally remembered where he'd heard the name before. Won Kwang—the father of Korean martial arts. And in a heartbeat he realized that Shim had convinced Waack that he was actually Won Kwang, thereby giving the man both color to his skin and a reason to follow the Korean.

"I am Won Kwang," Waack mumbled again as blood and teeth tumbled from his lips. "I have come back. And I will return again."

"I'll be waiting on you," Bolan said as he brought his fist down and drove it through Waack's throat.

Jerry Wayne Waack's eyelids fluttered twice, then fell to cover the light pink irises.

IT WAS TWO MINUTES before nine o'clock by the time the Thunderbird hit the Arlington city limits. Bolan had obtained the First Baptist Church's phone number from information via the cellular phone, called the church and arranged to meet the minister, Dr. M. Warren Dade.

Bolan pulled to a halt in the parking lot, leaped from the car, and bounded up the steps to the front doors. He caught several curious looks from the well-dressed churchgoers on their way to Sunday school classes. Covered with mud and still in his tank top and khaki shorts, and sporting three days' growth of beard, he looked like a man who'd had one hell of a Saturday night and decided that Sunday school might redeem his sins.

A shrunken, elderly man stood in one of the open doorways. He smiled at the Executioner, oblivious to Bolan's inappropriate apparel.

Bolan took the outstretched hand as he reached the door. "Good morning!" the old man said. "Glad to see you!" His eyes told the warrior he had no idea where he was.

"Where's the pastor's study?" Bolan asked.

The old man still gripped his hand, his face beaming. "Good morning! Glad to see you!" he said again.

The Executioner pried his hand away and hurried through the door to the church lobby as men, women and children dressed in their Sunday finest rushed toward the Sunday school classes about to start. A short woman in her early sixties, with well-kept gray hair was crossing the lobby. In a smart brown-on-brown tailored suit and carrying a teacher's lesson book, she walked like a woman on a mission.

Bolan stepped in front of her and saw a paper name tag pasted on the left side of the suit jacket. "Mrs. Cook," he said. "My name is Belasko, and I'm supposed to meet Dr. Dade immediately in his study."

The woman's smile was genuine, and while Bolan knew she had noticed his disheveled appearance, it hadn't disturbed her in the least. "Follow me," she said, barely breaking stride.

The Executioner followed the short little legs up a flight of stairs at a speed that would have made a world-class hurdler proud. They emerged onto a landing with glass windows, and on the other side of the glass Bolan could see the church offices.

Mrs. Cook opened the door, held it for him, then waved him through. She turned to a tall, slender woman a few years younger than herself who stood behind a metal desk. "Jo," Mrs. Cook called out. "Can you show this gentleman to the pastor's study? He's supposed to meet Warren."

The slender woman nodded and hooked a finger the Executioner's way. Bolan followed her down a short hallway, into a large office, then through another door into a wood-paneled room with bookcases circling the walls.

Dr. M. Warren Dade sat behind a large oak desk covered with open textbooks and loose pages. His eyes were closed tightly. A pretty woman wearing a red-and-white suit sat next to the desk on a short couch. Her eyes, too, were shut.

The woman called Jo nodded to Bolan and re-traced her steps down the hall. The Executioner stood quietly while Dade and the woman on the couch finished their prayers. He thought of the huge building he'd seen as he drove up, and the fact that he had no idea where the bomb might be planted. He glanced at his wrist. It was 9:15.

Taking a moment to let Warren Dade pray didn't seem like a bad idea at this point.

In unison, despite the silence in the room, Dade and the woman both said "Amen" and looked up. Dade smiled, a wide, hearty smile, and said, "You're Special Agent Belasko."

Bolan nodded.

"Mr. Belasko, this is my wife, Mary Beth. A good woman to have around in a crisis."

Bolan looked her way. He could see the spiritual strength in the woman's eyes, and sensed that she was probably as big a part of Dade's ministry as the pastor himself. These were good people, and they would be of help.

Bolan turned back to Dade. "Did you call the police?"

Dade nodded. "Or, rather, we tried. The entire phone system went out shortly after I spoke to you."

"Then—"

Dade raised a hand. "One of our deacons lives two blocks away," he said. "I sent him to make the call when we finally determined that none of the lines was going to work. In fact, you just missed him."

Bolan felt his eyebrows tighten on his forehead. Phone systems went out, sure. But it was curious that the lines at the First Baptist Church had decided to die at this moment.

Switching his mind back to the matter at hand, Bolan said, "What about Senator Christianson?"

Dade nodded. "He's here with his family. I sent one of the secretaries to get him out of his Sunday school class and bring him here."

Bolan looked Dade in the eye. "As soon as he gets here, we'll have to evacuate the church."

"Of course," Dade said, rubbing his chin. "The Lord helps those who help themselves, and I took the liberty of calling all of the Sunday school teachers in right after you and I spoke. They've gone back to their classes and will coordinate things without alarming anyone."

The Executioner smiled now. Dade was a smart, organized realist.

Mary Beth Dade crossed her legs on the couch. "You did say 11:55, didn't you, Mr. Belasko?"

Bolan turned back to her. "Yes. And if the guy who planted this thing was telling the truth, we should have plenty of time to get everyone out safely and maybe even find and defuse this thing. But I've got to tell you, the man responsible for all this was full of surprises." His mind drifted back to the dead phone lines. "If it comes down to the wire, we may have to get out and let the church go up."

Mary Beth Dade smiled a beautiful smile. "God helped us build this church," she said. "He isn't going to let it be blown up."

"I hope you're right," Bolan said.

"I am." She smiled again.

A tall, lanky figure appeared in the doorway, and Bolan recognized Peter Christianson from newspaper pictures. In his late forties with salt-and-pepper hair that nearly matched his charcoal pinstripe suit, Christianson turned pale as Bolan explained the situation.

"So I suggest you collect your family immediately and go home," the Executioner concluded.

Before Christianson could answer, a bell rang shrilly throughout the church. Dade stood up. "That's the end of the Sunday school opening exercises," he explained. "Even the stragglers should be in class by now. The teachers will be starting the evacuation."

The Executioner heard the rumbling of feet overhead as the class members above him began marching out of the rooms into the halls.

"I've got the deacons assembling in the chapel," Dade said as he circled the desk.

"No, pastor," Bolan said. "They need to get out of here, too. So do you and Mrs. Dade."

"But these men are the backbone of the church," Dade protested. "I've called them in to help search for the bomb."

Bolan hesitated. The dead phones meant a delay in the arrival of the bomb squad. And for all he knew, Arlington might not have its own explosives experts. If a team had to be called in from Dallas, they might be too late. Bolan reminded himself he couldn't search a building this size in that length of time by himself. He turned to Mary Beth Dade. "Mrs. Dade—" he started.

"Don't waste your breath even suggesting it," the woman said. Her eyes were firm, unbudging. "I stay with my husband." She paused, then added quietly, "And God."

Bolan turned to Christianson. "Senator, you'd better get going."

Some of the blood had returned to his face, but when Christianson spoke his voice had a nervous ring.

He shook his head. "I'm a senator," he said. "But I'm also a deacon."

Bolan looked back to the brave, dedicated eyes of M. Warren Dade and his wife. He saw no fear in either of these people, and knew the only way to get them to the front door would be to haul them there physically. He glanced to the ceiling of the church.

The Executioner wasn't sure that he had that right.

THE TWENTY MEN who sat in the chapel's first three rows ranged in age from their early thirties to the old man who had greeted Bolan at the door. Seated on the dais, to the side of the pulpit, the Executioner saw Warren Dade take the pulpit. Noticing the elderly gentleman in the front row, Dade moved to the edge of the platform and whispered down to a husky man in a navy blue suit.

That man nodded, turned toward the elderly door greeter and escorted his smiling face out the door.

Dade returned to the pulpit and said, "We need to make this quick and to the point. Some of you already know what's going on. For those who don't, there's a good chance that a bomb has been set to go off in the church this morning."

A few quiet gasps came from the deacons, but it was clear that most of them had already gotten the word.

"I don't want to waste any more time," Dade said. "So I'm turning the pulpit over to Agent Belasko."

Bolan rose, feeling slightly odd as he grasped both sides of the carved wooden podium. "Gentlemen," he said. "I need to correct something. I wouldn't say that there's a 'good chance' that there's a bomb here. I'd say there *is* one beyond any shadow of a doubt. What we have to do is get busy and find it. It's set to go off at 11:55.'' He paused to let the gravity of the situation sink in, then said, ''Anyone who'd like to leave right now should do so with no feeling of shame.''

He waited, but none of the men moved.

''Then let's get busy,'' the Executioner said. ''Dr. Dade told me each of you is responsible for a specific section of the building to check for maintenance problems.'' He saw several heads bob nervously up and down. ''I want each of you to search your part of the church. And I can't stress enough what I'm about to say next.'' He stopped for emphasis, then said, ''Do not touch anything that looks suspicious.'' He glanced down at his watch and saw that it was ten o'clock.

A hand rose from the second row.

Warren Dade stepped forward, leaned into the microphone and said, ''Question, Ted?''

A short, sturdily built man with a fringe of hair ringing his head dropped his hand and stood up. ''We'll do our best,'' he said. ''But I'm no professional at this and I don't think anyone else here is, either. We're very likely to miss this thing, if it's well hidden.''

Bolan stepped forward. ''Like you said, just do your best. I'll be conducting my own search of the areas I think are the most likely spots, but if you see anything you aren't sure of, come get me. Now, any more questions?''

Several heads shook.

''One more thing,'' the Executioner said, gripping the sides of the pulpit. ''Synchronize your watches by mine. It's exactly 10:04 . . . now.'' He waited while the men adjusted their timepieces. ''If we haven't found the device by 11:45, I want everyone out of the building. Is that clear?''

The heads bobbed up and down.

''Then let's roll,'' the Executioner said, and started down the steps of the dais.

AN HOUR AND fifteen minutes later the bomb still hadn't been found. Bolan had searched the sanctuary with the help of Senator Christianson, who was in charge of that section of the church. Learning from the senator that he and his wife usually occupied the sixth pew, to the left of the center aisle, he had assumed it to be the most likely place for Waack to place the explosive. But crawling under the pews in that part of the church had turned up nothing.

The areas around the main support structures of the building were also checked, on the assumption that Waack might be planning to simply bring the church down on Christianson's head. The Executioner's exploration had been interrupted several times by false alarms from the deacons.

Now, as Bolan and Christianson made their way down into the basement, the Executioner was beginning to think the deacons might have to be evacuated and the church allowed to blow.

Bolan reached the concrete floor of the basement and followed the senator down a long winding hall, wondering with every step where the Arlington police might be. Dade had said a deacon had left to find a phone that worked. That had been over an hour and a half ago.

Bolan stopped as Christianson pulled a set of keys from his slacks and unlocked the door to the janitor's room. The warrior's eyebrows furrowed in concentration. The phones had mysteriously gone dead. There had been no response from the cops.

Something was wrong. Real wrong. But he couldn't afford the time right now to find out what.

Moving past Christianson, Bolan scanned the room, seeing boxes, crates, cleaning supplies and several open shelves full of tools. Metal storm windows rested on their sides against the rear wall. A tall green metal box was set against the bricks at the rear of the room. Numerous black cables shot out of holes in the box, disappearing into holes drilled into the walls. The name AT&T was embossed on the front.

Bolan reached out, twisted the handle, and found it locked. He moved swiftly to the shelves, found a pry bar and popped the door. Inside, he found the answer to one of the questions that had plagued him since arriving at the church.

Spliced between the main phone line and the cutoff switch, he saw a digital timer with a twelve-hour clock. Lifting it to his eyes, he saw the clock had been set for 8:30. Just after he'd called Dade on the cellular phone.

The Executioner nodded silently. Waack had been many things, but stupid wasn't one of them. He'd set the timer so the phones would work until after it was too late to call a repairman who might find the timer.

Jerry Wayne Waack was reaching out from beyond the grave.

Bolan reactivated the main phone line and moved to a unit hanging on the wall. He got a dial tone, dialed 911 and a moment later a female voice asked, "Is this an emergency?"

"Yes," the Executioner said. "Where are the units who should have responded to the bomb threat at the First Baptist Church?"

"Bomb threat?" the woman said. "We haven't taken any bomb-threat calls this morning. Who is this?"

Bolan felt his heart bang against his chest. The call hadn't been made. "I'm standing in the basement of the church wondering why there's not a bomb squad with me," Bolan said. "A bomb's been planted somewhere in the church and it's set to go off at 11:55. Get some experts out here now!"

Bolan slammed the receiver back onto the hook, knowing it was too late. For whatever reason, the police had not been alerted. The fate of the First Baptist Church now rested in the hands of God. And the Executioner.

Bolan turned to Christianson. "Get the rest of the men out of the church," he said.

The senator looked down at his watch. "We've still got five minutes," he said.

Bolan shook his head. "You aren't going to find anything in five minutes you haven't already found. Now go."

Christianson turned and hurried out of the room.

Bolan closed the door of the telephone box and turned to the storm windows. Where was the bomb? Beside the telephone box he saw the huge natural-gas tank that powered the church. Even a small, properly set detonation here would ignite the tank and take out half the building.

A cold chill suddenly came over Bolan. He looked up at the high acoustical ceiling above him. Unless he missed his guess, the pews were directly above.

Bolan jumped at the ceiling, missing the movable tiles by an inch. A mop bucket stood against the wall next to the gas tank, and Bolan jerked the mop out and tossed it over his shoulder out of the way. He tried to pull the bucket away from the wall but it wouldn't budge. Frowning down, he saw the metal screws binding it to the bricks. At least ten of them. And the bright untarnished gleam around the heads told him they been installed recently.

Why would anyone screw a mop bucket into a brick wall?

Bolan dropped to one knee, knowing what he'd find inside the bucket before he looked. In the shadows beneath the rim, he saw a tangled mass of wires. Blue, green, red, yellow—the wires were of every color under the sun—and each started at a timer identical to the one that Waack had used to disable the phones. They ran from the timer to a small black box that served as the activating device, then into a lump of C-4 plastic explosive at the bottom of the bucket.

Bolan squinted into the bucket. Both the activator and timer had been screwed to the bucket with the same screws that held the bucket to the wall.

The Executioner looked down at his watch again. 11:44. He'd never be able to get all the screws out in eleven minutes.

Bolan reached down to the C-4 at the bottom of the bucket. It was held firm by some sort of adhesive, and moving it was out of the question.

Disconnecting the wires was the only chance, Bolan knew. But one wire was all it took to transfer the electronic impulse from the activator to the C-4, and Waack had spliced at least twenty to the plastic explosive. That meant that nineteen were decoys, and any or all of the decoys might well be booby traps.

In short, if he pulled the wrong wire, the First Baptist Church would become a fiery inferno of natural gas ahead of schedule.

The Executioner took a deep breath, then made his decision. The church would have to go. The deacons, Dade and his wife should be out of the building by now. Bolan would make a fast sprint through the building to double-check that it had been vacated, then get out before the bomb went off.

The Executioner was about to rise to his feet when he heard the raspy mumbling voice behind him. "Quite a complex little setup, isn't it, Sarge?" The voice coughed, then said, "Don't move."

Bolan's eyes rose to the storm windows leaning against the wall. In the reflection he saw himself kneeling next to the bucket.

And behind him, he saw the pale white face of a ghost.

JERRY WAYNE WAACK opened his eyes as soon as he heard the Thunderbird's engine roar to life. He lay still, deadly still, waiting for the car to back out of the parking lot. Every bone in his body felt broken, and now that he could breathe without giving himself away, he gasped for air through what he knew was a partially collapsed windpipe.

Waack had struggled to his feet, each movement an excruciatingly painful descent into hell. But enough hate-fueled energy still remained to start him toward the car. And even as the misery racked his body from head to toe, he felt a smile twist the shattered bone in his jaw.

Won Kwang was again rising from the grave to seek his revenge.

Waack opened the car door and collapsed on the seat in front of the steering wheel. He tried to catch his breath, but the sharp knives in his throat told him it was useless. He didn't care. All he wanted was enough air to get to Arlington, kill Bolan and watch the church go up in flames.

Waack twisted the key in the ignition and pulled out of the parking lot. He switched on the cellular phone and pushed the buttons to connect it to the transmitter he had hidden in the phone he'd given Bolan the night before. Arming the Executioner with a cellular phone, he had risked the man using it to call for help and monitored the line even when not speaking to the Executioner. But the fool had played by the rules. He hadn't even tried to call anyone.

Waack was less than ten miles from Arlington on I-30 when he heard Bolan call the church. He looked down at his watch and cursed, the low guttural noise shooting pain through his throat again. The bastard had beaten the timer on the church's phone lines by less than three minutes.

Waack had arrived at the church parking lot in time to see Bolan shaking hands with an old man at the door. He pulled the silenced Beretta .25 out of the glove compartment and was about to get out when he saw a man wearing a brown suit emerge from a side door. The man sprinted toward a Ford Mustang. He was leaving to find a phone that worked. To call the cops. That's what it had to be.

Pulling out of the parking lot behind the Mustang, Waack had started after the car when a station wagon pulled between them. The Mustang made it through a green light, then the station wagon screeched to a halt in front of him as the signal turned amber. Waack backed ten feet from the vehicle, cut the wheels and squealed around the station wagon as the light turned red. A camper-equipped pickup coming the other way hit both the brakes and its horn as it glanced off Waack's rear fender.

Waack accelerated, seeing the Mustang turn into a residential neighborhood at the next corner. He followed, making the turn as the car stopped in front of a two-story brick home. He guided the car up the driveway of the house next door as the man in the brown suit jumped out of the Mustang, then cut across the grass between the houses. Waack stomped the accelerator again.

The man in brown turned toward him in surprise. Waack's right front bumper caught him on the hip and the man spun off to fall on his grassy front yard. Waack ground to a halt as the man looked up in shock, and rolled down the window.

In silence, he had lifted the .25 over the side of the door and put two bullets through the man's brain. Then he backed the car off the curb and turned back toward the church.

BOLAN SAW THE TINY pistol in Waack's hand. A Beretta .25. Small. Not much stopping power. Except in the hands of an expert.

And Waack was an expert.

"Stand up real slow, Sarge," Waack croaked through his injured throat. "And turn around."

Bolan followed his instructions, turning to face the man. Waack looked like something that had risen from the coffin. The jaw Bolan had broken had swollen to three times its normal size, and a sharp sliver of white bone peeked through the compound fracture. Dried red-black blood covered his chalky face and accented the pink eyes. His black slacks and shirt were ripped and, all in all, Jerry Wayne Waack looked like he belonged at the cast party for the actors in *Night of the Living Dead*.

"I've got a surprise for you, Sarge," Waack said.

Bolan watched him. "You're just full of them, aren't you?"

"Yeah, but this one's the best yet." Waack turned to his side and waved the gun.

Senator Peter Christianson stepped from the hall into the large storage room.

Waack grabbed the senator by the arm and jammed the gun into the back of his head. "Looks like you and the senator are taking the same train to hell together, Sergeant Mercy," he said. He glanced up at the ceiling. "Seems like a funny place to start the journey, wouldn't you say?"

Bolan took a step forward but Waack shoved the gun tighter into Christianson's neck.

"You'll die with us, Waack," the Executioner said.

"I'm dying anyway," the assassin choked, and the choke brought on a series of raspy coughs. "I'm bleeding internally. I can feel it." A satanic smile took over his face. "You've killed me, Sarge. But you didn't win. I hate to admit it, but we're both going to have to settle for a tie ball game."

Christianson's eyes had become wide white orbs of terror. "We have doctors in the church," he pleaded through his trembling lips. "They could—"

"Shut the fuck up, you goddamn faggot!" Waack screamed. He raised the pistol and brought it down on the back of the senator's skull.

Christianson slumped to the floor, unconscious. Waack leaned over and jammed the .25 into the side of his head, then looked up to Bolan.

Bolan looked into the crazed pink eyes. Even now, one step from death himself, Waack knew what he was doing. He knew that under the circumstances Bolan might risk taking a shot or two from the low-powered .25 to get to him. So he was keeping the gun on the senator to keep the Executioner at bay.

"So what do we do now?" Bolan asked. He had caught a glimpse of his watch as the senator fell, and they had just a little over one minute before the timer hit 11:55 and the church went up like Hiroshima.

"We wait," Waack choked out. "Then we all report to Satan together."

The Executioner made the decision quickly. Although the odds were stacked against Christianson living through it, he had to risk the brain shot Waack would deliver the moment he moved. The odds any of them would survive the explosion were nonexistent.

Bolan had started to move when he saw a sudden flash of movement behind Waack. Suddenly the demented assassin was flying forward, a look of shock on his face. As he fell forward, the Executioner saw Dr. M. Warren Dade, his arms outstretched from the violent shove he'd given the madman. Dade lost his own balance and fell over the unconscious senator.

Waack's wild pink eyes opened wide in his ashen face as he fell toward Bolan, his thin snowy hair flying around him.

Bolan drew back as soon as the man fell, and drove the front knuckles of his fingers into the throat he had punched hours earlier.

Waack jackknifed in the air, hitting the floor in a sitting position. Blood spewed from his lips as if powered by a fire hose. Then he fell backward, his head striking the concrete with the sound of a watermelon dropped from a two-story building.

The Executioner moved over him and looked down. This time, the eyes were open, staring sightless up into eternity.

As Bolan hurried back to the bucket, Mary Beth Dade stepped into the doorway, grabbed her husband's arm and helped him to his feet. The Executioner looked down at the timer. "Get out of here," he said in a calm quiet voice. "This thing goes off in half a minute."

M. Warren Dade was as calm as Bolan as he shook his head. "That's not enough time," he said. He looked down at Christianson, still unconscious on the floor. "We'll never make it out of the building. Especially carrying him."

"I'll carry him," Bolan said. "Now go!"

Mary Beth Dade took her husband's arm. "We still wouldn't make it," she said, her voice even and in control. "None of us would. Can you stop that thing somehow?"

Bolan shook his head. "There are twenty wires here and nineteen of them are booby-trapped."

He looked at the timer again. Twenty seconds remained. The Dades were right. It was too late for any of them. Trying to run now would be an exercise in futility.

Dr. M. Warren Dade and his wife hugged and closed their eyes. "Dear Heavenly Father," Dade said, his face as intense as any Bolan had ever seen. "Where two or more are gathered in your name, you have promised to be also. We are four here, and we ask that you guide the hand of this man you have sent to us as your instrument of mercy and justice." He paused a brief moment, then said, "Amen."

"Amen," Mary Beth Dade agreed.

Bolan looked back to the timer. Ten seconds.

Dade smiled at the Executioner. "You can pull one of the wires now," he said softly.

"Which one?" Bolan asked.

Dade shrugged and the smile spread across his face. Next to him, his wife was beaming, as well. "Pick one," the minister said. "It doesn't matter."

Bolan took a final glance through the bucket to the timer and saw that four seconds remained. Without further hesitation, he jammed his hand into the bucket, grasped the first wire his fingers hit and jerked it from the bomb.

The Executioner watched the last three seconds tick away on the face of the timer.

Eleven fifty-five came and went.

And the First Baptist Church of Arlington, Texas, still stood.